Decorous' books
&
Presents

I0634114

Smooth Casanova

Smooth Casanova
A decorous' Books Collection

Published by Decorous Books
A Division of Decorous' Circle, Inc
Florida

Smooth Casanova is a fictional work. The names, characters, places, and incidents are either the product of the author's imagination or are used fictitiously, and any resemblance to an actual person (dead or alive), business establishment, events, or locales is entirely coincidental.

The Publisher does not control or assume responsibility for the author's or third-party Websites or their content.

First Edition
ISBN: 979-8-9922002-9-4
Printed in the USA

For information regarding special discounts for bulk purchases, don't hesitate to get in touch with the Decorous Circle Special Sales Department online at www.deezeebooks.com

The following Presentation is Rated

Book

M A
LSV

L – Language

S- Sexual Situation

V - Violence

This fictional work contains strong nudity for a Mature Audience. Viewer discretion advised.

Smooth Casanova

You could play any role in this fictional work, and the people from Decorous Films and Production knew that: that's why you have been chosen for this role in this project.

You had your makeup and costume on and stood beside a few other cast members inside the apartment; you were all positioned and ready to go.

The director looked at you, smiled, then took her seat. She requested: "Quite on the set!"

Everyone sealed their lips shut, including yourself. But you were excited. Your adrenaline raced, and you were eager to take on your role in the script. The camera crew was ready. You took a deep breath to relax. It worked.

Then, after a moment, you wanted to smile when the director shouted:

"Lights!"
"Cameras!"
"Action!!!"

Take 1

The verdict was in.

"So, what is it?" Ms. Nelson yelled, facing the bathroom door. "Tell me! What is it?"

"Yes!" Rebecca shouted from the other side of the door. "I can't believe it!"

"C'mon, Rebecca! Open the door and allow me to see it!"

"Thanks goodness!"

"C'mon–"

Rebecca swung the bathroom door open, holding a pregnancy test stick in her hand. "I'm not pregnant!" she cried joyfully, wrapping her arms around Ms. Nelson. "I'm not pregnant…"

"That's beautiful."

"I know."

"Let's go to the kitchen and let's have a seat."

Rebecca said, "I'm just Happy that I'm not pregnant," walking alongside Ms. Nelson. "Because I am not ready to bring a child into this world."

"At least not by him."

No comment.

Even though Ms. Nelson knew the truth, Rebecca secretly looked at her, hoping she might be pregnant. It seemed that Juan never wanted to stay home with Rebecca, but perhaps a pregnancy could help keep him there and let them spend more time together. While this might seem a bit desperate, Rebecca thought it was worth a try. She felt empty inside and just wanted to be noticed and loved by someone, as she used to be when she had a special man in her life—someone who would wake up beside her every morning. Sadly, he was no longer around, leaving her feeling lost.

Ms. Nelson took a seat at the kitchen table.

Rebecca approaches the countertop. "Would you like to have a cup of coffee with me?"

"I wouldn't mind."

"The usual?" she asked with her back facing Ms. Nelson while searching for the sugar jar.

"Yes."

The Kitchen grew silent, only for a hot moment. Okay, maybe for thirty seconds.

Then Ms. Nelson cracked the atmosphere with "Rebecca?"

"Yeah."

"May I ask you something?"

"Sure." Rebecca glanced over her shoulder, then returned to what she was doing.

"Are you on birth control?"

There was a slight stumble for words, then Rebecca finally spat it out: "Yes, sort of. At times, I might slip a day or two from not taking my pill by accident. But from now on, I will ensure I'll be on top of that."

"Rebecca."

She twisted around.

"You won't be hurting anyone but yourself if you don't."

Rebecca closed her eyes and cried.

Take 2

"**I still can't** believe she gave you all that money," Samuel began to say as we walked into a Georgio Armani clothing store. "Only for a massage?"

"Yeah," I said, emphasizing with sarcasm, "it was a massage, alright."

Samuel cocked his head towards me. "What sort of a massage did you provide her with?"

I looked away into the clothes rack and said, "A massage that landed with thirty-five hundred dollars." I started combing through a few Armani shirts. One after another, then stopped when I got to a peach-colored shirt. I pulled the shirt from the clothes rack. I liked it. I cut back to Samuel: He was combing through another clothes rack right across from me. Then I asked, "Are you not going to ask me how I earned the thirty-five hundred dollars, doing what sorta massage to her?"

"Nope." He didn't even look at me. "I don't want to know."

"Not even as to what she looks like?"

"Nope." He placed a lime-colored shirt back into the clothes rack and then pulled out a yellow one. "I don't care. If you're spending and treating, why should I ask?"

"Well, you should ask me how old she was."

"I have no interest in that." He raised a shirt to his chest, tried to visualize it on him, and tucked it back into the rack. He didn't like it.

"Well, what if I said she looks a little like that lady over there?"

He glanced over his shoulder, then combed through the shirt rack. "I wouldn't care."

"Well, what if I say she was at least twice her age?"

He looked over his shoulder again to better see the aging lady whom I pointed out to him. Then, after a quick observation, he said, "I wouldn't believe you."

Fine then! I started combing through another rack—the sportswear. Oh, yeah, I must get this one, too. I rested an orange Armani T-shirt over my forearm, then cut to my left. Two Hispanic chicks who appeared to be in their mid- or thirties walked past, eyeing me. I nodded hello. With long curly hair, the female on the right side smiled back.

"So, who was she?"

I turned back to Samuel. "Who was she? Who?" His question threw me off. "Who, them right there?"

"No. I'm talking about the lady you were with last night."

"Why? What about her?"

"Was she twice that lady's age over there?"

"Yeah. But you wouldn't believe me if I told you about her anyway."

"Are you kidding me?"

"About which part? The one you won't believe me if I tell you about her. Or the part about I slept with a sixty-seven-year-old lady last night?"

"Sixty-seven years old?" he tried to whisper.

A few people looked our way.

"Yeah." I turned back to him.

"Is she still alive?"

"Is she?" I made a face, whispering back. "She's well alive and active. She was like an Energizer battery last night: She kept going and asking for more even when I got soft down there."

Samuel almost laughed.

"Yeah," I went on, "at first, I thought she was a masochist because she wanted me to bang her, nonstop, for hours. But after what she put me through last night, having my toes curled up in the shower, I'm convinced she's a true nympho. One of a kind. A straight dick eater, too."

"At sixty-seven years old?"

"No. Correction: She's sixty-seven years young," I said. "There's no doubt about that either. Her little freaky-ass was acting like a twenty-five-year-old, if you ask me."

Samuel finally laughed, calling me a liar, as if I were making all this up.

"Say what you want. But she worked the hell out of me, draining me for everything that I had, while getting her money's worth." I looked over my shoulder, then back to him. I wanted to make sure that no one was close enough to hear our conversation before I continued: "I had to beg this lady to allow me to take a five minute break, because around four o'clock this morning when I had her out on the balcony, doing our thing out there, she wanted me to pull out of her and shoot my nut on her back. And when I did, only a drop oozed out of me. I was empty. Dead. My reserve tank was out of commission."

"You act like you're scared of her."

"Scared of her...? That's an understatement: I'm petrified of her. She can go the whole nine yards. And I'm not lying either."

"So, are you going to see her again?"

"I don't know. Probably not, unless I pop a Viagra pill and guzzle down a 5-hour Energy drink beforehand."

He laughed some more.

Then I said, "Even with that, I'm unsure if I want to see her again. She has called my cell phone since I left her hotel room this morning, still wanting more from me." I showed Samuel my iPhone. "Just look at this—twenty-three missed calls! This is only after I told Teresa, on her third phone call, that I was going home to sleep for a while and recommended that she do the same. She said OKAY at first, but then, about an hour later, I started receiving various phone calls from various numbers. Some were out of the area, while others were unidentified. But I knew they were all from her, so I didn't answer. As I told him about the unusual calls, my cell phone vibrated again. "Look at this! Another unidentified number."

"Answer it."

"Answer it? Are you crazy?"

"No. I'm not crazy. But take my advice on this," he said. "Just answer your call, and if she asks to see you right now, tell her that you are tied up for the moment, working on something important, and you won't be able to see her until tonight. With that being said, I can pick up a few Viagra pills, if you need some, to do the trick on her. Because, as I see it, if you don't answer your phone right now, she will keep calling you until you do."

That made much sense.

To which he went on to say, "I should have the pills ready for you at eight o'clock, so you could knock her back out and put her ass to sleep. It will be some time before she thinks of calling you again."

I wondered if that was true because it sounded too good to be true for a plan.

He nodded his head.

Oh, what the hell! I answered my cell phone on the fifth or sixth ring. "Hello?"

"May I speak to Casanova?" a woman said over the phone.

"Teresa?" I thought her voice sounded a bit different today.

"No, this is a friend of hers," the lady said. Then she asked, "Is this Casanova?"

I felt more trapped than confused. But for a silly reason, my stupid-ass said, "Yes, this is he."

"Well, my name is Emma Wolf, and I would like to schedule a massage with you sometime today, at your convenience."

"Hold on for a second." I pressed the mute button and brought my attention to Samuel. "It's not her: Someone else asking for a massage."

"A guy or a female?"

"A female."

"And what does she want?"

"She would like to schedule a massage with me today."

"That's it?"

"Yeah. That's all she said…"

"I don't see any hurt behind that, if that be the case," he said. "Go ahead and massage her just in case suspicion grows that you're not a masseur."

I released the mute button to open the phone line. "Yeah, hello? Ms. Emma?"

"Yes, I am still here. But please, call me Emma."

"Thank you, Emma. But I'm sorry to inform you, I'm booked for today." I intended to tell her I would be free sometime next week, but when I heard her gasp, I changed my mind. "However, could I be available tomorrow? Would tomorrow be fine for you?"

"Yes. Tomorrow would be fine under the circumstances."

I grabbed a pen from my pocket. "The time and place of your choice?"

"Uhm. Can we arrange it for tomorrow afternoon at two o'clock? At the Sheraton?"

"Two o'clock?"

"Yes."

"Two o'clock will be fine with me." I wrote her information down on a piece of paper. "And the room number?"

"Well, I would have to call you back on that," she said.

"Okay then, get back with me on this information, and I will see you tomorrow when—"

She hung up on me before I could finish.

I cut back to Samuel and said, "This one seems easy." I placed my cell phone back in my pocket. "It would be like putting icing on a cake. How hard can—" I froze when my phone vibrated again. I pulled my cell phone back out and looked at the front screen.

The name Lu Sang didn't ring a bell.

"Hello?"

"Yes," a female voice announced with a funny accent. "I would like to speak to Casanova Massage."

"This is he. How can I help you?"

"I would like a man massage right now."

"Pardon me?"

"I would like to have a massage."

"Do you wish to have a massage from me?"

"Yes, right now. I stress."

"Can you hold on for a second?"

"Yes. But not long."

"Yes, okay." I'm like, *Whatever*, as I pressed the mute button. I twisted to my left. "Sam!"

He looked at me while combing through a few trousers.

"It's another one, asking me for a massage," I said, then asked, "What shall I say?"

"Yeah, take it. It's only a massage. You can always use the extra money."

"But I don't even know how to give a proper massage."

"Buy a DVD on massage and learn."

I waited a few seconds before releasing the mute button on the phone and saying, "Hello?"

"Yes. What's wrong with you?" she sounded upset. "I waited one hour for you?"

Knowing that she was exaggerating, I still apologized. "It won't happen again, ma'am."

"It better not. Now, what time do I see you?"

I wanted to laugh. I found her accent a bit amusing. "What time would you like to see me?"

"Yes."

"Well, my scheduling for today is booked. However, I do have an opening for tomorrow night."

"Yes, I want it."

"Okay." I reached for my pen again. "May I have your info?"

She provided me with some information, mentioning that she lives in a gated community on Fisher Island. Then, she offered some unusual instructions for when I reach the security checkpoint at the front gate tomorrow. She instructed me to inform the security officer in the booth that I work for a satellite dish company and that I had left my toolbox at Sang's place the previous day, so I needed to retrieve it. She also mentioned that she dislikes it when Larry, the security officer, calls her home to confirm that she will allow me through.

Whatever floats her boat, I thought. Yet, I couldn't see the significance of me going through a firing squad to give her a massage at her house. Maybe it was just me, but I didn't understand the secrecy surrounding it.

When she hung up, I told Samuel all about what she wanted me to go through the next day, and he just laughed. But it was a different kind of laugh. It was a laugh that conveyed a hint of mockery. He walked away first, and I followed. We headed to the cash register several times. I paid for everything on my treat. I'm only … a man of my word. We hit store after store, purchasing a few more things, then headed to a health food store where Samuel wanted to buy some vitamins.

"Hey, Cassidy! Think fast!"

I twisted to him and immediately caught a small package of tablets that he tossed up at me. "What's this?" I asked, even though I read the label. "Energy booster." I tossed the small package back. "I don't need this!"

"Yeah, you do." He threw it back at me and added, "You would need it for your new friends you told me about earlier." He checked our surroundings to ensure no one was listening, then turned back to me. "The one who lives on sixty-seven street."

"Sixty-seven Street?" I felt lost.

"Yeah." He shot me a look that screamed that I was an asshole! "You know which one I'm talking about: the one from last night."

Oh, crap! I understand now. "Let me have a few more of those."

He did, then tossed me a few more packages of something else. "They might come in handy," he said.

The last two packages he tossed to me slipped out of my hands. They were much smaller than the energy booster package. I picked one up, and the first thing that caught my eye was the bright yellow bananas on the front cover. I read the content next to it: banana flavor. I smiled. I looked at the other package, which had orange, watermelon, and peach flavors. I instantly felt excited.

"Hey, Sam!"

"Yeah."

"Is there any kiwifruit over there?" I wished they did, because I wouldn't mind squirting a tasty sperm down Ms. Ginsberg's throat, even for Teresa's throat, too, since she was a swallower.

"Yeah."

That news brought joy to my soul. "Let me have all of them!" I stormed over to him to make sure he didn't leave any kiwifruit flavor behind.

The total cost was $539.73. I paid the bill. It will be worth it, especially in the long run. We walked out of the store and then the mall. By the time we reached the car, my cell phone had vibrated.

"Yes, hello?"

"May I speak to Casanova?"

"This is he."

"My name is Debra Bromberg," an elderly woman said. "And I would like to set an appointment with you."

"For what?"

"For a Massage."

I looked at Samuel.

Take 3

Cathy leaned over to pick another seashell. She placed it in a mug. That's where she temporarily kept her seashells until she got to the house. Then she picked up another one. This shell had a little more definition and depth. It had a nice shape to it. She cleaned the sand off it with her fingers.

It had a mucky feeling to it.

She hasn't always been a collector of seashells. The project only came to her recently, as a small hobby, to occupy her leisure time when she wasn't working. She enjoyed spending time outdoors, especially on the beach, to get some fresh air, before calling it a night. Every day was like clockwork for her, taking one day at a time, as the cliché goes. She wouldn't have it any other way.

A short distance away, she saw another seashell near a bunch of elderly-looking ladies. "Excuse me," she said to everyone nearby as she approached. "Do you mind if I disturb you all for a second to pick this up?" She pointed at a seashell.

Two elderly females cut their eyes at Cathy, paying her little or no attention.

"As I was saying," a heavy-set lady jumped back into the conversation with her friends. "Does he make house calls?"

"Yes, of course," a fragile lady, who looked to be in her early seventies, said. "So, I have heard."

"Oh, my," another one said with excitement in her tone, rubbing her palms together.

The heavy-set lady cut back in. "Did Martha say how big he was?" Her eyes veered toward the group before her.

"Well," the lady on the far left threw in her two cents, "from what she has told me, he's about eight inches long."

"I have heard it was nine inches."

They all cut to the lady in the sundress with the sunglasses resting on her head.

"I have," the lady in the sundress said.

"Well," another one claimed, "I have heard he's a foot long."

"Bullshit!" the heavyset lady joked, while getting excited. "I guess I just have to call him to find out myself, then."

They all gave each other a rich chuckle—all nine of them.

Cathy looked at her wristwatch and walked away with her seashells, realizing it was late. It was ten minutes after eight.

"Young lady!"

Cathy cocked her head around.

It was the heavyset lady, with her hand stretched outward. "Did you drop this?"

Take 4

"Look out, bro!" Joey shouted in front of the computer monitor, with Bluetooth in his ear, while playing some military-style combat video game with a few of his buddies who were logged in to the computer console. "You have the Talibans on your left. Make sure you get those motherfuckers before they get me." He paused, twisting the joystick in all sorts of directions. "Fucking, yeah!" he said with excitement. "Did you see that. Did you see how far he blew back? Look out! Look out! On your right! On your right side! No, not you, Matt. I'm talking to Wayne. On your right …! Yeah! You got him … Let's check out that other area over there … Yeah."

Melissa twisted her neck to the left and looked at Joey, his back facing her. A thought shot across her mind. She smiled, barely. Then she twisted back to her PC and signed off, placing her laptop on the nightstand. She stretched to allow the energy to flow through her body. She wasn't tired. At least not yet, she thought. She got off the bed, wearing only a pajama top and panties. Pink and black. Her panties were wedged on the left side of her buttocks. She didn't pull it out. She left it there and swaggered to the home computer. She snuck up behind Joey, surprising him with her hands rubbing against his chest. He didn't say anything. Nothing at all. He didn't even attempt to look at her. He kept his eyes on the computer screen, talking trash over his Bluetooth while enjoying a video game match with his computer buddies.

This excited Melissa to be in charge. She reached in, leaning over Joey's back, nibbling on his earlobe. He flinched. She went for his ear again, but he fought her off by applying pressure against her face, pressing his ear to his shoulder. She changed her strategy and maneuvered herself before him, hoping to steal a kiss away from him instead.

13

"Look out," he whispered, craning his neck in every direction to avoid her—first upward, then to the right, left, and back up again. "Not right now." After pausing for a second or two, he spoke to his friends through Bluetooth, saying, "No, not you. I was talking to Melissa."

At other times, Melissa would have been offended by Joey's comment for not identifying her as his wife to his friend, but that wasn't a central topic or concern that she wanted to address with him right now. Instead, she wanted him to entertain that sensitive itch between her legs. She was horny; wanted. She needed Joey's help to scratch his man tool inside her love hole. That was the only reason she tried pulling his flaccid muscle out of his boxer shorts.

"No, not right now," Joey said, pushing Melissa's hand away from his private area while keeping his eyes on the computer monitor. "I'm busy right now."

"Just allow me to play with it," she whispered, hoping his friends wouldn't hear her through the Bluetooth. "I want you."

"Not right now," he repeated, stumping over to shield her from him this time as he tried to continue playing his video game with his friends. Then he shouted: "Jesus Christ! Did you see what you made me do?! You messed me up!" He finally looked at Melissa, then back at the computer monitors. "No, not you all!" he backed into Bluetooth. "I'm talking about my friggin' wife here! She acting unusual; like she's in friggin' heat or something!"

Melissa got up and walked away. She headed back to bed.

"Yeah, right!" Joey joked about something a friend had said to him. "You must be crazy, bro. Go fuck your own wife." He laughed, then added. "I know you don't believe that shit...! Whatever you say, bro … Yeah, if you throw your mom in the deal." He laughed again. "Yeah, right!" he paused again. Then he said, "Hey, Matt! Do you hear this nutcase? Yeah, you know … And have you seen those pictures he posted on Facebook of his wife?" He laughed some more. "Yeah, you know…? Ahh, fuck you too, bro!" he laughed again, playing his video game in between. "But I could tell you this, though … No, not you, Matt … Yeah you, you asshole! Who else do you think I'm talking to…? Well, I can tell you this, bro." he paused and looked behind him to see where Melissa was.

14

Melissa cut her eyes from him and rolled over to her other side, with her back facing him. She grabbed a pillow and hugged it, setting her head into it.

"Hey, Wayne," Joey twisted back around to the computer monitor, while whispering into his Bluetooth, "if you throw in you-know-who in the deal, we might have something here … You know who…? No. your sister … Nineteen…? That's a good age, bro. What are you talking about?" he laughed. "You can't keep her under a lock and key forever, you asshole."

Melissa looked over her shoulder, expressing disgust.

Joey laughed. "I don't care what y'all say," he said to his computer buddies through Bluetooth, while playing the video game with them. "But I'm the best one at this shit!"

Melissa turned back to face the bare wall, her back to him. She felt nauseous as Joey's childish behavior annoyed her. His loud and obnoxious antics while playing his ridiculous video game were overwhelming. She tried her best to block out his constant chatter in the background. She even attempted to think about work, but quickly abandoned that thought since her job consisted of forty percent of her responsibilities. Instead, she focused on her friends. She reflected on how both her old and new friends seemed happy and content in their relationships, every single one of them.

Even big Sally, who regularly weighs about 375 pounds, was happy with the Black guy she was with. He must be doing something right, Melissa assumed, while also wondering of Sally's boyfriend had a big dick. Just being curious, without any sexual intention involved. Is it fat or skinny? Is it seven, eight, or nine inches long, as they say about a Black man's private part? She could only ponder that. No, she pondered these thoughts. Or better yet, was his dick the same color as his skin complexion or something much darker? It may resemble a darker shade of chocolate, like dark chocolate. Picture a Hershey's bar, but instead of being flat and square, it's thick and round like a sausage. Imagine a heavy, thick roll of salami – a meaty kind – that tilts slightly when you try to hold it straight out from the other end.

That would always remain a mystery to Melissa, unless Sally let the cat out of the bag.

Melissa wanted to smile, hoping for that day to come soon, but the timing was off today. *Waaay* off. She wasn't in a mood to even flirt with the idea of wanting to ask Sally if she could see her boyfriend's dick to ease her curiosity about it. The atmosphere smothered her with cyanide. Joey's appearance seemed to be the main ingredient in her discomfort. She barely shook her head, unknowingly, and somehow found a way to channel Joey out of her mind. She reminisced about her college days when she joined a local sorority group, the Zayin Sadhe Incorporated, while attending Florida State University—the Seminoles.

Okay, Melissa's frown started to fade away. She had dug up an old memory of this one guy, Scott Carson, whom her sorority sisters had introduced her to. He was a true honk: tall, white, and handsome. He had short, honey-blond hair, with a nice physique that made you pause to wonder if he had been genetically enhanced with African warrior traits. He had huge muscles all over him, especially below his waist. And yes, just the thought of him brought a bigger smile to Melissa's face.

She remembered how Scott used to work wonders on her. He would toss his tongue in certain areas, with her begging him not to stop. Or with him giving her a dip of his man stick, here and there, in all three of her holes, without any hesitation. It would go down in the backseat of his car, her car, in the back study room, on the second floor, in the main library at FSU, in Zayn Sadhe's house, in the girls' and guys' rest room. And finally, in a place she would never forget at Murphy's Cemetery home in Tampa, Florida, where she got banged the fuck out from the back by Scott, leaning over some woman's tombstone by the name of Erika something.

Those days were memorable.

Melissa closed her eyes to hold onto her happy memories, but she couldn't resist the sexual urge. It was beating at her front door. She stuck her hand in her panties to help relieve some of the tension. Her breathing escalated. She thought she heard Joey laughing in the background while communicating with his computer buddies. She didn't care anymore. She ignored him, trying to block out his childish play in the background. Her thoughts were on Scott Carson when she stuck a finger inside herself, then two fingers. She focused on her feelings for a moment, experiencing a growing sensation within her. She pumped faster and faster, waiting for release.

As she reached the peak of her climax, she was taken by surprise when the bed sheet was snatched off her and tossed aside. She looked Joey square in the eyes, disdaining him in disbelief, her mouth gasping, wishing she had the willpower to cry.

Joey spoke into his Bluetooth: "You won't believe what I have just caught my wife doing?"

Take 5

I climbed off Emma Wolf after I squeezed a monster load inside of her.

We were both drenched with sweat.

I rolled from her and tried to catch my breath, resting my arm over her potbelly. Her titters were huge. No, I need to correct that: her titters were humongous. At least twenty-five pounds each, and I say that with praise. I reached over and played with her left nipple, admiring her breasts. She cleared her throat to grab my attention. It worked. She had a cute face for a plus-size woman. Other than the lack of pigment in her skin, at five six, 273 pounds, she had a healthy glow for her late fifties. Fifty-eight, to be exact.

"Dories wasn't lying about you," Emma said, resting her hand on my shoulder. "You are strong down there, and magnificently, too."

"Thank you," I reached in for a kiss. "But I think you observed all the credits because your sex was incredible. And you forced me to give you everything to keep up with you."

"You're just saying that."

"But I'm not." I just wanted to keep it honest with her. "Because from what I had experienced with you a while ago, I enjoyed every second. It's like what I said, you were wonderful. And I would only like to be honest with you."

She blushed.

I took my hand off her nipple. "Do you see this right here?"

Emma nodded her head when she felt my hand between her legs.

So, I added, "This has a beautiful, tingling sensation about it."

She made a scoffing sound, giving me a wary stare, and then that same facial expression vanished. It seemed like something ran through her mind. She opened her mouth but then closed it.

"What is it?"

"Oh, it was nothing."

"So, tell me, if it was nothing to you." I removed my hand from between her legs. "I would like to know what's on your mind."

She stammered and then said, "I wish Nicholas could speak to me like this and do some things to me like what you have done for me."

"Whose Nicholas?"

"My husband. I thought I'd told you about him already?"

"Your Husband? No, you haven't." I tried to stay cool here. "This is the first time you have ever mentioned him to me."

"Oh, I'm sorry." She removed her leg from me. "Is this a problem for you?"

"Is it?" That's supposed to be self-explanatory. I faked a smile. "No, not really," I placed her leg over mine and stole a quick look at her breasts. "It's not a problem, unless it's one for you."

She made that scoffing sound again, but this time with a smile. "It's not a problem for me. Not at all." She then rested her hand on my tool, slowly brushing her thumb over the head of it.

"So, there you have it, we're safe to continue this then." I reached in and kissed her nipple – the left one – even though I had something else in my mind. "Because I just don't want to take that pussy from you whenever I think you need a good fuck."

"You see," she blushed again. "That's what I'm talking about."

"About what?"

"How do you know what to say at the right moment?" She looked at my chest, then went back to my face. "I wish Nicholas could speak to me like this. Make me feel wanted. Sexy."

"But he can."

"You just don't know Nicholas."

"But you do, right?"

"Yes, and that's why I can say that about him."

"He's still a man, is he not?" I kept rubbing my thumb over her nipple to keep it hard.

"Yeah." She had a look in her eyes as if she wanted to kill the small talk and fuck! "But what's that have to do with it?"

"A lot. May I ask you a personal question if you don't mind?"

"No. I don't mind, go ahead."

"Are you two sexually involved in the bedroom?"

"Well, other than his affair with one of his secretaries at the office, I can still say, yeah. But not so often like we were used to."

"But the two of you are still active in the bedroom, right?"

"I wouldn't describe it as being fully active in the bedroom. But if you're referring to our sex life, yes, occasionally, we are still sexually active, in the bedroom."

That's encouraging, I thought. If they're still intimate, there's hope for their relationship. This belief stems from a similar experience of mine years ago when I was a freshman at Broward Community College. It might sound childish, but I vividly remember that time, about thirteen or fourteen years ago.

Gosh! I was so much in love with Julie.

Julie, with the cute bootie. So, they used to call her behind her back. But for me, she was just Julie. Julie Sanchez, that is. My sexy Puerto Rican mami. She was short. She was shaped like that cute chick Demi Lovato, but with long, dark, curly hair that hung down her back. Her skin complexion was a natural suntan.

We had a little something going on until insecurity unexpectedly crept into our relationship, turning it into a tense situation. It was I who first started looking at Julie differently. It felt like she transformed overnight in the bedroom. She began doing things that raised questions for me, like how she knew how to do that, and what was up with her new sexual positions. I found myself wondering if someone else was involved. Then the unspoken accusations started, and we fell into a blame game.

Speaking for both of us, insecurity took a heavy toll on me, and then on Julie. It reached a point where insecurity began to play mind games with us. When Julie wasn't around, I could have sworn she was sneaking around and sleeping with other guys. Conversely, based on her perspective, when I wasn't with her, she believed I was doing the same with other girls. Unbeknownst to both of us, insecurity infiltrated our relationship, acting as a double agent and turning us against each other by raising doubts about our commitment.

The deception continued for weeks and then months, wearing us both down. First, there was suspicion, followed by unasked questions, distrust, doubt, and accusations. Eventually, we started having heated arguments, and our conversations grew cold—very cold. How can I put it? We were together, yet not connected. She was physically present but emotionally absent. Although we tried to work things out, the spark we once had for each other was gone. The intense passion we once shared had diminished, leaving us like two wet sticks in a rainforest, rubbing against each other but failing to ignite a fire.

Things didn't work between us anymore.

We stopped hanging out, and our sex life –if that's what you wanna call it– had deteriorated entirely for obvious reasons. The excitement was no longer there. It had vanished long before I knew it. We even stopped checking on each other. I don't remember who gave up or who left first, but from what I recall, it was over between us.

"Why are you shaking your head?"

"Huh?" I broke my concentration, focusing back on Emma.

"You were just shaking your head."

"It was nothing. I was thinking about the unfortunate situation you're currently in. That's all." Yeah, I lied to her. "But where was I again?"

"You'd asked whether Nicholas and I were still sexually active? And my reply was, yes, occasionally."

"Oh, yeah, that's right." I briefly lost my focus. "But before I continue, do you mind asking me how you know your husband is having an affair with someone at the office?"

"How?"

"Yeah."

"Well, besides someone anonymously notifying me about Nicholas's affair with this sleazy tramp at the office, I'd hired a private investigator to confirm it for me."

"And you are still with him?"

"Yeah." She nodded her head with ease.

"Wow … And you don't mind him cheating on you?"

"Yes, but of course. But now I kinda used to it," she said. "He will only sleep with her for a while, then get rid of her, as he has done to the other female in the past."

The other female in the past? What kind of sh— Never mind.

I wanted to stay focused on one issue at a time. "And that's why you're here with me now?"

"Yes, because if he could do it, so can I. The two of us can play this game."

"Well, let me be honest with you then. What you have here," I smiled, while resting my hand back over her mound, "between your legs, you have the potential of locking any man down. Even me!"

She laughed. "What do you mean by that?"

Take 6

I laughed. "Emma, I'm being truthful with you. Your pussy feels like a hot incubator that was made only for a purpose of pleasing a man, with a nice grip to it. Sorta like a nice pair of grip pliers to lock a man permanently. Better yet, it's more like a heavy-duty monkey wrench. And I would like to emphasize the heavy word here."

She laughed back. "You're just saying that."

"No, I'm not. I'm serious here." I didn't mean to, but I accidentally stuck a finger in her. I watched her eyelids drop as if they got too heavy for her. "Emma?"

She opened her eyes and looked at me. "Uh-huh," she moaned, as her breathing became intense.

"Emma, I need you to keep your eyes open for me ... Emma!"

She tried to look at me again, her eyes drowsy-looking.

"I need you to block out everything that I'm doing to you right now, as if you can't feel my finger penetrating inside you."

"But how?" she panted, through her hand

"Take control of yourself."

"But how?"

"Like if you have some fucking sense! You stupid bitch!"

She broke her trance and snapped out of it. She stopped panting like a porn start and tried to snatch my hand off her.

"Wait a second! Don't!"

"What did you just call me?!"

"No, no, no, no!" I stumbled with my words, fighting to keep my fingers inside her. "Let me keep them in there for a few seconds and stay still for me."

"But what did you call me?"

I ignored her question again and continued: "Do you know how you feel right now?"

"Yes! Disrespected by you!"

"There you go." I kept playing in her love hole. "Channel that same urge you have now to another area in your mind, and continue to block out what I'm doing to you." I kept my eyes on her. It seemed like she wanted to say something, but I cut her off: "I need you to follow me here." I lay her on her back and got on top of her. Her eyes were still on mine, lying there, as if she were a corpse. I grabbed the head of my man tool between her thighs until I found her entrance. I pushed it in her. "Emma."

She had closed her eyes but opened them again.

"I need you to stay focused for a second."

"Sure." She pretended not to be interested in what I was doing on top of her, while slightly grinding back on me.

"Now look. I need you to pay close attention here and stop moving your pelvis for me."

"To stop moving my pelvis?"

"Yeah."

"But I'm not moving my pelvis."

"Emma."

"Sure, then! Anything you say."

"Well," I said—thank goodness she stopped gyrating her pelvis because I was just about to deviate from my message and toss her legs over my shoulder instead— "the next time your husband is on top of you like this, I would like for you to ask something."

"Like what?"

"Honey, how much does it cost for a good divorce lawyer?"

"Why would I ask Nicholas something like that, while we are making out?"

"Because I need you to do it. But follow me here. I want you to pretend as if I were him and ask me."

"Why Nicholas?"

"Because I need you to. I need you to pretend I was Nicholas and ask about that divorce lawyer."

"Now?"

"Yeah." I push my tool deep in her now, slowly going back and forth.

"How much does a good divorce lawyer cost?" she asked.

"No. I need you to look me in the eye and ask me, as if you mean it. Pretend if I were your husband."

Silence took over, only for a short moment.

I kept my eyes on her.

23

Then she said, "Honey?"

"Yes." I played my role.

"How much does it cost for a good divorce lawyer?"

I smiled.

She smiled back, but it wasn't genuine. Then she asked, "But I don't see the purpose of asking him that while we're making out with each other?"

"It's not the question that might seem awkward for him now. It would be the seed that you will eventually plant in his subconscious mind that would bother him to the point that he would feel obligated to ask you why you ask."

"What shall I tell him then?"

"Well," –I kept penetrating my man tool inside of her, in slow motion, tapping on her back wall– "you need to send him a warning that if you even believe that he's fucking that slut at the office better than you, you will file a divorce against ass and take him for everything he owns."

Emma's eyes drifted off, then came back. "But he would only deny it, like always."

"Yeah. The chances are, he will like all other guys will do."

"Whenever I discuss this topic with him, we have a heated argument. He insists I'm falsely accusing him, even though I saw a photo of him entering a hotel room with another woman."

"But who says you'd be accusing him of cheating anymore?" I asked, then said, "You are beyond that level already. Now, you would be making it clear to him that you're aware of him cheating on you. But the thing is this, you just let him know that if you so believe that he's fucking that other girl better than you, you will file a divorce against his ass!"

"Do you think that would stop him from having an affair with his secretary?"

"Truthfully," I paused briefly when I got off her. "There's a yes and no to your question." I lay beside her, my legs over hers. "Because first, once he knows that you are aware of his sexual relationship with his secretary, in which you're not accusing him of cheating anymore, the chances are he would slow down. He would most likely take precautionary steps to cover up his tracks. Then, eventually, he would break it off with that other girl, completely, wondering what sort of information you have on him and what you are up to? What is your overall motive? He might even start playing the nice guy to you, hoping to get your mind off a divorce and give him another chance."

"Really?"

"Yeah," I tried to reassure her. "But there are a few other things you would need to do as well to have him head over heels for you."

"Like what?"

"When he is sexing you, you just make sure that you remind him of your warning that he better not to be fucking that other girl better than you or else you would file that divorce against him. And when he starts picking back up in the bedroom, you make sure you plant some more seed in his head."

"Plant more seeds in his head?"

"Yeah. Like, for instance, when he is having sex with you, have him claim this right here." I palmed the front gate of her pink paradise. "And if he's hitting you from the back, while you on all focus, ask him whose pussy he's fucking. And when he says it's his, yell at him, if needed, and tell him to say it like he means it. Have him scream it out for you a couple of times. Bring some excitement to the bedroom. Even have him to slap your ass a few times, here and there, while he is claiming his property. But most importantly ..." My voice faded down to a complete stop.

"What?"

I wanted the suspense to build before revealing it. "You have to make sure you put the four t's on him to seal the deal."

"The four t's?" She looked confused. "What's that?"

Take 7

"The four t's are the techniques that your sweet things can offer a man to hold him down."

"This sweet pussy here?" Emma tried to play back humorously.

"Yes." I cup my hand between her legs again and stick a finger in her. I felt her hips gyrating, so I went two fingers instead. I smiled. Then I pulled my hand away and sucked the nectar of my finger.

She looked at me as if I were weird.

"Here, have a taste."

She quickly wiped her lips clean with the back of her hand—and her arms, too—then looked at me with disgust. "You are so friggin' nasty."

I laughed, then got off the bed. "Just remember, it's your pussy juice, not mine."

She got off the bed and walked to the dresser in front of the mirror. She grabbed her checkbook, smiled at me, then turned back around. As she approached the dresser and began jotting down an amount she intended to give me, I couldn't help but notice her huge knockers hanging freely in front of her. She looked at me. I smiled, and she smiled, turning back to the dresser.

Yeah, she caught me looking at her ass, too. It was somewhat nice-looking for her age.

After a moment, she twisted around and handed me a check. "Thanks for the massage."

I almost fainted when I read the check, which stated, "Pay in the amount of $3,000." I cut back to her and said, "Thank you." I tried not to get excited as I put my shirt back on.

"But you know, you had never told me about those four t's?"

"The four t's?"

"Yes. What are they?"

"The four t's are the techniques a woman should know in the bedroom. The horseback, the rodeo, the milking-a-cow, and the hula hoop technique."

"And what do those have to do with me keeping my husband under control and stopping him from having an affair?"

"Because once you master these techniques," I stumbled with a slight pause here, hoping she wouldn't be offended by my metaphor, "your husband will most likely decide not to go out to get milk if he has a cow at home that could offer him more than just milk."

"A cow?"

"Yes. A cow." I think she caught on when I glanced at her breast, then back at her.

She smiled at me. "And how do I master these techniques you are discussing?"

"To be honest with you, it takes time to master all of them. But with a little practice, you can learn the basic skills quickly."

"Really?"

"Yeah."

"So, how can I start practicing these basic techniques?"

Damn! She threw a good question at me. I veered the room, then reached for her wrist. "I will show you something here to help you practice." I led her to the dining room table, then straddled a chair, facing the opposite way. She stood in front of me, watching. I held on to the chair rest and said, "Have you ever ridden on a horse before?"

"Yes. But that was a very long time ago."

"Well, this will be something like that horse ride you'd experienced back in the day. However, I need you to perform at a slower pace. Something like this." I rocked my hips back and forth in an awkward equitation motion, trying to keep my upper body stiff. "It's very easy once you get the hang of it."

She shot me with an uncertain yet questionable look.

"Don't feel like that. All you must do is pretend like you're horseback riding." I kept rocking back and forth in slow motion to show her what I was talking about.

She still wore that same facial expression of doubt.

"Here." I got off the chair. "Give it a try."

She did, after some hesitation. Then she said, "I can't do it right."

27

"You're doing just fine. That's why I said you must practice a bit until you get it right."

"I don't think Nicholas will like the idea of me wanting to sit on top of him the whole time while we make out with each other."

"But you don't have to. With these horseback techniques and the other three techniques, you can manipulate them in all sorta positions: While you are on top. On your back, or even on your side. The only focus here is on doing any of the four t's in whichever position you're in."

"Oh, okay." She took a short breath and asked, "What about the rodeo technique now?"

"Turn around and sit in the chair like you were sitting on a saddle."

She did, with her legs on the outskirts of the chair.

"Now grab the edge of the chair." I helped set her hands in front of her. "Okay. I need you to bounce a little for me now."

"Like this?"

"Yeah. Something like that. But not so fast. I need you to do it slower for me."

"Like this?"

"Yeah, sort of. But go a little slower for me."

"Like this?"

"Yeah. There you go."

She continued momentarily, then stopped, "So what about the milking-a-cow technique?"

"Well, that technique is a little difficult if you haven't tried it before. But once you learn and get the hang of it, it will be like putting icing on a birthday cake. However, to answer your question, that technique requires you to squeeze on your man's magic wand, with your vagina muscles, every time he pumps his stick inside you. Which I strongly recommended that you squeeze your vagina muscles on him when he's cumming. Because, with those technique, you can help drain every drop of his cum out of his whose pipe for him. It would sorta be like the same concept of milking a cow, squeezing on his tool whenever he's pulling out of you, but relaxing your muscles when he's sliding back in you … That would do the trick for you, having him begging for more."

She smiled.

"But remember what I've told you before; With a little practice, you'd have these four techniques down pack. And before you would notice, you would have your man jumping through flaming hoops to get inside your panties."

"That's good to know. But you only explained three techniques to me. What about the other one? I think you called it the hula hoop technique."

Oh, yeah, that's right. "I had almost forgotten about that one."

"So, what's that technique about?"

"Stand up for me, for a sec."

She did.

"Now," I stood before her, "I want you to follow my pace again." I gyrated my hips in a circular motion as if I were twirling an invisible hula hoop around my hips. "But keep your upper body stiff like this. I want you to stay focused right here and use nothing but your hips and stomach while winding your hips in small circles."

"Like this?"

"No." I just kept it honest with her. "I need you to keep your legs and upper body stiff." I decided to stand behind her, resting my chest against her back instead. "Follow my lead here." I gyrated my hips while holding onto hers. "There you go. Stay at that pace for a moment until you get the hang of it."

"Okay."

I kept twirling my hips behind her.

"Casanova."

"Huh?"

"Why don't you teach me how to do it correctly?"

"That's what I'm doing now."

She turned her to the side to get a look at me, with her back still resting against my chest. "I'm talking about teaching me the right way without all these analogies mess."

I kept quiet because I didn't want to hurt her feelings.

"C'mon, sweetie, don't have me beg here," she said with a desperate plea in her eyes. "I'd pay you for your time and service."

"But this is going to take some time to get them all right. You can't learn them all in one or two sessions."

"I know. That's why I want you to teach me everything I need to know. I'm willing to pay you for any number of sessions I'll take to get them right."

That's a big pill to swallow. I was just about to tell her to let me think about this and get back to you on it, but she cut me off with something soft and sweet.

"Please-eeee," she dragged, knocking about thirty years off her age. Then she said, "I would be under your total submission and do whatever you want me to do—any and everything. I'm a fast learner. I am." She kept her eyes locked on mine. "And if you want me to work on the rodeo technique first," she began, rocking her hips back and forth, "I would need your help to get it right." Then she switched her style up. "Or what about the hula hoop?"

Okay, that did it. She didn't need to say anything more. I was sure I could find a suitable time slot for her in my schedule. "When would you like to start?"

"What about now?" she kept gyrating her hips on me.

I smiled. It seemed like she had read my mind. I walked her back toward the bed, with my mouth over her nipple—the left one.

Take 8

As the hostess ushered Rebecca through the restaurant, several men in business suits were eyeing her. Some greeted her with either a nod or a soft hello as she walked past them. They all had that ogle look in their eyes as if they wanted to leave a good impression on her, hoping that one day they might perhaps bump into her to crank a conversation up.

Like, "Hey, you look familiar," or "Hey, I think I know you from somewhere," or "Excuse me, ma'am, but do you remember me from the Tout d Vous restaurant in Boca? "

Rebecca had heard about every single pickup line before. While passing by, they downplayed their greetings with a simple smile. Then she spotted Ronald and Linda a short distance away, and her smile grew.

Linda saw Rebecca approaching before Ronald did. She rose from her seat.

Then Ronald stood up.

"Oh, my goodness," Linda said with her arms wrapped around Rebecca. "I thought you were never going to show up."

"I ran into some traffic along the way."

Linda let go of her. "Where's your date?"

"Who, Juan?"

"Yeah."

"Uh, he couldn't make it. His boss has assigned him to work on a major project. But he promises to make it up to y'all."

"Oh." Linda didn't buy it.

Rebecca looked across the table at Ronald. He had just sat back down, with an ineffable look. She couldn't read it. And besides, it didn't stay there very long. It was only there for a second or two before it disappeared. She tried to encourage a smile.

Ronald attempted to smile back, but his smile quickly faded. Instead of saying "hello," "hi," or "how are you doing," he chose a different approach and spoke honestly: "It's been a long time, Rebecca."

"I'm sorry. I don't have any excuses for my absence. I shouldn't have done that–"

Linda cut in with a joke, saying "Damn right you don't have any lame excuse to give us," at the same time throwing a playfully punched at her arm.

Rebecca cowered. Her face had a frightened Melania Trump look, without bruises or scars. She was caught off guard, but then she relaxed once she realized who it was.

Linda was smiling at her. "You better not pull another disappearing act on us again."

"I won't." Rebecca tried to smile back.

Linda took a seat, then Rebecca followed.

"So," the waitress said, "are you ready to place an order now? Or do you all need some more time?"

Ronald looked at Linda, and she looked back at him. Then they both looked at Rebecca.

"I'm ready if you are," she said to Linda, then looked at Ronald.

With that, Ronald jumped straight to the menu and told the waitress, "I would like to have a beef tenderloin with a cucumber mango salad as a side dish."

"And you?"

Linda looked to her left. "Chicken?"

Rebecca barely nodded her head. "Sure."

Linda turned to the waitress and ordered, "Two apricot chicken with baked hash. And can you have the chef go light on the salt?"

"Sure. And would you like to have a drink with your meal?"

"Yes." Linda smiled. "Can we have a bottle of El Muga Prado?"

"Would that be all?"

"Yes."

The waitress walked away.

"What's the special occasion?"

Linda twisted back to Rebecca and said, "You ... It's not so often that I see my best friend. And I think this special occasion is enough to celebrate."

Rebecca was lost for words. She could only manage a smile, a forced yet painful expression.

About forty-five minutes later, while enjoying their meal, the waitress stopped by their table again and asked, "Would you like to have another bottle of wine?"

"No thanks. This would be fine," Linda said. "But you know what I would like to have?"

The waitress stood still, all ears.

Linda finished off her request with "A chocolate meringue pie." She then turned to Rebecca. "You must taste it. It's delicious."

"Sure. Why not?"

Linda looked at Ronald; he shook his head. She then twisted back to the waitress and said, "Just make that two meringue pies."

"Great choice, I will be back shortly." The waitress walked away again.

"It's just like old times," Linda said to Rebecca. Then she added: "Do you remember the last time we were here together, and that other waitress over there asked Cassidy if that was all he wanted to order, and he said no. But when she asked him what else he would like to have, he told her that he would like for her to bust that nasty zit on her forehead before she brings us our check, and we all burst out laughing."

"Yeah, I remember that." Rebecca was already laughing with Linda, but immediately stopped somewhere around here. It felt like an old kitchen knife stuck her in the chest.

"What's the matter?"

"It's nothing." Rebecca rested her fork, then slid her chair from the table. "Excuse me for a moment. I must visit the ladies' room."

"Well, let me go with you."

"No. You don't have to."

"Girl," Linda said as she stood up. "You're not the only one who has to go in there."

They both walked away and went to the restroom together. After they used the latrine, they went to the sinks.

"I'm delighted to see you again," Linda said while standing in front of the mirror, tracing eyeliner underneath her left eye.

"Me, too."

"So, tell me," Linda started decorating her other eye now. "What have you been up to?"

"Nothing really," Rebecca muttered, with water running over her hands, sort of in a trance-like state.

"Rebecca?"

"Huh."

Linda turned off the faucet Rebecca was using and grabbed her wrists. "Are you okay?"

"Yeah. I'm alright. Why do you ask?"

Silence hovered around them.

Then Linda said, "Rebecca…"

"What? Why are you looking at me like that?"

"Rebecca?"

"What?"

"I'm your friend. Please don't lie to me. Are you okay?"

Rebecca tried to hold that phony smile on her face as long as she could, but she couldn't; she gave in when she lowered her head.

Linda repeated: "Are you okay?"

Rebecca let go of her pride and began to cry.

"What's the matter?"

"I miss how we used to hang out together," Rebecca said. "All of us, me, Ronald ... Cassidy. And I miss him so much that I don't even know who I am anymore."

Linda wrapped her arms around Rebecca, Rebecca's arms around Linda, crying.

Linda saw their reflection in the mirror. Then she noticed something. Perhaps a livid, but she wasn't sure. She pulled away and raised Rebecca's sleeve. It was then that she saw a bruise on Rebecca's upper arm. "Is he beating on you?"

"Who, Juan?" Rebecca tried to play it off, pulling her arm sleeve back down. "Of course not. I hurt myself while I was at work the other day."

"Are you sure?"

"Yes, I'm sure."

It got quiet around them.

Then Linda finally broke their silence when she grabbed Rebecca by the hand. "Follow me in here," she said, leading the way into a stall. She then closed the door behind them. "Let me see it."

"See what?"

"Your legs."

"For what?"

"You know exactly what it's for. So don't play stupid with me." Linda knows plenty of women who were once in abusive relationships with a guy. And like all the cowards she's heard about, they would leave their trademark of bruises on a woman's body—when they couldn't get their way—by hiding the livid marks underneath the victim's clothes. "Now show me your legs."

"But why?"

"Because I wanna see them."

"Girl, you are crazy." Rebecca tried to laugh it off and went to open the stall door, but Linda stopped her.

"We're not leaving here until you show me your legs."

Rebecca looked Linda in the eyes. She knew Linda was serious. It was written over her face. Rebecca exhaled, dismantling her phony smile. "Linda, please don't do this."

"Show me..."

"Linda."

"Show me!" Linda shouted, but didn't mean to.

Rebecca considered it for a moment before finally relenting. She lowered her pants, letting them fall to her knees, exposing her thighs.

Linda's bottom lip shivered. "That fucking bastard." She cried.

Take 9

"**Why don't you** stay the night with me?" Lisa Sang said with a funny English accent. "Because there's a lot more where that comes from?"

"I wish I could, but I can't." I took my eyes off the personal check she had just given me. Fifteen hundred dollars. I folded it in half and then tucked it into my shirt pocket. "It's getting late."

"It's only eleven o'clock."

"I know." I wanted to laugh because I had been with her for the past four hours straight. "But to be truthful with you, I have a lot of work to do in the morning."

"Are you sure you don't want to stay till then? What can I say to convince you to stay here with me?"

"Nothing. I doubt it. But I must go." I fasten my belt buckle.

She paused, giving me that dejected look again. Then she said, "I can't believe you're bypassing this opportunity to take advantage of me. Full advantage."

"And you're wondering if I'm sure about that?" I slid my shoes on, starting with the right one, then the left.

"Yes." She nodded softly, her face breaking into an ingenious smile.

Very tempting, but I had to pass up on that offer. "Yeah, I'm sure of that."

She looked disappointed.

"Don't do that." I took a step toward her. She lowered her head. I raised her chin and looked into her eyes. Beautiful Asian eyes slanted slightly upward. I could only imagine how sexy she must have looked back in the day if she looked like this now at sixty-one years old and five feet tall. She still held onto her youth. I leaned in for a kiss. She pushed her tongue into my mouth; I pulled back. She couldn't kiss that well, but she gave it her best

36

shot. I broke free from her because I knew where this would lead us: to somewhere I would be forced to finish. "You know what I can do for you?"

"What's that?"

"Give me a day or two" – I reached in for another kiss, I don't know why I did that – "and I'll make it up to you."

"A day or two?"

"Yeah." I kissed her again. Oh, now I know why I kissed her a short moment ago. She had little lips. Then I said, "If you're good until I get back, I might have a nice surprise for you."

"Like what?"

I thought about slicing kiwifruit with a glass of martini. I know that would do the job for her, turning her little ass out. I want her from the back, while she's on all fours, with her face pasted on the bed.

She playfully slapped my arm," Why are you smiling at me?"

"Oh, it's nothing."

"So, tell me what sort of surprise you have in mind for me?"

"It wouldn't be a surprise if I told you now. Would it?"

"I guess you're right."

I kissed her and reached for my blazer hanging over the sofa armrest.

She walked me to the front door; I opened it.

She slammed the door shut. "Don't go out there like that." She seemed a bit paranoid. "I need you to tuck your shirt in before you step outside. Because I don't need the neighbors speculating about anything over here."

"But this is a flannel shirt. This is how you're supposed to wear it."

"I know. But you must tuck it in front of me. Just this once."

"Okay. But only under one condition."

"Under what sort of condition?"

"You have to tuck my shirt in for me."

She smiled, then unfastened my belt buckle. I didn't have any underwear on. She knew that. My pants dropped to my ankles.

Nine Days Later

Sometimes, things remain unchanged.

Take 10

For Juan, there's no doubt about it, he would rather be waiting on Shakira, J. Lo, Sofia Vergara, or better yet that sexy-ass white chick Iggy Azalea from Australia that to be waiting on this stupid southern bitch!

He blew his SUV horn the moment he saw Rebecca exit Powell's Gym. She smiled when she spotted him sitting in his black, tinted-out Hummer—a H2 2003 model. He cracked a smile back. She put a hop in her step and headed to the SUV.

"Alright bitch, I got my eyes on you."

Rebecca twisted to the left, glancing toward the sidewalk. "Hey!" she smiled.

It was Jahmal, standing next to his partner, Corey, sporting a rainbow-colored Obama smile. "Girl!" he started with a slight drag before he said, "You better stop stealing my clientele."

She said, "I can't help it if they like what they get from my aerobics class."

"And we both know why."

"Yeah" – she blushed – "because I'm more flexible" – she flirted a bit when she tapped her index finger against her hip – "and hot … You tramp!"

He laughed back. "Whore."

"Ouch! That one hurt."

Jahmal and Corcy both laughed when Rebecca rested her hands on her chest. The left side, over her heart.

Then Jahmal said: "Well, I'll see you tomorrow, girl. Have fun because I know I am."

Rebecca smiled back, tittering. "Tomorrow." She then turned back toward the waiting SUV. Seconds later, she popped the passenger door open and climbed in. She reached for a kiss from Juan, but he remained still. He even puckered his lips toward her.

There was nothing there. There were no feelings or emotions involved. *Nada.* It was like kissing the back of one's hand. Go ahead, give it a try.

"What's the matter?" she asked when she saw the disdainful look on his face. "Have I forgotten to do something for you?"

Nothing.

If a look could kill, it would have been a homicide crime scene.

Then Juan finally broke his silence to ask, "Who the fuck was that?" He barely shook his head to the side.

"Who?"

He looked through the windshield. "That motherfucker right there."

"Who? Jahmal?"

Juan cut back to Rebecca.

She made a scoffing sound. "Sweetie, he teaches one of the aerobic classes in there: a few doors down from mine. Believe me, you don't have anything to worry about him. He's gay."

After a slight pause, Juan mocked: "He's gay, huh?"

"Yeah."

"Do you think I'm fucking stupid to you?"

"What are you talking about?"

"I saw how he was looking at you. And you were just standing right there, teasing him right back; just like a little fucking whore that you are!"

Rebecca wiped the little expression she had on her face, looking more stoic now. "You are overly reacting about this," she said, twisting toward the windshield, then to the passenger window. She didn't want Juan to see her tears.

Juan pulled out of Powell's Gym and drove silently, not saying a word to her.

And it bothered her.

She didn't know what disturbed her more: the silent treatment or getting her ass kicked by him. Either way she looked at it, she hated when her feelings were ignored. She wanted to turn around and say something to him, just about anything. But she didn't know where to start. Periodically, she glanced at Juan and then back at the passenger window. It was like clockwork, hoping he would eventually look back at her, but he didn't. Not even a glimpse from the corner of his eye. There was nothing at all. He kept driving. She had no choice but to listen to the reggaeton he had on the whole ride home.

She broke their silence only when Juan pulled up in front of her apartment building. "Are you not coming inside?"

Juan kept his eyes on the windshield, not wanting to give a response or look her way.

"Juan?"

Nothing

"Juan, can we at least go inside and speak about this?"

Juan sucked his teeth and turned the music volume up on her.

Rebecca stayed still and kept her eyes on him, not knowing what to do from here. A crazy thought came to mind. Then, another one. The first thought that came to mind was to tell Juan if he leaves, never to come back again because she was through with his bullshit! The second thought: she wanted to spit in his face, because he deserved it.

But she decided not to go with either of them because she knew where that would lead. A straight ass-whooping! She broke down and did something different. She reached over the console and tried to kiss him on the lips, but he pushed away. She felt trapped, left out in the wilderness. She looked at the clock on the dashboard. It read 5:52 pm.

She cut back to Juan, then kissed him on the cheek instead. "I'd be in the house waiting for you to return whenever you get in."

Still, no response. But the message was well received, loud and clear: he had her in the palm of his hand.

Rebecca pulled the door hatch and got out.

Juan drove away.

Take 11

"What do you think so far?" Ms. Ginsberg tried to whisper with her back facing me. "Do you like what you have in front of you?"

I carried four bags in one hand and three in the other, while walking through Aventura Mall wasn't hard enough already when people were constantly bumping into you –now imagine here– I had to keep my eyes focus on her buxom ass without losing sight of it.

"So, tell me." She began to ask, "What are you going to do with this when we get home?"

No comment. I kept it to myself.

Ms. Ginsberg twisted her neck to look at me. "Why are you smiling?"

I broke my focus on her rear when she stopped walking. "There's no reason, ma'am."

"Are you lying to me?"

"Yes."

She laughed. "Now tell me," she began to ask, but then froze right there when three bystanders walked past us. Then she finished off what she was saying as they walked ahead of us; "What are going to do with all this ass in front of you when we get home? Now dazzle me, hon."

"Can I be honest with you?"

"Yes." She smiled.

"I'm gonna tear that ass up, only if you allow me too."

Her smile changed into something perverted. "If," she sounded a little offended by my comment. Then she made a scoffing sound before adding, "That's a bit of an understatement. But yes, I will allow you to, only if you are man enough to handle it."

I kept quiet because –beside the point that she's playing on dangerous ground right now, so to speak– that other day when I had her in a doggy-style position, I was plunging my dick so far up her ass, she was begging me to stop. But I wouldn't. She shitt'd all over my dick, crawling and squirming all over the bed as if she was the Amazing Spider Woman fighting to get the hell away from my Gotham dick. Especially toward the end when she felt off the bed and landed flat on her stomach; in which, I grudged fucking her right there on the spot.

I swear, I tried to tear her little freaky-ass up that night, as if tomorrow wasn't promised to me. She was slipping and sliding all over the marble floor. And the only reason why I stopped ponding my dick in her so hard, was because, I busted a heavy nut inside of her love tunnel after –which I want to emphasize on this word after– she stopped squirming. She allowed her sphincter to milk me dry while doing the rodeo technique on me.

"So be careful now," I warned jokingly. "Because if you're not careful what you're asking for, I would toss your ass up in one this dressing rooms to teach you a lesson or two."

"Hmm, I think you're bluffing," she said, twisting back around and starting to walk again. "Let me see if I can find you a dressing room to put you to the test."

So be it: She was the one who would feel it. Every bit of seven and a half inches of man steals inside her.

"What about in here?"

I looked over at the Armani shop. "Nope! We can't do it in there," I said, while trying to keep up with her. "They kicked us out of there last week."

"What about over there?"

"At the Nautica?"

"Yeah?"

Even though she had her back toward me, I still shook my head. "That's one place we can't go. After that little episode you pulled in their dressing room, I think they have completely banned us from that store."

"Well," Ms. Ginsberg said, taking a quick peek at me and spinning her head back around in front of her, "if you had stopped when I told you to, the security guards wouldn't have kicked the door open on us."

I would rather not comment on that one, because how could I have stopped myself when she was the one who was doing all the work, pumping back and forth, with her evening dress lifted over her rear, her panties down at her ankles, screaming "Don't stop."

"What about over there?"

I followed her head movement and looked to the right. A naughty smile grew on my face when I saw a rose-colored fluorescent light hanging over the department store's entrance: *Victoria's Secret.*

"Are you sure?" I asked because I was down for whatever.

She looked at me to say, "Please don't insult my sexual urge," before spinning her head back around. "Of course. I'm sure." She started to veer off to her right.

"So, you don't need to say anything more because–" I shut the hell up when I felt a heavy slap across my face.

At the same time, I heard someone say, "You dirty motherfucker!"

I was caught off guard for a few seconds—okay, maybe about two seconds if you want to be technical about it. I didn't know whether to let go of the bags or punch the instigator in the face with the bags in my hands. But when I turned to face this perpetrator, I couldn't believe what I saw.

It was my long-lost buddy, Brad. "I knew that way you!" he said. Then he asked, "What the hell have you been up to?"

Take 12

I was still in shock!

Brad wrapped his arm around me; I dropped my bags and hugged him back.

"It has been a long friggin' time, dude."

"I know." And I was serious about that.

Brad was the first one to pull away. He kept his eyes on me, smiling. "What's up with the new look? I like it."

I felt like a little kid, wishing he would stop playing with my hair. "Shit, look at you." I studied him back.

He unloosed his ponytail so his hair could hang free, just a little, posing on his shoulders. "It's about the same length as yours," he said, combing his fingers through his hair. "So honestly, what have you been up to?"

"Nothing. I'm just working here and there to save money before making my next move."

No response.

Brad kept quiet, as if his mind had drifted off somewhere, looking at me.

Then I added: "What about you?"

"What about me?"

"What have you been up to?"

"Oh." He snapped out of it, throwing a smile back on his face. "Other than living my life to the fullest, I still play around with the stock market while doing little gigs at the clubs."

"Gigs?" I was puzzled, but then again, looking at his body frame wouldn't surprise me a bit. "So, you work as a bouncer?"

"Nah." His smile widened. "I striptease at a few nightclubs down here."

"Get the hell out of here!"

"I'm not lying to you." He looked over his shoulder, then back at me. "I strip dance with my friends over there."

I looked over his shoulder. I saw two black guys with a child standing beside them. I cut back to Brad. "You're pulling my leg."

"Dude, I'm not gaming you here. I even go by the stage name as Mikey."

"Mikey?"

"Yeah."

I still didn't believe him. That wasn't his character. Better yet, I doubted if he even knew those people over there.

"I'm not lying to you."

I looked over his shoulder again. I'm sure of this now: he didn't know them. The little girl who was with those two guys had an annoyed expression on her face every time I looked their way. She seemed bothered by it.

I cut back to Brad, but before I could say anything to him, he said, "Allow me to introduce you to my friends anyway." He twisted around and beckoned them over.

Yeah, right. I was still in doubt. I wanted to see how far Brad was willing to go with this. But he hadn't waved those people off yet as they approached us. I twisted around to check on Ms. Ginsberg; she was watching me. Our eyes met, and we looked at each other. She tapped her wristwatch, indicating that I needed to pay attention to the time. I was. That was the only reason I raised my index finger to about shoulder length, essentially telling her that I needed another minute. I smiled when I saw both of her hands shoot up in the air as a hopeless gesture. She looked upset at first, but then nodded her head while rolling her wrist in a repeated circular motion, signaling that she wanted me to hurry up. By the time I turned back to Brad, the people he claimed to know had approached us.

"Hey, guys, this is my friend Cassidy," Brad said to them. "The one I was telling y'all about last week. We go back a long way with each other." He then turned to me now. "Cassidy, this is my friend Kevin."

"It's nice to meet you," I extended my hand.

"The same." He shook my hand.

Brad cut in, telling me, "This DaShawn."

"It's nice to meet you, too."

"Likewise."

Brad cut it again: "This young lady's name is Destini."

46

"Hello." I extended my hand to her, but she didn't meet me halfway. There was no handshake. Nothing at all. I looked at the guy who stood beside her. "Is she your daughter?"

"Yeah." DaShawn began to say, "She's my little princess."

"She's a spitting image of you." Besides their eyes, to me, they both had the standard features of each other.

"I hear that a lot."

I cut back to her.

She just stood there, with a repulsive look, as if I had said something awful about her.

Then DaShawn added, "Please excuse her manner. She tends to get a little grouchy around this time of the day." He looked at his wristwatch, then at Brad. "On that note, it's already seven forty and I have to drop her off at Aunt Enid's house before it gets too late." He paused, then added: "I'll see you at the club tonight."

"Cool."

DaShawn twisted back to me and said, "It was nice meeting you."

"The same here."

Kevin nodded his head; I backed.

Then they walked away, leaving me and Brad to ourselves.

I just shook my head when Brad looked at me. "I can't friggin' believe it," I scoffed out a little laugh. "You're a male stripper?"

"Yeah. For the past two years, ever since I left."

We both fell into silence.

Then I broke it: "I'm sorry for what you had to go through about Monique. You didn't deserve that from her."

"Bro, that's old news. I'm way over that now. I'm just happy that I saw her for who she was behind my back: a floozy trick, with nothing going for herself."

I wanted to share a similar story with him, but I decided not to.

We fell into silence again.

Oh, what the hell! "You know–"

He cut me off: "I heard about what happened between you and Rebecca."

That was all he said to it; nothing less, nothing more. He let it linger in the air.

I stood there stunned. His words and facial expressions caught me off guard. It felt like a punch. I didn't know if I wanted to stumble backward or hold my jaw instead. But what I did know for sure was that after swallowing my pride, I asked him, "How did you find out about that?"

"Ronald had told me about it."

"Ronald?"

"Yeah."

"So," I asked a silly question, "you two are back in contact with each other?"

"Yeah, but of course. Shouldn't that be obvious since he told me about you and Rebecca?"

"Yeah. I guess you have a point there." That was something I was afraid of: Being exposed, for others to know about.

Take 13

"If you don't mind me asking," I began to question Brad, trying my hardest to hold a smile on my face. "But how did you and Ronald start talking again?"

"How?" he made a wry face as if my question sounded foolish. Then he mocked: "How did we start talking again?"

"Yeah?"

Brad sorta shook his head with a smirk before he said, "About a month ago, a friend of mine by the name Ciara was checking out her Facebook page in which one of friend sent a message to everyone she knew on her friend list, asking them to write a lovely elegy or join the memorial service over the web for you. And when she asked—"

I cut him off because I could have sworn I received that wrong. "For whom?"

"For you." He laughed.

Damn! My old friends have written me off just like that, by pronouncing me dead to forget about me.

"But check it," he went on to say, "when Ciara asked me to help her with an elegy, I read the obituary over the Facebook page to see what I could say. But I broke down in tears when I found out it was for you." He punched me in the chest. "I thought you are friggin' dead, bro. I did. That was the only reason why I called Ronald to see what had happened to you. But that friggin' bastard tricked me, telling me he didn't want to discuss it over the telephone. And you know me already, I immediately shot over to his house to find out what had happened to you. But that slick-fucker then told me that he wasn't sure whether you were dead or not, only telling me that he had Linda and one of her girlfriends to come up with something conniving to fish you out." He barely shook his head humorously. "But instead, I fell for the bait. So,

49

there you have it, that's how we got in touch with each other again."

"Oh." That was wishful thinking.

"But seriously, bro," Brad dared to tell me, "You shouldn't be cutting your friends out of your life, especially Ronald. He's worried about you." He paused and then added, "Don't look at me like that. I had my reasons for staying away."

We fell back into our quiet zone again.

Then my iPhone vibrated.

It was a text message from Ms. Ginsberg: "Get rid of him and let's get on with it."

I twisted around to look at her. She was paying attention to her cell phone, punching in the keys. I twisted back to Brad, smiling.

"We have to stay in touch," he said. Then he pulled his wallet out from his pants, drawing a business card from it. Then he asked, "Do you have a pen on you?"

"Yeah." I passed him a Sharpie instead.

He crossed something out on the card and started jotting something else. Then he said, " Here," passing a card to me. "You have all my information on that. Just make sure you stay in touch with me."

"Sure thing." I looked at his card. It appears that he crossed out the name 'Mikey' and wrote his name near it, along with a few more telephone numbers. "I'd make sure to do that."

He then pulled out his cell phone. "So let me have yours," he asked.

"What, my info?" I wasn't sure about that.

"Yeah, what else do you think I would be asking for?"

My iPhone vibrated again. I looked at the cover text message.

It was from Ms. Ginsberg again: "What the hell's going on? I'm waiting for you. Now get rid of him and bring your ass over here!!! Just watching you from a distance makes me horny. So, hurry up!"

When I cut back to Brad, he said, "I'm not leaving your sight until you give me your info."

I twisted around to look at Ms. Ginsberg, then at Brad again. I gave him my number, and he keyed it into his cell phone. And before I could say anything to him, my iPhone vibrated again. I looked at the front screen. I was confused. It wasn't from Ms. Ginsberg this time. It was from someone I didn't know. A female. Someone by the name of Ciara McKinney.

"Are you gonna answer that or what?"

"Nah, I'd let the answering machine grab it instead."

"Bro, answer your damned phone. It might be important."

Yeah, he might have a point there. So, I answered it: "Hello."

Nothing. The phone line is clear, but I can hear some background noise. I wasn't sure who or what it was.

I repeated, "Hello?"

Then Brad raised his cell phone to his ear and said, "Hello," back to me.

"You asshole!" I pretended as if I was about to punch him in the face. "Why would you do that?"

He laughed. "I wanted to be certain that you gave me your right telephone number," he said. "And I can't wait to tell Ronald and David, and let them know who I saw in the mall today."

"No. Don't!" I nearly panicked, which sounded more like a desperate plea than a request. "You can't allow anyone to know that you saw me."

"Look, we are all friends here. How would it look if I hid this from them? Especially Ronald?"

I kept quiet.

Then he added, "You eventually must come out of your shell. I know I did."

Why did I come to the mall today? I pondered.

"Look," –Brad wiped the smile off his face, looking more serious– "I'm being honest with you right now. You should give Ronald a call; he's worried about you. And if you don't call him to let him know that you're safe, I will."

"Just let me think about it."

"Alright. That's your choice. As you already know, friend or no friend, I love you like a brother. But if you don't call him soon to let him know that you're doing alright, I will have to make that call for you."

I swallowed hard. "I would need a little time to myself. I'll call him."

"Cool. You have until Tuesday."

"Tuesday? That's less than a week away."

"That's more than enough time for you."

I swear, I wanted to tell Brad to *Go fuck off* for putting me in this unwanted predicament. But I settled for something different: "Alright. Give me till Tuesday, then." I reached for my bags. "But in the meantime, let me get out of here because I'm in a bit of a rush to get somewhere."

"Yeah, me too. But make sure you stay in touch."

"C'mon, dude. That's a must." In the back of my mind, I had intended to call MetroPCS and have them disconnect my cell phone number and provide me with a new one.

"Alright then," he said. "It was nice seeing you again."

"The same here." I gave him a dap, with the bags in my hand.

We both went our separate ways. He veered off to the right; I went straight ahead. I took a quick look behind me to see if he was watching me. Yup. He was, with a smile on his face, as he put his cell phone to his ear. I twisted back around and walked over to Ms. Ginsberg when Brad made a right turn by a concession stand to exit the mall.

"What's the issue with you?"

"Nothing."

"Well, whatever it is." Ms. Ginsberg began to say when she hooked her arm over mine, walking me into Victoria's Secret. "I know the perfect remedy to make you feel better again."

Take 14

Rebecca placed the telephone back in the cradle.

Juan advised her that he would be home shortly.

She looked at the clock on the wall. It read 7:15 p.m. She started placing a dinner plate on the table. She knew he would be pleased with the meal she had prepared for him. It was one of his favorites: smothered pork chops and yuca, along with white rice on the side.

She waited ten minutes, then twenty minutes. By now, it was five minutes after eight o'clock. Juan still hadn't shown up as he promised. She called his cell phone. No answer. The answering machine picked up, directing her to leave a message. She decided not to. He must be on his way home, she thought. She hung up.

She waited for a few more minutes—still no sign of Juan. By now, an hour had gone by; then another hour, then another hour. She looked at the clock on the wall again. It read 11:42 p.m. Just when she was about to pick up the dinner plates and put them away, she heard a key rattling in the door lock. She smiled, positioning herself as a sex symbol, with one hand resting on the table. A carnal thought came to mind. She slid the left side of her robe down her shoulder to expose the negligee she wore underneath it. She wanted to entice him. It was red.

Juan opened the door and froze just as he was about to enter. He smiled when he saw Rebecca standing there and asked, "Were you waiting up for me?"

No words.

Rebecca just nodded her head while lowering the other side of her robe to expose the top part of her negligee to him.

Juan's smile widened as he stepped inside the apartment, leaving the door open. Seconds later, a dark-complexioned

53

Spanish guy entered the apartment behind him. She quickly covered up and twisted around, her back facing them.

Juan walked over toward her. "You cooked dinner," he said, while wrapping his arms around her from behind. "And it smells good too." He kissed her on the neck. Then he asked, "What is it?"

She could smell the liquor in his breath. "Pork chops and yuca," she said, then lowered her voice for Juan to hear her alone: "Why did you bring someone over here with you? I told you I had a surprise for you."

"Uhh, don't worry about him. He only stopped over for a few seconds. He's gonna be leaving soon."

"Well, let me change into something more appropriate so I can fix you a meal."

"Give me a kiss before you go."

"Later," she whispered while trying to escape his grip. "When your company leaves."

"C'mon," he dragged with a slur, "it's only a kiss."

She gave in and kissed him—only a peck.

Juan held onto her wrist and said, "Gimme another one."

She did, holding her lips against his a second longer than the first time. But when she pulled away from him, her curiosity rose. She stood on her tippy toes again this time to smell his neck. Then his shirt collar. She was sure of it: she smelled a woman's perfume that wasn't hers on him. "Let me go."

"What's the matter?"

"Let me go!" she snapped, freeing her wrist from his grip.

"What's the matter with you?"

"I'm not stupid!" she stormed away, heading toward the bedroom. "You were with that fucking bitch again!"

"What the hell are you talking about?!" he followed behind her. "I wasn't with her, I swear."

As soon as Rebecca stepped inside the bedroom, she tried to slam the door behind her, but Juan prevented her from doing so.

He pushed himself into the bedroom and approached her. "What's the hell is your problem?"

"I know you were with that stinking bitch again!" her voice broke into a cry. "You have her scent all over you!"

"Rebecca, I told you that I swear already. I wasn't with Sandra when I went out tonight."

"So how in the hell do you have her smell on you then?!"

He stammered, then said, "Okay then. I'm not gonna lie to you."

Rebecca was all ears. Although she wanted to hear the truth, she was still hoping he wouldn't drop the bomb on her that he was sleeping with her.

He continued: "I visited my friend Alfredo's house today, where we argued at your workplace. That's who's out there right now. He is a good friend of mine. We had a few beers and decided to go to a bar in Palmetto afterward. Then before I knew it, one drink led to another."

"But," she cut him off, "were you with her?!"

"Who, Sandra? No."

"So why do you have her scent all over you then?"

"Sweetie, I just told you that I was at a bar. There were a few females in there, and perhaps one of them might have worn the same perfume Sandra wears, leaning against me. This happened at least once or twice, but it was only accidental. You know you're the only one who can satisfy me sexually. I mean, mentally."

Rebecca lowered her head, slowly shaking it.

Juan raised her chin, then said, "You know I won't sleep around on you. So don't think foolishly. Your mind is only playing tricks on you."

"But how do you expect me to act when you come home with that smell on you?"

"I don't know," he stammered. Then he asked, "Don't you trust me?"

No comment.

She lowered her head again.

Juan raised her chin once more. "Don't you trust me?"

She broke down and said, "I want to."

"And you can."

Before Rebecca could respond, he kissed her. It was something regular, nothing out of the norm—just a regular peck on the lips, but much softer. Then he reached in for another kiss, and then another until she eventually gave in and kissed him back. He cupped the back of her neck and kissed her again. She welcomed it by wrapping her arms around him, whispering his name softly every time she had a chance.

"Juan..."

His hand dropped from her neck to her back, then her buttocks. He squeezed both, while pulling her closer to him.

"Oh, Juan...," she softly whispered his name again.

He nearly slammed her back against the wall and pulled her robe off, exposing her negligee, as if she weren't anything. It was transparent. He lowered his head to the left side of her breast, and at about the same time, he pulled it out of her negligee. He sucked on her nipple first. Hard. She held onto the back of his head, wanting more. He carried her to the bed, then laid her flat on her back. He got on top of her.

"Juan, what about your friend out there? We should wait till he leaves."

"He's not gonna come in here."

"But what if he hears us in here?"

Juan hesitated for a split second, then said, "Dame un segundo, mi amor," in his Spanish tongue just before he jumped off her and ran out of the room.

Rebecca smiled, then eased over toward the center of the bed.

About a minute later, Juan returned to the room, very anxious to get where he left off. He climbed back on top of her, with an eight-inch dildo in his hand.

"Did he leave?"

"No", Juan said while trying to take her negligee from her. "He was out there watching a movie. So I turned the TV volume up and told him I would be here talking to you for a while." And just when she was about to say something, he cut her off by resting his index finger over her lips and said, "Make love to me."

He didn't need to say anything more. Rebecca twirled her tongue around his finger. Juan removed his finger and placed his tongue in her mouth instead. Then their tongues wrestled, as she helped him take his pants off. By the time he managed to slide his man tool inside of her, her pink paradise was soaked and wet. He pushed it deep inside her. Her head sank into the pillow.

"Ohh, yes," she moaned. "Don't stop…"

Juan kissed her.

"Don't stop."

He didn't. He kept pumping his tool inside of her, giving her everything he had on every drive. She couldn't hold out any longer. She started rocking her pelvis back on him. She felt her climax building up. Her pussy was on fire, and she needed to cum to put her flames out. But then she was thrown off when Juan stuck his tongue back in her mouth. Her tongue fought back.

Then Juan switched it back up on her, placing his finger back in her mouth, slowly pumping it in. "Keep sucking it for me." He panted with his finger still in her mouth. "Pretend like it's my dick in there." He swallowed hard, grinding his man tool inside her love tunnel at the same time. "Suck it for me. I want you to pretend like I had two dicks in you. One in your mouth and other one in your pussy … Now I wanna cum in both of your holes."

She couldn't take it anymore. She was on the urge of cumming now. "Don't stop," she managed to say with Juan's finger in her mouth.

"Suck it for me."

And just like that she tightened her lips around his finger, sucking on it, as if that was his secondary dick.

"That's it," he whispered in her ear. "I want you to suck on this dick for me."

She moaned, tell him not to stop, "I'm about to cum."

"Just suck it for me. I wanna cum with you."

She applied more pressure to his finger, maintaining a better grip, and pumped her head back and forth over it while increasing her pace.

Then, suddenly, Juan pulled his finger away, tantalizing her with it. She stretched her tongue out. She wanted his finger back. No, his secondary dick back in her mouth. And he gave it back to her, pumping his finger back and forth in her mouth while slamming his man tool inside her.

She moaned that she was about to cum.

"Suck on this dick for me … Suck on it."

She took his finger in her mouth and sucked it.

He started giving her a better fuck, going deeper in her, tapping on her back wall. He whispered in her ear. "I want you to suck it for me."

She moaned.

Juan whispered in her ear again just before he pulled his finger out of her mouth again. "I want you to suck it for me; as if it was my dick in your mouth."

"Ohhh, Juan, I will. I will do it for you … Ohh yes, you know I will suck it for you. Just put it back in my mouth."

Then, within seconds, she felt a sensitive sensation travel through her body, especially over her lips. She knew it wasn't Juan's finger anymore because it felt heavier and wider. Much broader, she thought about that huge dildo that Juan had in his hand just a short moment ago when he came back inside the room to her. The same dildo he used on her last week, and the week before. That same black artificial dick he had purchased from an adult's toy store on Broward Boulevard the previous month. She was sure that it was. She stuck her tongue out to catch that secondary dick in her mouth, but it just brushed against her lips. She thought Juan was toying with her. Then, about a second later, *if that,* that plaything shot across her mouth again, but this time with a light tap against her lips, then another tap.

"Suck it for me," Juan softly whispered in her ear. "I want you to suck on that dick for me, as if it was mine." He then started fucking her with a strong arch in his back. "Put it in your mouth and suck on it for me."

She flicked her tongue out and started playing back with that secondary dick of his, using the tip of her tongue against it. And just when she was about to cum, she opens her mouth to take this hopeful, make believe dick in there. She sucked on it for a hot second, probably for about four seconds before she cocked her head away to get it out of her mouth.

"What the fuck is going on?" she snapped after realizing that wasn't a dildo in her mouth but rather someone's dick. It was a real dick. She knew the difference.

To which Juan practically begged, "No, baby. Don't stop. I want you to suck it for me."

She tried to break free from Juan, but he had her pinned down. He was on top of her, still pumping his man tool inside of her.

"Juan!" she shouted, trying to push him off her. "You're fucking friend is in the room with us! Get the fuck'd off me!"

Juan kept pumping.

Take 15

"Rebecca, listen to me first," Juan said, while lying on top of her, pumping his man tool inside of her. "Listen to me." He began gyrating his hips, reveling in the sensation. "It would mean so much to me if you would do this for me?"

"Juan, do you know what the fuck'd you're saylng to me?"

"Yes, Rebecca. But I love you. I swear I do. I need you to do this for me."

"Juan." She couldn't believe what she was hearing from him. Her voice broke into a cry. "Not like this."

"Please…" He then eased his mouth to her ear and whispered: "Just this one time. That's all I ask for." Then he sucked on her earlobe as he kept sticking his tool in her.

"Juan…"

"Ohhh, Rebecca … You feel so fucking good."

"Juan…"

"Please, my love. Just do it for me this one time."

"But I can't."

"Yes, you can," he whispered in her ear. "I love you, just do it for me … Ohhh, fuck. Your pussy feels so good … Rebecca, you can do it. Do it for me," he pushed for a hot moment, panting in her ear. Then he added, "Just close your eyes and pretend like it's my dick in your mouth. Because you know how that excites me."

"Ohhh, Juan…" She wanted to cry.

"Just do it for me, Rebecca. For me." He sucked on her earlobe again. Then he added, "Close your eyes for me, and don't think about it. Just do it for me and make me happy. I love you."

Nothing.

She kept quiet.

Then Juan repeated, "I love you," in her ear. "Do it for me."

Rebecca broke her silence with a moan: "Ohh, Juan..."

"For me. Please do it for me. I love you."

She started gyrating her hips in a slightly circular motion to counteract his.

"Do it for me."

"Ohh, Juan..." She closed her eyes, feeling him picking up his speed, going deep in her.

Then she heard Juan say, "¡Date prisa, Alberto, vuelva a meterlo en la boca!" in his native tongue.

She could only assume that he had told Alberto to hurry up and go to her mouth again because within seconds, she had Alberto's dick in front of her; up and close. It was dark and meaty, not to mention long, too. It looked about the same size as an eight-inch dildo; if not, stronger. She tried not to entertain the thoughts of another man's tool in her. In this matter, another man's python was at the entrance of her mouth like this. She closed her eyes and left her mouth open for him to get his rocks off on her.

Alberto started rattling the head of his snake over her lips, then lowered it into her mouth. Rebecca laid there flat on her back, her head tilled to the side, her mouth opened, as Alberto slowly pumped his dick in there.

About two minutes of that, Juan then decided to maneuver Rebecca around so he could fuck her from the back. She went for it. Straight doggy-style. On all fours.

Then within a short moment Alberto was up on his knees in front of her, with his swollen dick rock hard. He was ready now. He grabbed the back of her head, hoping to position her right. She shook his hand off her head, throwing one hand over his pelvis area to push him back. He grabbed her hand and rested it on his dick. She was cool with that. She tried to jerk it off for him. She was no longer on all fours but only on three, yanking her hand back and forth over Alberto's dick, hoping that he could get off like that instead. But when Juan started pounding her from behind, she lost her balance and fell forward. Her head rested on Alberto's pelvis area, forgetting all about his dick in front of her.

She tried not to moan out when Juan revved her pussy up to the maximum, but she couldn't help it. She let go. She moaned out loud, very loudly! She tossed her head away from Alberto's body, straight to the mattress. Ass up, face down, she moaned like she was in labor but in a good way. A perfect way.

Smooth Casanova

She was on the verge of cumming this time. Any second now. She felt Juan going in and out of her, faster and faster, while beating on her back wall, with his thumb over her asshole. She couldn't hold back any longer –to hell with the moaning shit– she screamed with joy when she started squirting. Her pussy muscles spammed with one strong contraction after another one. Juan kept drilling inside her. Then, seconds later, she felt another orgasm building up inside her. It felt like a big one. A huge one. But she knew it would take some time to get there again. She couldn't wait. She started pumping back on Juan, biting her lower lip, making an ugly face.

Alberto felt left out. He wanted to participate, too. So, he lay flat on his back, picking Rebecca's head up a little to rest on his pelvis. It wasn't long after that he grabbed his dick and groped it around her lips until he found an opening. He barely pierced his way into her mouth before she let him in. Just the head of his dick. Her mouth felt good and warm to him. He wanted more. She opened her mouth a little wider this time for him, resting more than just the head of his dick inside there. And when he felt her head going to work, barely working her way down on him, he pumped his dick in her mouth, trying to get a little more of his rod in there. It worked. He pumped again, hoping to get her mouth more active. That worked, too.

Rebecca raised her head, in an upright position, with Alberto's dick in her mouth, slowly bobbing her head up and down. She used both her mouth and tongue to pull and suck on his rod at the same time as she went to work on him.

Alberto finally relaxed and let her take over. She eased up a bit to suck on his dick right, in a much better position for both, while Juan doing her from the back.

"That's it," Juan said to Rebecca, pumping his dick in her, as his balls slapping against her ass.

Rebecca's head started picking up more speed, bobbing her head faster over Alberto's dick as she applied a little more squeeze of her jaw muscles around him. She gripped her mouth over his rod, with a little tug each time she stroked him with her mouth. He burst off in her mouth only when Alberto couldn't take it any longer.

Rebecca realized what she had done for this stranger and felt dirty about herself. Her conscience bothered her. She had already swallowed half of his cum but not all of it. She spat the rest of his semen on the bed.

"What's the matter?" Juan asked her why she had just suddenly leaped off the bed. "I didn't cum yet!"

"I don't care." She tried to reach for her robe on the floor near the end of the bed, hoping to cover herself. "I can't do this anymore."

"The hell you can't!" Juan tried to grab her.

But Rebecca shook her arm loose from his grip.

Juan leaped from the bed, naked below the waist, his shirt open, and he tossed her to the corner of the room. He charged after her with his palm raised, hand raised facing the opposite direction, as if he was about to backslap her across the face around the same time. Alberto walked out of the room. The doorbell rang. He stopped himself. Then, a second later, there was heavy rapping on the door.

"Bitch!" Juan grabbed his pants off the floor. "We aren't finished with this yet!" he quickly got dressed and walked out of the room to find out who was at the door. He opened it.

It was Ms. Nelson: she wanted to know why the TV volume was so loud.

Juan ignored her as he and Alberto walked out of the apartment together.

Ms. Nelson felt a terrible vibe. She stepped inside the apartment and shouted: "Rebecca!"

Take 16

"Remember," Samuel threw an ideology up in the air just before midnight, as both of us sat outdoors in the backyard, watching a few pedestrians on the beach, "history shows that people condemn what they didn't understand."

I thought about his statement for a second. I paused. I shook it off. I thought about it again, then grabbed a cold beer.

"I saw that!"

I turned back to him, feeling lost. "You saw what?"

"That damn look you gave me a second ago when I said people condemn what they didn't understand. Do you disagree with a known fact?"

I almost shot him with that same reproving look again. "I wouldn't say that he statements you made are a known fact about people. However, to answer your question, yes. I would have to disagree with your point that you made a short moment ago."

"What are you, an idiot or something?"

I'd rather not answer that, as it might lead to an argument as well.

Then Samuel said, "I don't know how you can contest that. I can easily name you about a million events off the top of my head to back up what I'm saying to you."

Okay, that did it. "Go ahead and name one."

"You want me to name you one?"

"Yeah."

He stabbed me with a piercing stare, as if I put him under the spotlight, and said, "Fine then." He took a deep breath, then asked, "Have you ever heard of over-the-counter medication? Prescription drugs?"

"Yeah. And your point?"

"Well, my point is this for your information: these prescription drugs are either made from herbs, plants, insects, or animal parts."

"Yeah, so they say. However, I'm not a pharmacist to contest that. But what does this have to do with people condemning what they don't understand?"

"A lot has changed since the sixteenth century. Back then, when Africans were found to be using certain herbs and animal parts to create their medicines, they were labeled as witch doctors and deemed savages. Many people condemned them for their practices, even going so far as to burn them at the stake. Ironically, the very same groups that once called these Africans practitioners of the devil now use the same ingredients in their own medicines. Today, those who once condemned the African practices refer to themselves as pharmacists instead of witch doctors, highlighting their hypocrisy." He paused to take a sip of his beer. Then he added, "Now isn't that a bitch?"

"That doesn't count." I grabbed a few cashews from the bowl. "Name another one?"

"Another one?"

"Yeah." I nodded my head while chewing on a cashew.

"Okay. What about females then?"

"What about them?"

"What about them?" Where in the hell have you been for the past decade or so? Because not only what's going on right now, but history shows how females have been mistreated throughout the ages, compared to guys."

"I don't buy that."

"Yeah, I expected you, out of all people, would say something like that to me," he said. "But just look at it. Females' integrity and essential qualities have been assassinated by men nearly from the beginning. For example, Mary Magdalene in the Bible. It claims that she was a whore. But ask yourself, was she really?"

"I mean no disrespect, but I do not believe in the Bible. I only read the Torah."

"But you've heard of the story of Mary Magdalene and Jesus, right?"

"Sort of. But I'm not all that familiar with them, though."

"Well, the Bible painted Mary Magdalene as a whore because they wanted to discredit Jesus as the son of god. But the question we should ask ourselves, was she a whore, or was she Jesus's mate? As we both know, the Romans did the same thing with Cleopatra and Marc Anthony. They said that Cleopatra was a whore. But was she? Of course not. They tried to discredit her as a whore in hope to destroy her reputation among the people of Rome, because right after the senate assassinated Marc Anthony, his inheritance falls in the hands of his children who Cleopatra bore for him. But here, the senate refused to allow any African descendant to play a role or any role in white Rome."

"But what does that have to do with condemning what they don't understand?"

"Everything," he said. "In today's arena, women like Hillary Clinton and Nancy Pelosi are often rebuked because we don't know what to expect from them. Why is that? Are we afraid or intimidated by the strength of women's intellect and unwillingness to understand it? Or are we simply too insecure to accept a woman in a position of power?"

"C'mon, man, you're taking this a little too far now."

"Oh, am I?"

"Yeah." I nodded my head again.

"So, other than me throwing up the fact that in synagogues and mosques alike, females are required to sit in the back while the men sit up front, why don't you tell me why you disagree with the concept that people condemn what they don't understand, then?"

"And you want me to counteract your argument by giving you my opposition to yours?"

"Yeah, just one."

I smiled. "I can sum it up in just two simple words for you."

He scoffed with a short laugh. "I would just like to see you do that. Go ahead. Let me hear it."

I did when I said, "The Holocaust."

"I knew you were going to say some shit like that!" He got up from his seat, heading for the glass doors. "Every damn time you would have a Jew in the corner; they always scream out the holocaust to you..."

I laughed when he stepped inside the house, going off at the mouth and saying he should have used the Black card on me first.

My cell phone vibrated.

It was from Emma Wolff.

I smiled. I wanted to take the call, but I decided to let her leave a message instead. She always does. Then, about a second later, my cell phone vibrated again.

65

This time, the call came from somebody else by the name of Ciara McKinney.

The name looked familiar. But where? A client, I thought. Nah, I know all eight of my clients' names by heart. So, I let the answering machine pick up the call, too. Then it dawned on me: That missed call was from Brad.

I cracked a smile, only a small one, while shaking my head. Then a thought occurred to me, and then another.

What the hell!

I dialed an eleven-digit number while blocking out my telephone number. After the fourth ring, I heard a weary voice dragging across the phone.

"Hello?"

I kept quiet.

Then the voice said, "Cassidy, is this you?"

Without saying a word, I hung up on Ronald.

Take 17

By the time Maggie grabbed her bra off the floor, the alarm clock went off.

It was after 4:00 a.m. Four twenty-seven to be exact.

She walked over to the night table beside the queen-size bed and hit the snooze button on the hotel alarm clock.

But it was too late, Juan had woken up. "Are you leaving already?"

"Yeah." She kissed him. "I have to go home before Kyle expects something."

Juan looked at his wristwatch and then back at Maggie. She had a body frame built like an hourglass –like, *Wow!*– a perfect 10. She was well-developed in all the right places, with a milky white complexion that gave her a healthy glow.

"But I thought you said he went out of town for the weekend and told you to have fun at the club?"

"Yeah, he did. But I told him that I would be home by three o'clock, but it's already after four. I don't want him to call the house to check on me and find out I'm not home."

"Well, he did tell you to enjoy yourself, right?"

"Yeah."

"So, take his advice." Juan reached for her wrist, then pulled her back toward the bed. "Another hour won't hurt you."

"No, Juan." She was already back on top of him. "Not right now. I need to go home before he calls the house. Why–" Juan kissed her on the mouth to shut her up, but she managed to continue anyway: "Why don't you call me later tonight so we can meet up here again?"

"Shhh ... You talk too much," he whispered. Then he gave her another kiss before saying, "Let's not waste any more time. We have the room for a few more hours."

Maggie's breathing grew stronger when he started nibbling on her chin and lips. "Juan…" she panted, hoping that she could control herself.

"Shhh …" he kissed her again; she kissed him back. Then he added, "Let's not talk. I want you to enjoy yourself."

He went for her panties; she helped him pull them off. She couldn't take it any longer. She grabbed his bent sausage and groped it between her legs until she found an opening. The head of his dick slipped in her. She then gyrated her hips to get the rest of his man's tool in her, but Juan took over. He flipped her over in a kitty position, straight on her back, with her knees spread high. He had about six hours to play with her. He pushed himself deep into her raw.

She dug her fingernails into his back, begging for more of him.

He gave her his all, even though he heard his cell phone vibrating on the night table beside him. He knew the possibility that the phone call was coming from only one person. *Rebecca.* The reason behind that was that she had been trying to reach him all night long.

"Fuck me from the back!"

Juan agreed. He immediately flung Maggie on all fours because that's what he intended to do anyway. He didn't waste any time thrusting himself back inside of her. She grabbed onto the bed sheet in front of her –her hands balled up into fists, her back arched– as if she were on a racing horse, throwing herself back against him every time he pushed himself deep inside of her.

He slapped her across the backside and shouted, "Whose ass is this?!"

Maggie stammered at first, but managed to say "It's yours! It's all of yours!" while throwing her ass back on him.

Another slap. "Say it again!"

She did.

Take 18

"Oh, but of course," Ms. Ginsberg said while on the telephone, sitting at her desk. "As the saying goes, those who control the food control the population." She paused for a short moment. "Uh-huh." She paused again. "Oh, sure. So let's buy four thousand shares of Ethanol that you're referring to." She paused again. "Uh-huh." Another pause ... "Okay, but what about adding six more thousand on corn and three ... On wheat ... Yes ... Yes." She paused again. Then softly moaned, "Ohh, yes ..." She straightened up in the chair. "Oh, no. I wasn't talking to you. I was thinking out loud about something. So where were we?" She paused again, but this time it was a little bit longer than the other ones. "Oh, I see." Another pause. Then she asked, "Which option do you think I should choose...? Hold on for a sec." She shook her leg to grab my attention when she said, "Hon."

I looked up at her, with her big toe in my mouth.

Then she continued: "I need your help on something."

"On what?" I sorta babbled with two of her toes in my mouth now.

"On which stock to invest in."

She must be joking, I thought. I knew nothing about the stock market.

She asked: "Ezchip or Radware?"

I shrugged my shoulders, and at the same time, went to work on her other toe.

"Just pick one. Anyone. It's yours anyway."

I pointed between her legs with her pinky toe in my mouth, sucking on it.

She blushed. "I'm serious. I need you to pick. The first or the second one?"

I went with the first thing on my mind: "The second one."

"Pardon?"

"The second one."

She seemed to have liked the idea when she jumped back on the phone and said, "Yeah, let's go with Radware for now." She paused, "Uh-huh … Uhhh, let's say about two thousand shares … Yeah ... Uh-huh …Tonight?" She paused, looking back at me.

I looked back at her, keeping my eyes on her. She smiled when I slowly dragged my tongue over the top of her foot.

"Snookum," she jumped right back on the phone, "tonight is a bad idea, it's not going to work." She laughed richly. "No. No. It's the timing for me. That's all. I have already made dinner arrangements with someone, and it's likely to be a long night… No. It's no one you know… yes, a guy." She paused with a slight laugh, then said, "No, you don't know him ... No, of course not. It's strictly business… Uh-huh… Well, don't allow me to hold you up then… Uh-huh, tomorrow. Whew!" She looked at me again and quickly jumped back on the phone. "Snookum, I must go. Something has just popped up … Yeah. Okay, tomorrow." She hung up smiling.

I slowly parted her legs, with my hands positioned on both of her legs, with me in between. She adjusted herself in the chair, scooting a bit downward. I looked up at her again. She gnawed on her bottom lip, watching every move. When I reached in, she started moaning, and I hadn't even licked my tongue across her golden spot. I heard my cell phone vibrate on the floor beside me; I ignored it. Then I went in for the kill.

Ms. Ginsberg closed her eyes the moment I sucked her pussy.

My cell phone vibrated again.

Take 19

Rebecca opened the apartment door just as Juan was about to stick his key inside the lock. "I'm sorry," she said, while wearing tiny spandex shorts that nearly looked like a little boy's briefs. "I didn't mean to get you upset."

"Don't worry about it. It was nothing." He tried to smile, admiring what he saw. "But I was in the wrong, too, because I should not have snapped at you."

"No," she said, really believing it was all her fault. I shouldn't have tried to embarrass you like that in front of your friend last night." She took a step closer to him and asked, "Do you forgive me?"

"I don't know," Juan painted a phony look of deception on his face, trying to be humorous about it. "Should I forgive you?"

"Yeah," she enticingly bobbed her head, taking another step towards him. "I think you should. Because I stayed up all night, waiting for you to come back home to make it up to you."

"Oh, did you?"

She bobbed her head again, then rested her hands on his chest.

He kissed her; she kissed him back. She tried to unbutton his shirt, but he stopped her.

"I would like to take a shower first," he said. "I slept in the car all night, and I have a terrible odor on me."

"I don't care."

He gave in when she started nibbling on his neck, working her way down to his chest area. Then further down. She went for his zipper; he helped her. As quickly as she wrapped her mouth around his flaccid muscle, she promptly took it out of her mouth when she smelled a distinct odor that wasn't hers. She wanted to puke, but rather, she spat whatever he had on him on the floor.

"How dare you?!" She hit him as she got up. "How can you do this?!"

Juan caught the second blow the moment she threw a fist at him and asked her, "What the hell are you talking about?"

"You know exactly what I'm talking about!"

"Wait a second!" he grabbed her arm when she tried to walk away from him. "I wasn't with anyone last night."

"You're a fucking liar!" she shook her arm loose from his grips. "Just get out of my face! I'm tired of all your fucking lies!"

"Rebecca!"

"Get off of me!" she broke free again. "And go back to that bitch, where you have just come from!"

He grabbed her arm again when she tried to run into the bedroom. She tugged; he pulled her back toward him. Then, based on an instinct, she swung her other arm back at him, hoping to knock his hands off her. It worked, but her roundhouse punch socked him in the face. His face was out of all places. She didn't mean to hit him—she swore she didn't—but it happened so quickly. Technically without any exaggeration here, this loser, low life, womanizer, woman-beater, spic, or whatever the heel you want to call him, literally snapped!

He let go of her arm and threw her in a headlock instead, with his chest against her back. "You stupid bitch! You wanna put your fucking hands on me!"

"Get off of me!" She tried to mule kick him with her heels when he raised her off the floor. But even that didn't work. He had run her into the bedroom door, busting it straight open. She cried: "You are hurting me!"

"Shut the fuck up! You fucking puta!" he tried to toss he on the bed to bit on her like a punk that he was, but they both fell on the bed together, with him on top of her. Their legs dangled off the edge of the bed.

"Get the hell off of me!" she shouted, acting more hysterical now than before because she was flat on her stomach. "You're choking me!"

Juan tried to snatch her off the bed, with him on top of her. But they fell back on the bed again, with both of their knees slamming to the floor.

"Get off of me!"

Juan tightened his grip.

"You stupid motherfucker! You're choking me!"

They both started squirming and twisting.

"You know what, fuck this shit!" was all Juan said when he loosens his choke. He held on to her, using only his forearm now on the back of her neck to pin her down. With his other hand, he tore her spandex shorts to the side and went for his dick. He grabbed it around her meat loaf while straddling her legs apart. She was crying. Dried as a wool blanket.

She screamed, "Don't!" and tried to fight him off her. "Get the fuck off me! You sick bastard!" She fought some more until she felt that first punch on the back of her head.

She saw a flash of light. Juan's punch didn't knock her out; it only dazed her.

"You stupid bitch!" he pushed himself in her.

Then she felt another punch. Darkness shadowed her, but only for a second, or maybe for two seconds. She was dazed again. She barely got her vision back. A short moment later, she felt her body rocking back and forth, slumped over the bed, with Juan drilling her from behind. It felt like a broomstick was plunging inside of her. She didn't know why, but that's what it felt like. Dry and hard.

All she could say without uttering a single word to Juan was "Please. Stop!"

She felt a slap over her head this time.

"Don't."

Another slap.

"You're hurting me. Stop!"

Then there was a punch on the side of her face. Probably over her temple area, she thought. Well, at least that's what she believed his first hit her with since darkness blanketed her, knocking her straight to sleep.

The doorbell rang.

Take 20

I kissed Ms. Ginsberg before I stepped out of her penthouse.

"Make sure you call me to let me know you've made it home safe."

"Now, don't I always do that?"

She extended her hand and pulled me toward her, gripping my waist. "Now," she joked, inches from my face, "don't you start getting sassy with me?"

I smiled and reached for a kiss.

Ms. Ginsberg nearly panicked. She stepped back inside the penthouse, then craned her head out into the hallway, hoping that no one would see us. "All right now," she seemed relaxed. "You better be careful."

I took a step closer. "Or, what?"

She took a step back. Then another step.

I took the bait, taking another step towards her.

Then she grabbed me and tried to slam the door shut behind me. But I stopped it just in time.

"Why don't you spend the night with me?"

"Claire, what did we agree on from the beginning?"

She kept quiet.

"It's only best this way."

Then she broke her silence: "For Whom?"

"For both of us." I wrapped my arms around her. I reached in for a kiss. "Let's not spoil the fun."

"Alright." She gave in. "But just make sure you're here first thing in the morning."

"Like clockwork."

She patted me on the ass. "Now get on out of here before I get horny again."

I gave her another kiss. "Tomorrow morning?"

"Tomorrow." She finally shoved me away. "I need to get some sleep anyway."

I stepped out into the hallway, looking at my wristwatch. It was after ten o'clock. I cut back to her. "I'll see you in the morning."

"Fine. Now get out of here, I said."

I walked away, and she watched me the whole time. Even when I stepped onto the elevator cart, its door closed behind me. I blew a sign of relief because I couldn't wait to get to my cell phone. I had twenty-nine missed calls and sixteen messages left. I knew seven telephone numbers from my fast dial, but the other four were confusing. I didn't know who they belonged to. But I still listen to all messages on my way to the first floor. All the messages had the same thing: My service was needed. I called Lisa, Emma, and Nicole as soon as I got in my car. The others would have to wait until Tuesday night when I'm free.

"Okay," I said into the receiver, then cranked the car up. "Well, I would see you tomorrow at eight o'clock." I paused. "Okay then. Later."

Nicole hung up.

Our date was set for tomorrow night. She wanted to go out to grab something to eat first, then straight to the hotel afterward.

That was something I couldn't refuse. She loved pulling her denture out of her mouth when we got to business.

I pressed the END button, then froze. My curiosity arose. I hesitated at first, then shut the car engine back off. I dialed another eleven—digit telephone number. Someone picked up the phone on the third ring.

A long moment of silence past between us, then a voice shot over the phone line: "You fucking prick! You better not hang up on me again."

No response.

Then Ronald added, "I can't wait to get my friggin' hands on you! You fucking asshole!"

I finally said, "Whatever…"

The phone fell back into complete silence.

Then, after a moment, Ronald said, "Cassidy…?"

"Yeah."

"How long would it take to reach our old stomping grounds?"

"I don't know," I hesitated a bit because I knew where this was leading. "Probably about half an hour, why?"

"Alright then. Meet me there," he hung up.

Davis Zebrowski

I called him back, hoping he would agree to postpone this meeting arrangement. I needed a little more time apart from him. But when he answered his phone, he hung up on me again.

That shit pissed me the fuck off!

I threw my cellphone against the dashboard.

Take 21

It took me about forty minutes to get to Fort Lauderdale pier. I could have gotten there much quicker, but I wanted to stake the parking lot out first to ensure Ronald came by himself. And by the look of it, he did. He stood in that same spot, slumped over with his forearms resting on the wooden rail, for about twenty minutes straight.

"Hey!"

He twisted his head around first, then his whole body. Then he stood straight up, looking at me. He seemed lost for words.

So, I said, "What's up?" hoping to play everything down.

I didn't know what to expect when he took a few steps toward me. A punch? A slap? A headlock? I was prepared for whatever he threw at me. But when he took his last step, he hugged me. I hugged him back.

"Man," it sounded like he was about to cry, "it's good to see you again." Then he broke free from me when I let go of him. "What have you been up to?"

"Just taking everything slow."

"Dude!" he smiled. "What's up with the new look?"

I didn't know how to answer his question. But I settled for something that couldn't be contested? "I needed a little change."

"A little change my ass!" he began to look again, scanning me up and down. "You don't even look like the Cassidy that I once knew. But I like it, though."

I didn't respond to his compliments because, knowing him, they were all feigning—a phony front. I stepped away because it was my turn to rest my forearms on the rail. I kept my eyes out for the ocean in front of me. Then, seconds later, he took his place beside me, on my left side. We stood there in silence, listening to the ocean waves together, clashing against the pillars beneath us.

Then I asked, "How's Linda doing?"

"How's Linda doing?" he mocked me with a bit of anger, twisting toward me. "I can't believe you would have the audacity to ask me that question!"

I kept quiet. This was the Ronald I knew.

He continued with, "Do you have the slightest idea as to how many friggin' nights I stood up waiting on a call, while praying that I didn't receive any bad news about you? Well, do you?!"

I looked at him, then at the ocean again. "You don't understand."

"Understand what?!" he shouted, while standing straight towards me. "That you run away from the people who loved you?"

I had to look at him again, hoping my statement, "You don't understand," would resonate with him.

"Understand what ?!"

"Man!" I shouted back, standing up to face him. "I fucking loved her!"

He toned his voice down: "So that's the main reason for you to run?"

"Yeah," my voice dropped low, too. Then I cut back to the ocean.

"So, whatever happened to us?"

I kept quiet.

Then he said, "I thought we were like bros?"

I murmured, "We are."

"Well, you have a good way of showing it." He cut to the ocean, using only one hand on the rail.

The sound of the ocean waves took over again.

Then I asked him, "What would you have done if that were Linda?"

"Linda?"

"Yeah."

Without any hesitation he said, "I would have been over at your place, sleeping on your friggin' couch until I sorted things out first. But I would have never jumped up and left, without telling you anything first."

I kept quiet.

Then, after a few seconds, he broke the silence between us: "So, how are you making it?"

"I'm doing alright."

"And financially?"

"I'm good."

"Are you sure? I brought some money with me until I hit the bank tomorrow."

"I'm good. Believe me."

He cut back to the ocean after I did.

Then I asked, "How is everything with you?"

"Everything is alright. It's the same shit. Things haven't changed much since you left, other than these bustards in Washington, D.C. kept raising our taxes so that they could live off our hard-earned money."

I almost laughed at the thought of this new life, where paying bills and taxes are the least of my worries.

"What's so funny?"

I cut back to him. "Nothing. I'm just happy to hear your voice again."

"Yeah, fuck you, too!" he nudged me in the side.

I laughed.

He laughed back when he punched me in the chest.

"You asshole!" I kept a smile on my face.

"Well, that makes us both about even then."

"Whatever…"

We looked at each other briefly before he shook his head and said, "I can't believe I'm standing beside you."

"The same here." I gave him another hug—a much longer one this time. I let go of him first. "So, tell me," I started to ask, "what the hell has been going on since I left?"

"Man, where shall I begin?"

I barely wried my neck to the side, about the same time I said, "Anywhere."

And he did when he said, "David got fired from work again. But—"

I cut him off: "For what?"

"He got into a fist fight with Joey. But I got him his job back."

"What the hell did they get into a fight for?"

"Which one, the first or the second one. However, either way you look at it, both fights were about you."

"About what?" I was confused.

"As you know, Joey already said some fly-shit about you, and David decked him in the face a few times. And we both know how David can get when he hears people talking smack about us."

"How is he doing?"

"Who, David?"

"Yeah."

"Man, it's the same old thing with him," he said. "He's taking one day at a time. Other than that, nothing much has changed about him."

"And Linda?"

"The same with her. Movies, parks, et cetera, et cetera. The same old routine as her, too. You haven't missed anything."

I smiled when I cut to the ocean again.

"And from what I have been told," Ronald began to say, "Rebecca has been getting the crap beat out of her by the guy she is with. She probably shows up to work about two to three times a week. She even looks to have hit rock bottom from the last time—"

I cut him off: "I don't want to hear about her." I shot him a serious look. "That's her problem. Let her live with it."

"I guess you're right."

We both fell into silence briefly, until we started talking about David again. Ronald initiated the topic, and I laughed my ass off when he told me that David finally got the chance to have sex with Sharon. I wish I had been there to hear firsthand from David himself. From what I vividly remember about him, he probably thought he was the man after being with Sharon, the golden stallion. I could see him now, talking trash and claiming how he had Sharon in that position, while bragging about himself nonstop.

Ronald told me about a new guy named Marcus at my old workplace who is involved with several women in the front office— Vanessa, Jennifer, Tiffany, and Sandra, for example. Marcus has reportedly had relationships with nearly all the women at Powell's Roofing and Shutters, including Henry's wife. It all made sense to me after Ronald explained that Henry, whom we both knew from Powell's Roofing, mentioned Marcus to his wife during one of their company picnics to belittle him. According to what Ronald heard through the grapevine, Henry had told his wife that Marcus was involved with several women at work, and they were all aware of each other but didn't mind.

This information, to make a long story short, must have intrigued his wife Alice about Marcus' sexual ability in the bedroom because – other than Ronald had personally saw Alice snuck off with Marcus at least twice during and after the company picnics – rumor has it that they have been coming out of hotel rooms together on a few occasions.

I could honestly admit I missed certain aspects of my old life.

When Ronald's cell phone rang, he nearly panicked, telling me not to say a word. Then he answered his phone. "Hey, sweetie. What's up?" He paused, then said, "No. I'd met up with an old friend of mine ... No. Just an old friend ... I don't know. Probably about five more minutes ... Yeah, I can do that for you. Would you like to have one or two of them ...? Okay. I love you, too. I'll see you in a bit." He hung up and told me, "That was Linda. On the way home, she asked me to stop by the store to grab a box of Fig Newtons because she has the munchies for something sweet."

I stammered with my words at first, then finally spat them out. "You won't tell her you have seen me, right?"

"Man, of course not. This is me you're talking to."

"Exactly. And that's my point."

"I'm not gonna tell her, if that's what you're worried about."

"Thanks." I was the first to move up the pier, heading toward the parking lot.

Ronald caught on and followed me. "When am I going to see you again?"

"I don't know. That's on you."

"What about this weekend? On Saturday? We can hang out a bit to catch up on lost time."

I glanced at him, then back in front of me. "I'm cool with that. But not over here: Let's meet up in Miami."

"What about David?" I know he would be furious if I didn't tell him I saw you."

I smiled, even though I wanted to laugh. "Yeah, he might as well come along with us, too. And, in the meantime, I will call Brad to see if he's also willing to hang out, for old time's sake."

"Hold up! Are you referring to Brad? Our old buddy Brad?"

"Yeah."

"There goes my friggin' surprise to you. But how did you get in touch with him?"

"I ran into him the other day in the mall."

"When?" Ronald's whole facial expression changed before my eyes.

"A few days ago. Why?"

"Because that asshole didn't tell me a friggin' thing about it!"

81

I felt like an idiot when I pulled my key chain from my pocket. "That was sort of my fault. I'd told him to keep it secret that we bumped into each other until I reached out to you first."

"I don't care about that or the little secret you all made with each other. He was supposed to tell me about this … that friggin' bastard! Just wait till I get a word with him: He's not going to hear the last of this shit!"

I hugged Ronald and pressed the button on the small device attached to my keychain to disarm the car alarm.

Ronald got excited when I approached my Audi—not just because he heard the car alarm deactivate, but also because of where I was headed.

"Get the heck out of here!" he said, cupping his hands over the windshield to get a look inside the car. Then he looked over at me. "Is this car stolen?"

"Are you insinuating that I'd be driving in a stolen vehicle to come see you?"

"Yeah."

"No, of course not. This car is not stolen. It's clean."

That said, Ronald snatched the driver's door from my hand, pulling it open to get a better look inside. Then he asked, "Is it yours?"

If I tell him *Yes*, the next question would be about the nature of my activities. I chose not to disclose the source of my car, as further inquiries might follow.

So, on that note, I lied to him instead: "It belongs to a friend of mine."

"What kind of friend do you have to allow you to borrow a car like this?" he asked. Then he said, "Just keep it to yourself because I don't wanna know. However, be cautious with this ride and try to avoid any scratches on it. Because I don't wanna hear about some Mexican drug cartels having you pinned down in the Everglades, feeling you to those hungry alligators out there."

"Nah. It's not like that."

Ronald's cell phone started to ring again. He read the caller ID and looked back at me. "Speaking of the prick, this is Brad right here." He took the call.

Take 22

Ms. Nelson asked, "Who is it?" just before she looked through the peephole and immediately opened her apartment door.

Rebecca had a forlorn look on her face. Her hair was pushed back in a ponytail. Strands of hair were scattered and looked wild.

Ms. Nelson could see Rebecca had been crying, perhaps not long ago—maybe within an hour, but not more. The bottom of Rebecca's eyelids was not only puffy but reddish-looking, from the look of it, from wiping her eyes.

"Come in and close the door behind you," Ms. Nelson said. She walked away so Rebecca could follow her lead.

They headed to the kitchen.

"Have a seat. I'd make you a cup of coffee."

Rebecca sat at the far end, slouched over a bit, her elbow resting on the table. Her palm was at the center of her forehead, holding her head up.

Ms. Nelson looked at Rebecca, then back at the coffee maker. She poured two scoops of Taster's Choice coffee into it and added water. Then, she headed to the table area to take a seat. "Honey, look at me." She waited. Then she said, "I can't tell you how to live your life, but I can tell you this…" She paused, just a bit longer than before. Then she added, "You deserve much better than this."

Rebecca's bottom lip started quivering at that moment; her tears began to flow.

Ms. Nelson proceeded anyway, delivering it to her unadulterated: "You can go ahead and cry all you want. Because at the end of the day, you are the only one putting yourself through this mess, day after day. It's the same old thing with you and him. And I just don't get it." She pierced Rebecca with a curious stare.

Then she said, "You can't be that naïve and blind not to see it. Or perhaps it is that you don't wish to see it?"

Nothing. No response.

Rebecca kept quiet.

Ms. Nelson continued: "He's breaking you, and you don't see it. I don't understand. How can you be so blind not to see what he is doing to you?"

Again, Nothing.

Then suddenly, Ms. Nelson's eyes became watery. "Do you see this coffee here?" she asked, raising her cup.

Rebecca slowly nodded her head.

"I have had this mug for at least seventeen years now, and I have never gone without it, because it has served its purpose for me without any problems." Ms. Nelson staggered in her seat with slight hesitation, then twisted to the side and slammed her coffee mug on the floor. "Seventeen years I had that damned cup! Seventeen years!" she nearly cried. She then left the table, walked to the kitchen counter, and opened a cabinet drawer to grab something. It didn't take her long to find what she was looking for, because she returned to the table with it and asked, "Do you see this?"

Rebecca nodded her head again, but this time she looked confused.

"Do you see it?"

"Yes."

Then Ms. Nelson slammed a roll of masking tape on the table and asked, "Now do you think I can fix my damn coffee mug with this, to get it back to where I once had it?!"

Rebecca barely shook her head. "No."

"So, how in the hell do you think you can fix that boy after he then violated you when he put his hands on you?"

Rebecca didn't respond.

"Tell me!" Ms. Nelson shouted at her. "Tell me how in the hell you can fix that?!"

Rebecca's right hand began to shiver on its own.

"Tell me!"

Rebecca cried. "What should I do?"

"I can't tell you what to do. I can only support you by pointing out certain things that I believe are not in your best interest. That's all I can do as your friend. And that's why I can easily say that boy is not the person for you. You deserve so much better than him, other than being his punching bag. At your age, and given how beautiful you are, guys are supposed to fall at your feet, begging you to marry one of them. But hey! What do I know? I'm just a lonely fool without a man in my life, right?"

Rebecca opened her mouth, closed it, and opened it again. Just as she was about to speak, the coffee began to drain behind her, causing her to shut her mouth once more.

Ms. Nelson cut her eyes to the shattered coffee mug on the kitchen floor, then back to Rebecca. "Go ahead, say it."

Take 23

I pretended not to notice Cathy Swartz standing at a small café counter, a few steps ahead of me, placing her order with the cashier. "Yeah," I bumped Cathy on her side, trying to place my order over hers, "I would like to have–"

"Hey, excuse me!" Cathy cut me off, looking distraught at first. She twisted to her right. Then she smiled when she realized it was me. She nudged me back.

"Hey!" I immediately joked, turning back to the cashier. "I hope you saw that. She assaulted me. Can you please call the police for me? I want her to be arrested."

Cathy joked back: "Well, they might have to arrest you, too, since you hit me first."

"Just save it for the judge, ma'am."

"Well, I just might do that."

I kept quiet, smiling with her.

Someone faked a cough. Then another cough.

Cathy and I both twisted around, caught off guard by the gesture.

The cough came from an older white gentleman; he appeared to be in his mid-eighties, judging by the numerous wrinkles on his face and neck. He wore a blue and brown Knickerbocker golf suit, green socks pulled up to his knees, and black and white shoes to match. I briefly hoped that I wouldn't dress like him when I reached his age. Because–

The older gentleman interrupted me by asking, "Are you going to order your food or just stand there?"

"Oh, I'm sorry."

Cathy and I quickly placed our orders. She went first, then I. I ordered a French cappuccino and a hot bagel. Then I stepped aside and walked over to Cathy.

"What brought you out so early?"

I pulled the cup from my lips and said, "I wanted to grab a few things" –I barely raised the bag in my other hand since her eyes were focused on it– "before I start my day off right."

"The same here."

"Oh, that's why I didn't see you this morning?"

She made a cute face. "Were you looking for me this morning?"

"Yes." I joked back. "But of course."

"I hope you're not a stalker."

"And what if I am?"

She tried to pinch me on the arm.

I laughed. "But seriously, I haven't seen you jogging this morning."

"I took the day off. But perhaps you'll see me tomorrow morning."

"Tomorrow morning?"

"Hmm-uh," she nodded her head just before she took a sip of her coffee.

I nearly fell into a trance watching her. She had one of the prettiest sets of lips I have ever seen, rivaling those of Demi Lovato, who would give Cathy a run for her money.

Cathy snapped her fingers a few times in front of my face, trying to break my concentration while smiling at me.

It worked.

I tried to laugh it off, then shook my head. "Do you mind if we take a walk?"

"Uhhh…," she stammered, then glanced at her wristwatch.

So, I threw at her: "Only for a few minutes."

No comments. She stared at me, her face devoid of expression as she thought.

"Well," I used a little persuasion, "what about a block or two?"

She hesitated at first, then agreed, "Why not?"

We strolled, shooting the breeze about anything that came to mind. We started talking about the cappuccino I held in my hand and the coffee she had in hers. From there, we gradually shifted to a related topic: which country we thought produced the best coffee beans. I said Cuba, for sure; she claimed Venezuela, of all places. But we later agreed –hands down– that Haiti produced a better grade of coffee. Then our conversation switched from coffee beans to the Free Trade Agreement that the United States government had made with other countries.

Now, this was the crazy part about this topic that I agreed with Cathy on: she made plenty of sense with an exciting political statement about how the greed in Washington D.C., going back to the Clinton Administration, when they signed that Free Trade Agreement without any stipulations regarding what is allowed and what is not. Since then, besides the FTA harming our economy and blaming it all on the Bush administration, many companies pulled out of America to take advantage of cheap labor elsewhere. Then these same companies that left this great country because of the loopholes in the FTA dared to sell their products back to us as if we were a bunch of idiots.

The nerve of those conniving bastards on South Capital!

Kathleen delved deeper into the topic of prison labor camps in our country, specifically discussing UNICOR. I realized I was unaware of many aspects of prison industries. For instance, I didn't know that after the government imposes high taxes to cover the costs of housing federal inmates, the same legislators who approve these taxes then profit from the labor of these inmates. They compel inmates to work in factories that produce government goods, and subsequently, Congress passes a Defense Spending Bill to purchase these products back at a higher price, splitting the profits with their lobbyist friends.

Now this helps explain why Republicans are so persistent in starting unnecessary wars with other countries, only to cry out for the Defense Spending Bill, claiming they need more troops there. Because, as Cathy puts it, the more active U.S. troops were over there, the more government products were required.

As we approached the third block, I was amazed at how much I had learned in such a short time. Cathy looked like she wanted to cross the street, but stopped, which disappointed me. I suppose that was the end of our conversation for now.

So, I asked her, "Do you have any plans for this Thursday night?"

"Why? Are you asking me out on a date?"

I remembered to smile. "It all depends."

"On what?"

"On your reply."

She let out a short, soft scoffing sound and said, "I'm available on Thursday night."

"Well, to answer your initial question, yes, I would like to go on a date with you."

She smiled. "A date it is then."

Just like that! I smiled like a child in front of her. "What time would you like to meet up?"

"I don't know. Perhaps around seven o'clock would be fine for me, if you don't mind?"

"Seven o'clock would be perfect."

She parted with a smile, promising to meet me at the beach house just before we separated. For some unknown reason, as I crossed the intersection, I turned around to sneak a peek at her. She caught me looking as she tried to sneak a peek back at me, too. She smiled, and I did the same, but only briefly until I realized I was running late for my appointment.

I nodded goodbye and quickly walked away, the bag of goodies in my hand.

Take 24

"Good morning, ladies," Samuel greeted two older women, holding the door open for them as they exited the building. But then they stopped.

The woman on the left, Pamula, asked Samuel, "Where is that young man who usually spends the day with you?"

Samuel appeared to contemplate her question briefly before turning toward Sean, who stood a short distance away, assisting one of the residents with their bags.

"Not him," the other female said, her name was Elena. "We're talking about the young lad who usually washes cars out here."

"Oh, you're talking about Cassidy?"

Pamula quickly turned to her friend Elena and whispered, "I thought you said his name is Casanova?"

"That's what Alice told me."

Pamula twisted back to Samuel. "Yes, we were talking about the same young fellow here."

"Well, if it's him that you are looking for, he went on an errand for one of the residents here. He'll be back shortly."

"Ohhh…"

"But," Samuel started to say, "if you would like to leave a message for him, I assure you, I will inform him that–" his voice faded low. Then he said, "Speaking of the devil. There he goes, right there."

Pamula and Elena turned simultaneously, smiling. They looked at each other and walked away without saying a word.

Samuel thought it was unusual that they would walk past Cassidy without saying anything to him.

Take 25

"What the hell is the matter with you?"

Nothing at all. Not even a glance.

I glanced behind me and then back at Samuel, a smile on my face. "Look at you, you're checking those two dames out over there. I know you still had it in you."

Samuel finally shifted his focus to look at me. "They were inquiring about you."

"Yeah, right?" I took another look at them, then at Samuel again. "You play too much. I don't even know when to take you seriously anymore."

"Well, I'm serious now. They were asking about you."

"Yeah, okay." As if what he had just told me made a difference: I still didn't believe him. "But in the meantime, I have to take this bag upstairs to Ms. Ginsberg before I get yelled at again."

"Alright then. I'd see you later."

"Yeah, later." I walked away and jumped aboard the first available elevator cart to the top floor.

As soon as I approached Ms. Ginsberg's door, her attendant and housekeepers walked out of the penthouse and shouted, "Claire!"

Ms. Ginsberg shouted back: "I'm in here! In the den!"

I made my way toward her and paused at the doorway when I noticed she was on the phone, behind her desk, discussing business as usual. She glanced over at me.

I showed her the brown paper bag.

She smiled and got right back on the phone. "Okay, that's a fine job, Snookum. But hey! I have to go right now; something important has just come up. A package that I was waiting on has just arrived… Okay." She hung up without saying goodbye. Then she asked me, "Did you get everything you need?"

Without saying a word, I reached into the paper bag and pulled out a bottle of Martini and two kiwi fruits.

She smiled even harder this time while getting up from her desk.

I smiled back when I noticed she wasn't wearing any clothes below her waist, not even a skirt or panties. She walked around her desk and grabbed my hand. I admired her backside as she led the way to her bedroom.

Take 26

"Let's go! We only have a few more moments left!" She raised one knee, dropped it back down, and then immediately raised it back up in the air again for her participants in the aerobics class to follow. "I need y'all to keep up with me!" She switched to the other leg now, kicking her knee up and dropping it down again, periodically alternating between legs. "That's it, Shirley! I want you to keep going! You too, LeAnn!"

Even big-butt Michelle kept pace with the class.

"And at the count of three!" Rebecca shouted, "We're gonna start breaking it down." She paused to take a deep breath. Then she began her countdown: "One... Two... and–" she choked. Well, at least that's how it felt when she looked over at the doorway of her aerobics class and saw Juan standing there, watching her. She returned her focus to her participants and dared to say, "Three!" with the bit of strength she had left. She simplified her aerobic exercise to something easier and more comfortable. She began doing Alf's dance from that hit TV series in the late eighties, throwing both of her fists downwards at an angle, repeatedly, from one side to the other, while barely pumping her shoulders and raising her knee at the same time. Just one knee at a time, not two. It was a solid burning exercise for her aerobics class.

"That's it, Jessica!" Rebecca smiled, though it was a fake one, as she pretended not to notice Juan heading straight toward her. "I need you to pick your pace up for me!"

Jessica put forth all her effort.

"Rebecca..."

"Not right now," she said to Juan, displaying a warm smile to her class, not wanting to look at him. "I'm busy."

93

"Rebecca." He tried to catch her fist, but she quickly pulled it away from him while performing Alf's dance, pumping her fists downward and raising each knee one at a time towards her fist.

"Rebecca?"

She ignored him.

But he was persistent in getting her attention when he got down on one knee, "Rebecca..."

The whole class stopped exercising.

Shirley, LeAnn, and big-butt Michelle all had their hands over their gaping mouths, even skinny Jessica, too.

Rebecca felt embarrassed. She stopped doing Alf's aerobic exercise and turned to Juan when he grabbed her wrist.

"Rebecca, will–"

She cut him off, saying, "Not right now," because she would rather discuss the incident from the other night when he demonstrated against her by forcing himself on her from behind while slapping her around. "I mean that: Not right now."

However, Juan proceeded anyway.

LeAnn and the other girls in the class were utterly shocked when he pulled an engagement ring from his pocket and attempted to place it on Rebecca's finger.

They all expressed a soft, *"Oh, my god,"* in unison, then began chatting about the size of the diamond that Juan had presented to Rebecca. Some claimed it was a full carat, while others argued it was only half a carat.

When Juan started to propose to Rebecca again, the room grew immensely.

Rebecca said, "Not right now, Juan. Please don't do this."

"I just want to do what is right by your side. That's why I need you to be my wife and me to be your husband. I truly mean that."

She wasn't sure about that, barely shaking her head while Juan slid the ring onto her finger.

Then a few girls in her class chanted, "Say yes!"

Rebecca glanced at the spectators. Most of them, around ninety percent of the class, were smiling at her.

"Rebecca, will you marry me?"

She turned back to Juan. He remained on one knee, gazing up at her.

"Marry me," he said with a more apologetic tone, as if he wanted her to forget about what he had done to her the previous night. "Things will be so much better between us. I swear."

Smooth Casanova

Rebecca had her life flash before her eyes: the movies, candlelit dinners, and strolls in the park while holding hands with a significant other. She recalled playtime, good times, cuddle time, and the naughty time, which she definitely couldn't forget—all of those moments she missed and longed for.

On that note, she said, "Yes," out of respect for his image. However, she immediately added, "We still need to talk about something when I get off work."

"Whatever you say." He got up and kissed her; she kept still.

People in the class were cheering and clapping.

"I'm serious," Rebecca whispered to Juan. "We need to talk."

"Sure, mi amor," he gave her another kiss. "You won't regret this."

Rebecca attempted to smile at the spectators, but her grin felt too burdensome to maintain.

"Give him another kiss!"

Rebecca twisted to the cheering crowd, trying to figure out who would say such a foolish thing.

"Go ahead!" Jessica made it clear that she was the one who said it. "What are you waiting for? Give him another kiss! I wanna see!"

"Yeah, what are you waiting for? Give me another kiss."

Rebecca turned back to Juan, her doubts lingering.

Then he continued saying, "Give me a kiss and show them how much you love me."

Take 27

"Whether people like it or not," I began, lowering my voice to Ms. Ginsberg as I stepped out of the shower and walked into the master bedroom naked, drying my hair with the damp blue towel she had left on the bathroom counter for me, "because as I see it, I don't care how they feel, as long as you are happy."

"Happy?" She made a sarcastic scoffing sound of a fake upper-class laugh while lying on the king-size mattress, resting on her side. A thin bed sheet barely covered her nakedness, her left titty exposed. "That's a bit of an understatement." Her smile widened as she kept her eyes on my flaccid muscle that hung freely in front of me. "Because, to the contrary, I'm overjoyed spending my time with you. Blissed. Ravished away, living in paradise. The seventh heaven –the bed sheet slid from her upper body, exposing her breast completely when she started throwing her arms backward– "doing backstrokes on cloud nine."

"Can you be serious, for once?" I almost laughed when I took a seat on the edge of the bed, drying my feet. I admired her thick nipples. They had a pretty peach color to them. "But seriously, I think everybody in this building has some sort of suspicion about what's going on between us."

"Does it bother you?"

"No. But of course not."

"So why bother yourself by mentioning this to me then?"

"Because, I feel like, hey, what the hell!" I reached for my underwear. "Why shall we keep sneaking around like this? If we were just open about it that we're having sex with one another, the chances are they would move on to someone else's matter and leave us alone. And to be quite honest with you, I don't see the significance behind us wanting to keep our relationship a secret anyway. Because, as we both know already, one way or the other, they all know that something is going on between us." I stood up and slid my underwear on.

"And without concrete facts about us, they don't know anything. Now should they?"

"No."

"That's my point," she explained, "Because as we both know, rumors plague our curiosity to seek out the truth about something or someone, even when it's none of our business. And when we obtain the needed information to support our accusation or to discredit the rumor that is out there, we tend to move on to something different to talk about." She paused, smiling. Then, she added, after watching me slide my pants on. "So why not play this game of theirs to our advantage to plague their curiosity about what we're doing up here, without revealing anything to them. Because, beside the point that, our business is our business as to what we do with each other; in which it intrigues other people to the point of wanting them to dig into my personal life as to whom I choose to fuck and suck."

I chuckled and went for my shoes, taking my seat on the edge of the bed again.

"Cassidy?"

"Huh?" I looked at her.

"Sometimes we worry about what others think or say about us, rather than considering how they criticize themselves. We should not indulge in their pointless curiosity about us or share our private matters with them. If they find out about our relationship, so be it. But until then, we shouldn't let them control how we feel about what they might know. Besides living our own lives, what really matters is focusing on what brings us happiness instead of worrying about what they might say or think behind our backs. All of this shows my point: they go out of their way to pry into our lives to gossip, whether through criticism or sarcasm, simply because they want to live our lives, either wishing they were us or trying to hide their dull, unfulfilling lives. Why else would they care about our lives instead of their own? But there's something else we need to remember: when we start caring about what they say or think, we give up on ourselves, trying to maintain an image of someone we're not, living our lives for them instead of for us." She paused, then continued talking.

I barely understood what she was saying because my mind wandered, thinking about Rebecca for some unknown reason.

Ms. Ginsberg waved her fingers in front of my face a few times. "Snap out of it!"

I did. I came back, unaware of how long I had been zoned out before her.

"What's the matter? You drifted off somewhere."

I remembered to smile. "I was listening to you."

"No, you weren't. What were you thinking about?"

"Okay," a false smile spread across my face, "you caught me. I was thinking about something a friend mentioned to me recently."

She appeared to accept my harmless lie.

Then it occurred to me: "I had almost forgotten to mention something to you as well."

"What?"

"I made plans for this upcoming Saturday with friends to catch up on old times. So chances are, you and I would have to meet on Sunday if that's okay with you." I paused, waiting for her hangdog facial expression to fade before continuing. "Or, only if you want, we could spend some time together on Saturday before I meet up with them. I'm cool with either day. The choice is yours."

Although she said she didn't mind, I knew it still bothered her. But then she asked, "What sort of plans had you made with your friends?"

"Nothing out of the norm." I just wanted to be truthful with her here. "We will probably hang out on the beach for a little while or perhaps go fishing. It all depends on the mood that we're in."

"So why don't you take my yacht out this Saturday? You all can enjoy the weather and do both."

Now that sounded like a brilliant idea. "Are you sure about that?"

"Of course. I'm sure." She then sat up, kicking her legs off the edge of the bed to sit beside me while blanketing herself with a bed sheet. "I will contact Eddie tomorrow morning to ensure he prepares the yacht for you on Saturday."

"Thanks." I reached in and kissed her; she welcomed it.

"So, make sure that you go down to the dock around noon sharp, and I will have everything arranged for you," she said. "And if you be good to me, I might have a surprise on the yacht for you."

"If I'm good to you?" I tried to mock her back, joking.

"Yes." She barely tilted her head to the side, acting spunky yet conceited.

I smiled. I'm not going to lie. All sorts of things ran through my mind—a case of beer? Imported Champagne? A few bottles of rum? Will her private chef cook for us on the yacht? Oh, who knows?—because she's always surprised me in some way or another. "So, don't be surprised if I might have something for you too." I then searched in my pants pocket for my keys.

"You? You have something for me?"

"Yes, me." I looked over at the nightstand beside the bed, then got up.

She grabbed my wrist. "What is it?" She kept her eyes on my pocket.

She likely thought I had something in my pocket for her. So, of course, I played along with it: "I'm not telling you."

"Why?"

"Because, as I said, it's a surprise for you."

"Okay." She smiled; her eyes still locked on my pocket. "I'm surprised. So let me have it now. "

"Are you sure you want it now?"

She quickly nodded her head, then looked back at my pocket.

"Are you sure?"

"Yes," she nodded again. "Now give it to me."

I thought about something and looked at my wristwatch again. It read 4:20 in the late afternoon. I had plenty of time to play with her before my dinner arrangement with Ellen tonight, so I stuck my hand in my pants pocket. "But you must close your eyes first, for it to surprise you. "

She seemed bothered by my request.

"I'm serious. You need to close your eyes for me first."

She pretended to have done so, with one eye still half open.

"I'm serious, Claire." I looked at my wristwatch again. "You must close your eyes for me. Both, or I'm not going to show it to you."

"Alright then."

I pulled my hand out of my pants pocket and said, "Keep your eyes shut for me. And don't open them until I tell you to. Okay?"

"Uh-huh." She got excited.

"Let me have your hand."

She flung her hand outward.

I grabbed it.

About a second or two later, a smile grew on her face when she realized what she was holding in her hand.

"Oh, my…" she had already opened her eyes without me telling her to do so, while wrapping her fingers around my dick with a better grip. "What a surprise."

I then positioned myself in front of her. She looked up at me, then at my growing muscle in her hand. I brushed her hair aside from her face and held it behind her head to look at her lips when she opened her mouth.

I felt loved. You should have seen me. It was my turn to shut my eyes when she slowly bobbed her head once, twice, three times, and then I gave up counting as she put her head in motion.

Slow motion.

Take 28

"Pssst!"

Rebecca turned around just before unlocking her apartment door.

It was Ms. Nelson. "He is in there," she tried to whisper, "inside your apartment."

"Who? Juan?"

"Yeah," she kept her voice low, "So come over here and let him sit inside by himself to show him how it feels to be alone for a night."

Rebecca paused and smiled, appreciating Ms. Nelson's concern for her. "Thanks for the invitation," she said. "But I invited him over to talk with him."

At first, Ms. Nelson stammered over her words, as if she wanted to respond but stopped herself, taking a deep breath. Then, finally, she said, "Well, you just be careful in there. Do you hear me?"

"Yes. I hear you." Rebecca entered her apartment and was immediately struck by a savory smell—something tasty.

Juan must be cooking, she thought.

Soft Latin music was playing in the dim background: bachata. Juan was singing along to it.

When Rebecca placed her keys on the table by the door, she left the living room lights off, as a faint glow was coming from the kitchen area. This gave her enough light to navigate the room without bumping into anything.

Usually, she would head straight to her bedroom for a shower, but this time, everything felt different — truly different. Instead, she found herself heading to the kitchen. Her mind was cluttered with thoughts, and she felt a strong need to share her feelings with Juan. She wanted to talk to him about the upsetting experience he put her through the other day when he crossed a line.

Juan had promised Rebecca that he wouldn't get physical with her again, but he did. He assaulted her brutally, treating her as if she were a new inmate in a state penitentiary, violating her in every imaginable way. Along with slapping and punching Rebecca, he held her down against her will and forced himself on her from behind. To make matters worse, he casually walked out of her bedroom, which felt like a prison cell to her that night, leaving her slumped over the bed, crying to herself as if she were just a victim in a cruel environment.

The next day, if Juan had returned to the apartment, Rebecca probably would have killed him while he was asleep. Everything was planned from start to finish, but he didn't show up. She even tried calling him a few times, hoping to convince him that it was all her fault so he would come back, but he never answered her calls. For two whole days! Then, suddenly, he just showed up at her workplace unannounced, asking her to marry him.

If that's not a dysfunctional order, it's pure fucking insanity!

Rebecca stopped at the kitchen entrance when she saw Juan dancing to a Latin song while stirring a wooden spoon into a cooking pot over the stove. She cut her eyes to the steak knife on the countertop and then returned to him.

"Juan?"

He twisted around, looking at her with a childish smile on his face, still singing that Spanish song before her as if he had forgotten about all the *Putas, Perras,* and *Rameras* he had called her the other night just before he walked out on her.

"Juan," she repeated, hoping that he would stop singing.

And he did when he said, "You've come just in time. I need you to taste this for me, *mi amor*. Tell what you think." He turned back to the pot.

"Juan" –she wore a serious look– "we need to talk!"

"Yes. I know," he glanced at her, then back to the pot. "But I need you to taste this first." He shook his head to the side at the same time he said, "Come over here and taste it for me," while stirring the spoon in the cooking pot. "Please."

She took another look at the cleaver, then back at him.

"C'mon," he said with his back facing her. "What are you waiting for?"

Take 29

Sometimes it's best to take a step back to make a better leap forward.

"And that's what I have been trying to tell you all this time," I said to Ellen as we sat across a table from each other at an elegant restaurant on key Biscayne "Because before you know it, if you don't make a stand for yourself, you are only subjecting yourself for all sort of attacks from him."

"Like what?" The ridges on her aging face made it appear that she was desperate to know.

"Like the bickering. The constant complaining that you don't have the same comparison to other people. Particularly, to other females in general. There are also the ignoring and isolation stages, as well as the hanging out and cheating stages, if that hasn't started yet."

She barely nodded her head. "It has already," she whispered, then looked to her left and right to ensure no one at a nearby table was overhearing us. Then she cut back to me, looking identical to actress Judi Dench, who was known for her role as M, the head of intelligence in the James Bond films.

"You know," I began to tell Ellen when I saw that rejection look painted in her eyes, "I can give you two suggestions. I strongly recommend that you pick one of them. But it's all up to you if you choose to do either one of them or none at all."

"Which is?"

"My first suggestion is," I wanted to keep it honest with her. "I think the two of you need a little space from each other so you can breathe."

She didn't need to respond to that: her silence alone gave it away that there was something they had already done with each other when she slowly took her eye off me, combing her fork through her untouched plate of food. After a moment, nearly thirty seconds later, she whispered with her face tilted downward, doodling a fork in her string beans: "And your other suggestion…?"

"My other suggestion?" I tried to play stupid, as if I didn't know what she was talking about, hoping to get her attention off her plate.

It worked. She looked at me and said, "Yes. You stated that you have two suggestions for me, but you only gave me one."

"I only gave you one of them?" I fought hard to hold that confused look on my face.

"Yes."

Then a smile broke across my face.

"What is it?" she smiled back, seeming more intrigued than before. "Tell me. I would like to know: What is your second suggestion?"

"Are you sure that you would like to know about it?"

"Yes. Now tell me."

"Well. My other suggestion to you is" I wanted to laugh without holding anything back from her, "we can go to that small hotel that we passed up, on our way over here, so I can fuck the hell out of you!"

She seemed shocked yet astonished by my other suggestion. She acted as if she wanted to say something, but closed her mouth. She veered her surroundings again to make sure no one heard me, and then she cut back at me.

I asked, "What do you think about my other suggestion?"

She laughed self-deprecatingly and said, "It sounds interesting yet tempting," as if I were joking. Then, with a charming smile appearing on her face, she added, "But what should we do afterward?"

"What should we do afterward?" I mocked, wiping that smile from my face to let her know I was serious. "We could go for another round afterward of some good hard fucking, if you're up for the challenge."

That was her cue.

Without hesitation, Ellen raised her index finger in the air and shouted, "Waiter! We would now like to have our check, please!"

It took us about twenty minutes to drive to that small resort off Key Biscayne beach. And as soon as we popped our hotel door open, I went straight for her dress, then her panties next. I pulled her Fruit of the Looms down her legs. She kicked them aside. I twisted her around, with her back facing me, my manhood was in her. Not all of it, but at least half of me. She couldn't take it all at once. But after about fifteen minutes of playing halfway in her pussy she welcomed me.

I gave her not one but four massive orgasms. However, on her second climax, I felt a little uncomfortable when she started saying that she loved me. Especially that one time when I had her in a missionary position –flat on her back with her legs wrapped around me– and I kissed her on her mouth.

She grappled me and pulled me in closer, crying in my ear, begging in me to cum inside of her.

And you'd best believe it, Ellen's cubbyhole was sorta like a Goldilocks preference; not too tight, not too loose, but just right. I shot a good load inside of her.

Only when we finished fucking did she say, "I would like to see you again."

"The same here." I reached for my shirt.

"Oh, that's right." She leaned toward the nightstand and grabbed her purse. "I have almost forgotten about this."

"About what?" I reached for my pants.

When she pulled a cashier's check out of her purse, she tried to hand it to me. "This is for you."

"No." I barely shook my head, refusing to stretch my hand toward her. "This one is on me."

"But I insist."

"Well –I slid my left leg inside my pants, then my other leg– "hold it for me then."

"Are you sure?"

"Yeah." I latched my pants button together.

"So, when will I be able to see you again?" she sat at the edge of the bed, using the bedspread to cover her body.

"That's on you." I slid my shoes on, then I cut back to her. "Because I would like to see you again, too. But I would only do so under two conditions."

"Which are?"

I smiled. "For one, the next time I see you, I would like you to wear something a little tighter and sexier. Sorta sleazy looking. Perhaps consider a black mini-skirt or a more revealing skirt to show off your lovely legs. And wear that same garter belt the next time I see you, with a fishnet stocking on."

"Are you serious?"

"Yeah."

"I can't do that."

"Why?"

"Other than I find that inappropriate, I don't want to look too provocative to give Douglass the impression that I was sneaking around him."

"So?" I began to tuck my shirt into my pants.

"So?" she tried to mock me. "He would find out that I am sleeping around him."

"So?" I leaned in and kissed her, hoping to soothe her anxiety. "But do you know what I prefer?"

"What, for Douglass to friggin' divorce me and brushing me crumbs off the table?!"

"No. Of course not. But I prefer that next time, if your husband is getting ready to go out late at night, claiming to be going somewhere he chooses not to disclose to you, I want to get started on getting dressed, too. Throw something provocative in front of him, then come visit me."

"But he would probably suspect some kind of adultery about to be committed by me and ask where I'm going like that?"

"That's even better. Because if your husband asks you where you're going dressed like that, tell him that you will enjoy the evening out by yourself. And suggest that he should do the same."

"But it would look obvious that I'm sleeping around on him."

"Hell. What goes around comes around." I barely tilled my head to the side before continuing: "And if he says that you can't go out of the house looking like that, just tell him to give you good reason why you should stay home by yourself while he goes out to enjoy himself … Then ask him to give you a better option."

Her troubled facial expression changed into something more acceptable. "I like that idea," she whispered, then smiled.

I smiled back.

"Now, what about the second condition?"

"The second condition?"

"Yes. You said you would only see me under two conditions. You gave me one, so what is the second condition?"

"I can explain that to you the next time we meet."

"No. Tell me now. I would like to know what it is?"

"It's something to do with your mouth," I almost laughed. "We must find a way to keep ourselves occupied. And I think I have the perfect solution for that."

"What might that be?"

"Let's wait till next time." I reached down and gave her another kiss. "Because I would rather show you than explain it to you."

"To show me?"

"Yeah. Show you."

"So, show me now."

"No. Let's wait."

"No," she was persistent. "I would like you to show me right now."

Suit yourself then. I reached over and softly glided my left thumb over her lips. She closed her eyes. I slowly slid my thumb back to the other side of her lips. She took a deeper breath, panting. I slumped over and gave her another kiss, with my thumb still resting on her lips, standing between us. I kissed her again. She kissed back with her eyes closed. I kept playing on the coastline of her lips with my thumb. Back and forth. Her mouth agape, begging for another kiss. And I did when I stuck my other hand inside my pants. I stood straight up and took a closer step toward her. I removed my thumb from her mouth and replaced it with my meaty manhood, slowly rubbing it back and forth over her lips.

I don't know what gave me the courage to say it, but I told her, "Open your mouth for me."

She did, while craning her head outward –watching me, watching her– sitting on the edge of the bed, with me standing in front of her. She took nearly half of my dick in her mouth.

I closed my eyes and thought about Queen Elizabeth.

Take 30

"Oh, fuck!" Rebecca was on her back, one leg over Juan's shoulder as he munched down over her pussy. "Don't stop!"

He didn't.

Within seconds, she came heavily, shivering like a wet puppy who got caught outside in the cold.

Juan tossed Rebecca's leg over his head, wanting to put her in a doggy-style position, but she was drained. She was still trembling. She just lay there on her side, her back facing Juan. He eased up and inserted his dick in her anyway, spooning her from the back. She kept her eyes closed, feeling him inside her. Her pussy muscles contracted.

As he worked her from the back, he whispered in her ear: "I love you…"

"I love you, too."

He reached his hand ever her and played with her clitoris, while pumping his dick in and out of her pussy, so she could create a new motion for him to follow. And he did when he shook two of his fingers faster. She moaned louder while pressing her head back against his head to kiss him. It wasn't easy at first, but they managed to connect their tongues. Juan slowly eased his other hand over to her breast, then to her nipple. He pinched her left nipple, then her right one. He squeezed it. Her moaning grew stronger while she cracked her mouth open.

Within seconds, he ran a finger over her lips. She tried to parry his finger away from her mouth, cocking her head to the side. She was pretty sure of his intentions. She remembered what had happened the last time he had done that. But this was much different, though: he followed pursuit, chasing after her lips.

She tried to buck again, while on the verge of another climax. She was right there, right at the heart of it.

But Juan didn't back down with his finger. "Suck it for me," he tried to whisper in her ear, rubbing his finger along her lips.

"No…" she begged.

"Please," he whispered back, "Just suck it for me."

"Uh-huh," she dragged with a moan, swaying her mouth away from his finger.

He pushed his dick deep in her, pumping faster while picking up more speed. "Do you like how this feels in you?" he panted in her ear. "Do you like it?"

"Yes … Yes … Don't stop!"

He kept pumping in her and ran his finger along her lips and said, "Pretend like I'm in front of you. I want you to suck it for me."

"Oh, don't …" She gasped for air. "Don't…Don't stop! Don't stop!" She rested her hand between her legs to feel his dick plunging inside of her.

Then, the opportunity presented itself this time, and Juan went for it. He stuck his finger in her mouth, sliding his finger back and forth. "Suck it for me," he said.

She moaned, leaving her mouth open for him. She didn't pay any attention to what he was doing with her mouth because she was on the verge of cumming.

He repeated once more when he felt her pussy contracting again over his dick, "Suck my finger for me, Rebecca. Suck it for me. I want to cum, too."

After a split second, she gave in and twirled her tongue around his finger. She imagined his finger was a dick she once knew, while bobbing her head back and forth, feeling Juan thrusting himself inside of her.

"That's it, Rebecca. There you go. Suck it for me … Suck his dick for me."

She did. She sucked his finger as if it was a dick: His dick.

Take 31

"Would you get upset with me if I'd call you a stupid ass?"

"No. Not really." I took my eyes off the beach and turned to Samuel. "It wouldn't bother me a bit how you felt about me. Because at the end of the day, I will still be me: Cassidy Zimmerman."

"Oh." He took another sip of his beer, then cut back to the people on the beach.

"But to be quite honest with you, I'm a bit curious to know why you would ask me that."

"Ask you about what?"

"About your question, just a moment ago?"

He looked at me as if he were clueless. "I don't understand what you're talking about?"

"You just asked me if I would get upset with you if you called me an asshole."

"No. Correction: A stupid ass!"

"Yeah, whatever. But why would you ask me that?"

"Like you said, it would make a bit of difference with you. So, why bother to ask why?" He took another sip of his beer, his eyes still looking at mine. Then he added, "I would be just wasting my breath about it. Because, as you said, at the end of the day, you will still be you. Cassidy Zimmerman." He cut back to the beach. "It's pleasant out here tonight. Don't you agree?"

"Are you serious?"

"Yeah. Of course, I am." He looked at me again. "It's beautiful out here."

"You know what the hell I'm talking about."

He acted as if he was confused by my statement, then he sprouted: "Oh, you're referring back to the stupid ass part?"

"You know exactly that's what I'm talking about."

"So, what about it?"

"Are you not going to tell me?"

"No, so you might as well leave it alone."

I nearly let some foul words slip when he glanced back at the beach, but I held them in. I waited a moment, then a few seconds more.

From the look of it, his mind was made up, and he wasn't going to tell me.

"Fine then." I grabbed a cold beer and popped the cork. "I didn't want to know about it anyway."

"Oh, sure you didn't."

No comment.

I rather not indulge in his bullshit tonight. I kept quiet and watched the scenery with him. I glimpsed at my wristwatch. It read 7:42 pm. And like always, there were few people left on the beach around this time of the night.

Samuel broke our silence: "It feels good out here tonight, doesn't it?"

"Yeah. I was thinking the same thing."

He glanced at me, then looked away.

I cut back on the beach.

"May I offer you some constructive criticism?"

"Sure, why not?" I glanced at him as he continued to stare straight ahead at some pedestrians passing by. "It's valuable to hear what others have to say from their perspective."

"Oh..."

We fell right back into silence.

Then, just as I was about to question him about his inquiry, he said, "So what are you acting like a stupid ass?"

"Why do you say that?"

Because look at you, you're still young with plenty of years ahead of you, but you'd rather waste your life out here, being a fool like me.

I'm lost here.

Then he went on: "You only have one life to live, and you must utilize it to the best of your ability. Capture every moment of your life, day in and day out."

"But I am."

"With me?" he tried to be sarcastic. Then he added, "Oh, that's right! It makes a lot of sense to me now."

"You know what I meant."

"Yeah, I do, and that's why I'm sharing my insight with you about life in general, because it's for your good."

"What are you trying to say?"

"Cassidy, I like you as my friend. But a friend is not someone who holds back another friend from going further in life just because, for example, someone like me who gave up on life a long time ago."

I'm still lost here.

Samuel put his beer bottle down. "You see," he spoke with a little slur, "I was like you many years ago. Roughly about ten years ago. Lost in every direction yet running from my fears. The fear of moving on with my life, being afraid of what I must go through all over again with someone different. A different woman, with a different attitude about life. A different personality. A different outlook on things. Just about everything else that is different from the last person I once shared my life with. But now, I'm taking a chance to share my life with someone new. That's an unforeseen obstacle, if not a challenge.

The whole thing about remodeling yourself for specific changes after being with someone different for so long. Changes that you would probably like, and some changes that you might not. But you must remember: the purpose of life is not only to know and master yourself by pushing yourself to the limit, to the unthinkable challenges that life has to offer you, but to enjoy life itself…"

I'm receiving a mixed message here.

He kept talking: "Just look at them two over there."

I did. "Yeah. What about them?"

"That's a life worth dying for."

I turned back to him. "For whom? For them or me?"

He looked at me, retorting a question without answering mine: "How old do you think they are there?"

"I don't know. However, they appear to be in their late fifties or early sixties. Why?"

He cut back to them with a smile. "They're about my age. Aren't they?"

"Yeah. I guess."

He cut back at me, wearing that same smile on his face. "The greatest gift to man is a woman," he said. Then he asked, "Don't you agree?"

"Yeah. Sort of." And that's only if you're not counting my Domino Pizza in the house.

"So why are you wasting your life here with me?"

It felt like he was charging at me with a rusty kitchen knife with his question. My only defense was, "I'm not wasting my life here with you."

Yeah, *that* one blew over his head.

"You see," he began with a confident smile, "when I was about your age, I was in a good relationship with the most beautiful lady that you could imagine. I used to cuddle up with her every single night."

"I'm well familiar with a relationship," I admitted. But then again, I didn't like talking to him about relationships either, especially when he's drunk. "Just remember, I used to be in one before."

"Oh, yeah, that's right. With the young lady named Jessica, who caught you cheating on her."

"No. You have it wrong. Her name was Rebecca, and it's the other way around: I caught her cheating on me."

"Are you sure about that?" he asked in a way as if he doubted me. "Because I could have sworn–"

"Yeah," I cut him off. "I'm sure about that."

He made a scoffing sound from a drunken laugh. "You have so much to learn about life."

"What else do I need to learn about life that I don't know already?"

"Everything. And I'm not just talking about the fundamentals of life: Eat, shit, and sleep. I'm talking about the joy of life and being with your significant other, looking back at the old memories you two shared while revisiting the good times you had together. That's what life is about. Moving forward to the next chapter, getting over the stumbling blocks with each other ...," his voice faded away.

"Why are you looking at me like that?"

"There's no reason," he said, then asked, "How have you ever thought about getting your life back together again and finding a decent girl to settle down with? Someone to grow old with, without you cheating on her like you did that other one."

"Which other one?"

"That young girl Jessica."

"Her name was Rebecca," I corrected him again. "And for the hundredth time, she cheated on me."

"Are you sure about that?"

"Yes, I'm sure. But to answer your question about finding a female to settle down with … I'm still searching. I haven't found one yet."

"What about Ms. Ginsberg?"

"We're just friends."

"So why are you smiling then?"

"Because you are making me smile. You're smiling at me."

"Yeah, whatever," he kept his eyes on me. Then he asked, "Have you ever thought of starting a relationship with Ms. Ginsberg?"

"No. Not really." I lied. "But in a way, she would rather keep our friendship like this."

He hissed. "You're a better man than I am, then. Because if I were you, I'll do my best to fuck the shit out of her until she changes her mind, of wanting to take y'all relationship up another level."

Only if he knew.

"Shitting me!" he went on. "I'll be over there right now if I were you, tearing her ass up all through the night. And by morning, I'll give her a good morning fuck to start her day off right."

Been there, done that.

"So," he began to ask, "what about that other girl then?"

"Who?"

"That other lady who has been calling you regularly?"

"Who, Emma Wolf?"

"Yeah. That's it. What about her?"

"She's married."

"Oh." He looked disappointed. Then, he found some inspiration. "What about that young lady I saw you speaking to this morning?"

"Who, Cathy?"

"Yeah, what about her?"

No comment.

"Yeah," he dragged out with a smile. Then he said, "You must have a thing for her because I see that look on your face again."

"Because you have that big grin on your face."

"Yeah, whatever!"

"I'm serious."

"All jokes aside," he said. "Are you working on her?"

I hesitated a bit, then admitted: "Yeah. But she is playing hard."

"Just ask her out on a date."

"That's already set."

His smile widened again. "But whatever you do," he began to say, "When it works out for you two, don't cheat on her like the last girl."

I damned near snapped by accident: "Why do you kept insinuating that I cheated on Rebecca?"

"Because you have."

"No, I haven't.

"You have."

"How?"

He leaned back in his chair to get comfortable, as if his explanation was going to take some time.

I was all ears.

Take 32

"Look," **Samuel** **started** speaking casually at first, but then spoke with authority, "sex is not the only form you could use to cheat on your significant other. Because there are many other forms of cheating." He paused for a split second. Then he started back again: "Yeah, but of course, having sex with another person outside of your relationship is probably the most ultimate form of cheating that one could do to someone behind their back, but still, that's only one form of cheating; there are many other forms out there."

"Like what?"

"When we first meet a female, we tend to put on a false persona. Sometimes, this persona might even be genuine, in a sense. We treat her like a God-given trophy, as we did when we first met, excited beyond measure. We start by spending long hours on the phone, chatting about everything that comes to mind. Then, we take her to restaurants, movies, parks, museums, and even shopping, going out of our way to impress her.

Sometimes we even take the extra step to introduce her to our friends and family members, placing her on a high pedestal, saying she is the only one for you or me. Here, not only would your friends and family members believe you, but she would believe you too, because of the time spent with her. The attention she received, along with the lavish gifts as a future investment, how could she not believe in the relationship she has with you? But then, suddenly, you stopped giving her the attention she was used to. Just like that!" he snapped his fingers, then continued: "We all get tired of the same old stuff.

So now you take that masquerade off and show her the real you, while tossing her up on the shelf like she's some cheap trophy that you won from a pimp convention. You don't want to spend the same quality of time with her that you used to share when you first met her. Essentially, depriving her of all the joy you two once shared puts everything on hold until you're ready to give her that time again. Because now you want to spend that same quality time you used to give her, you're giving it to your homeboys or something else."

"But that wasn't me."

"Yeah, it probably wasn't you. Or probably it might have just been you."

"You don't know what the hell you are talking about. You're drunk."

"Yeah, I might have had a few beers, but I'm not a fool! I could see it all over you."

"See what's all over me?"

"All the hurt and pain that is inside of you."

"You're drunk."

"And you're the fool here because you know what I'm telling you is the truth."

"For one, I'm not in some type of pain here … Two, I don't even think about that whore anymore."

"You, see?"

"You see, what?"

He scoffed again. "Every time you mention your ex, you get upset, calling her all sorts of foul names."

"What the fuck! She cheated on me for goodness' sake! On our anniversary day!" I paused to get a good look at this drunk idiot. Then I asked: "Do you have the slightest clue as to how many friggin' nights I had to work overtime to pay off that engagement ring that I intended on giving her?"

His eyes perked, as if he was interested to know. "How many?"

"Over a friggin' year!"

"A whole year?"

"Yes, a whole year."

"So that you have it!"

"Have what?"

"As to what caused her to cheat on you."

God damn it! I swear that if he were about twenty years younger, I would have slapped him across his mouth!

He almost shouted, "What?" It seemed as though he was trying to instigate an argument. "You know I'm telling you the truth here!"

I sighed, then took another deep breath. I had to remind myself that he was under the influence of alcohol. "So, you're telling me that by working overtime to pay off an engagement ring, she cheated on me?"

"No. Correction: To cause her to cheat back on you."

Okay, I got up from my seat. I had enough of this bullshit!"

"Where are you going?"

I stopped.

"Sit back down and hear me out." He paused. Only for a short moment, if not for a few seconds. Then he repeated himself: "C'mon, sit back down and stop acting like a puss."

"I'm not a pussy." But then again, I sat back in my seat.

Then he continued: "The only reason why I say that you cheated on her first, is because, while you were working overtime at your job, that was just as you were sneaking around on her, behind her back, without explaining why you were depriving her of those same hours you used to share with her; all because you were planning on surprising her with that ring."

"But even if I choose not to tell her about my surprise, that still shouldn't give her the right to cheat on me."

"Probably you're right, or probably you're not. But the truth is that you cheated her by not spending the time with her that you used to…"

I glanced away from him while he was rambling on with his nonsense. I couldn't believe how he tried to convince me that it was my fault that Rebecca had cheated on me. Well, to me, that was total bullshit! He couldn't pin this one on me. But for some reason, I drifted back to that argument I had with Rebecca in the shower when she told me –after she spoke to that fucking spic– that she couldn't make it to the movie theater with Ronald and me because, of all things, supposedly, she had to fill in for one of the aerobics instructors at her job who didn't show up for work. I vividly remember that day she threw it in my face, disputing: *You don't even hear me bickering about it when you work overtime.*

That fucking tramp!

She didn't have the right to go to bed with somebody else because I wasn't spending enough time with her!

Samuel chiseled his way into my thoughts as he kept talking to me: "… and I just think you're going about this in the wrong way, if I might add–"

"What?" I cut back in. "What the hell do you mean by you think I'm going about it the wrong way?"

"It's like what I said, if you had been paying attention to me, you would have understood what I was saying."

"So, tell me this, then," I began to ask, because it is evident that I must have missed something: "What would you have done if you were in my situation after catching your fiancée cheating on you?"

"Would you like to know what I would have done in your situation?"

"Yeah."

"You didn't hear a damn word I have just said to you a second ago," he said. "I would have found some sort of closure from all of this."

"You would have found some sort of closure?" I had to look at this damned fool. "That doesn't make any sense. What sort of closure do you need to seal the deal from what you've discovered about your fiancée's infidelity?"

"Well, first of all, based on what you've told me, if I had caught the old lady hanging out with another man in an adulterous way, I would have driven right back home and waited for her to get there after she was done doing whatever with him."

"For what? To kill her?"

"No. Of course not."

"What else would you possibly be waiting for her?"

"To give her an option to pick either him or me."

"You're telling me that you would have given her an option to pick you or him?" Okay, I shook my head this time after a quick pause. Then I asked, "Are you friggin' crazy?"

"No. I'm not. But sometimes we tend to make mistakes: mistakes that temporarily blind us for a moment and might mislead us astray. It sort of forces us to do things out of the ordinary, which might belittle our character in ways we have never imagined. So, by giving her an option, me or him, I would only help her refocus back on what she's willing to give up or sacrifice."

"Now, what if she denies the fact that she's having or had a sexual affair with someone else on the side?"

"I would have found my closure right there that same moment when she would have lied to me about him."

"So, you're telling me that if she's up front with you and is honest about it, you would have given her another chance?"

He looked at me like a child and said, "Don't we all deserve second chances?"

"Yeah. But not that bitch Rebecca!"

"Where are you going?"

"I'm not gonna sit here to listen to that bullshit! I have to get some sleep. I have an appointment later tonight."

"Well, just think about what I have told you."

"For what?!"

"Because the next time you get into a relationship with someone worth dying for, I hope you don't cheat on her, too, like the last one."

"Go to hell, Sam!"

"Where are you going?"

"The hell away from you." I stepped back inside the house. Then my cell phone rang, and I smiled.

Take 33

Melissa had a soft, sensational itch below her waist, and she needed Joey to scratch it for her.

She stepped back into the bedroom wearing a peach-colored nightgown. Her pajama top was unbuttoned, exposing part of her black lace bra. Joey was playing a video game match on the computer with his buddies again. She approached him from behind and wrapped her arms around him, leaning in to whisper in his ear.

"Are you coming to bed soon?"

"Yeah. But give me another minute."

She nibbled on his earlobe. "Are you sure?"

"Yeah." He turned his head away from her and spoke into his Bluetooth. "No. Not y'all. I'm talking to my wife here." He laughed at something that was said and added, "Whatever, dude."

Melissa hoped to persuade him to do otherwise by slowly lapping her tongue around his neck, then to his earlobe again. She whispered, "Put the game up. I want you." She then grabbed onto his private area and tried to massage it through his pants.

"Not right now, Melissa." He swiped her head off his Johnson. "I'll be with you in a bit."

"But I want you right now." She sucked on his earlobe some more. Then she added. "Why don't you stop what you're doing and come to bed with me?"

He jerked his neck to the side harder this time, forcing her to stop. "Just give me five more minutes! That's all I need, five minutes, and I'd come straight to bed with you."

"You promise?"

"Yeah," he said to her. Then he spoke into his Bluetooth. "Go to hell, you're an asshole!" He laughed about something someone said to him, then added, "In your friggin' dreams, dude."

Melissa kissed Joey on the side of his face. "In five minutes, right?"

"Yeah." He shook his head away, then quickly focused back on the computer monitor. "I promise."

She kissed him once more on the cheek and trudged to the bed. She dimmed the night light and propped the pillow behind her. She glanced at the alarm clock, which read 10:39 p.m. Her eyes drifted toward Joey, more specifically the back of his head, as he chuckled at something his friends had said to him on Bluetooth. An idea struck her. She wanted to keep herself entertained for the time being until Joey came to bed. She reached over and pulled open the drawer beside the bed, grabbing one of Joey's private adult magazines.

When she flipped the magazine open from the center, hoping to breeze through the pages, she blurted out: "Oh, my, God!" she couldn't believe how this one girl in the magazine by the name of Heather could take not only two or three dicks all at the same time, but she had four of them in her. Melissa was astonished. Her eyebrows slowly relaxed, showing a sign of curiosity now. She went to the next page.

"Mmm…" she was intrigued.

She turned the page again, seeing Heather in different penetration positions from each other as Heather's sex partners. All of them had controlled facial expressions of pleasure.

Melissa glanced over at Joey, who laughed about something. She returned to the magazine and settled in for bed. Gnawing on her bottom lip, she flipped to the next page—page 54. Her breathing quickened; adrenaline coursed through her. She glanced at Joey, then back at the magazine. Rubbing her legs together, she then separated them, spreading them apart. A twitch formed between her legs, up the middle. It was a pleasurable twitch. She reached a hand down to investigate. Besides the warmth of her front entrance, she felt wet. She looked back at Joey, then at the alarm clock again. Thirteen minutes had passed, and he still hadn't come to bed yet.

She let out a soft moan, glancing at the back of Joey's head again. He was still focused on that stupid video game!

She returned to the magazine; her panting intensified. She turned to the next page. Page 55. She felt something inside her that made her twitch again between her legs. She moaned. It was very brief, not loud or low, but just right. She glanced at Joey with a contorted expression, then quickly shot back to the magazine. She couldn't endure it any longer. She pulled the bedspread over her –up and over her breast area– then slowly stuck a hand in her panties, sticking a finger inside of herself. The middle finger. She closed her eyes and kept grinding.

She wanted more.

She slammed the magazine against her breasts over the bedspread when she felt another twitch between her legs. She held onto the magazine tightly before that twitch got away from her. Her contorted facial expression was painted with ecstasy. She opened her eyes and took another look at Joey. She wondered, *Why the fuck he's not over here yet?*

She couldn't take it anymore. She pulled the bedspread over her head, eyes closed. She went to work on herself. She slowly ground her finger, then slipped another finger inside of her.

She wanted it.

She needed it.

She humped on her fingers, penetrating them deep in her, going back and forth in slow motion. She didn't want to stop. She remembered Heather was wide open on page 57, taking all four guys at once. She remembered all their faces: she wanted to have Heather's facial expression. Melissa remembered it clearly. Heather's mouth was agape while she kept eye contact with her sexual partner in front of her.

Melissa wanted more.

She inserted a finger into her mouth, gripping it with her lips and moving her head back and forth, like Heather did for that guy on page 53. It felt so surreal to Melissa. She continued. Both of her openings were exposed. She wanted—no, she needed more.

"Melissa?"

She felt the bedspread pull away from her. She didn't care. She continued, picking up her pace as she went on.

Joey slowly crawled into bed with her. He wanted a piece of her now, but as soon as he touched her, she let out a loud grunting sound and started cumming.

"No-ooo! Please don't touch me right now! Wait!" She grunted some more. "Uh, fuck!" Her body kept trembling. She tried to hold on to that feeling as long as she could. Then she felt a twitch, followed by another. She felt drained.

Joey attempted to touch her again.

"Wait," she whispered, breathless, her eyelids heavy. "Let's wait a second till the shaking stops." She then grabbed the bedspread and wrapped herself in it. She closed her eyes and turned onto her side.

"Melissa?"

Nothing.

"Melissa?" Joey dived under the cover and lay behind her in a spooning position.

"Wait, baby," she whispered, closing her eyes. "Allow me to rest for a moment."

But the more she tried to prevent him from poking his thing in her, the more persistent he was at it. He kept pumping behind her. She gave in and removed her hand. Joey finally slid in her.

She was wet and hot.

He whispered something to her. It was probably a compliment, but she wasn't sure. Whether he said it or not, it felt like it was tossed over her head and out the window; gone with the wind. She would rather not chase after it because it held no importance to her.

She had the thought of that guy's dick on page 56 on her mind when she stuck her thumb in her mouth, slowly bobbing her head to it.

Take 34

It was ten minutes to eleven when I spat mouthwash into the bathroom sink. I then looked at myself in the mirror once more.

The rebirth of Alexander the Great.

I exited the bathroom, grabbed my blazer, and headed for the door. "Hey, Sam!" I stopped just before I walked out of the house.

"Yeah!" he responded from one of the back rooms.

"I'm about to head out! So don't bother waiting for me!"

"What the hell are you telling me that for?! Do I ever wait up for you?!"

"Go to hell then!"

"All right, I'll see you when you get back!"

"Later!" I felt the night breeze slapping me across my face as I headed to my car.

Collins Ave was teeming with people. Everyone appeared to be having a great time, whether they were heading to restaurants or nightclubs. I started the car engine, then revved it once and then twice. My Audi roared like a lion awakened from its slumber. I revved it again.

Welcome to the jungle of Miami.

Turning left, I drove down Collins Ave toward Bal Harbour, branching off to my right. I checked the navigation system to ensure I was going the right way. I was. I drove a little farther, crossing over a small bridge, then made another right turn when I reached Bay Harbour Islands. I slowed down to double-check the address because it indicated that I was in front of the designated house.

The house number read 405.

It was the right house, of course. I was impressed. It was a decent-sized house, with at least three or four bedrooms.

However, judging by the appearance of the neighborhood, it was well out of my budget.

I pulled into the driveway and parked. Only a few lights remained on in the house. I looked toward the second-story window. I could have sworn I saw someone standing there just a moment ago. Or perhaps my mind was playing tricks on me. I approached the door and rang the bell.

No answer.

I pressed the doorbell again. Then immediately afterward, I heard something behind me. I twisted around.

One of the neighbors across the street, an older white gentleman in his mid-sixties, stepped outside his house with a dog — a Cocker Spaniel.

He nodded. I nodded back, then quickly turned around when the door swung open.

"Welcome to the Beckford's resident," a Black man said, who appeared to be a butler or something along those lines. How can I help you, Sir?"

"Yes, may I speak–"

At that moment, a woman shouted from inside the house: "Winston! Send him upstairs to me!"

This presumed butler turned back around. "Can you follow me, Sir?"

I did once I stepped inside the house.

He led the way, guiding me up a massive, elegant staircase that curves toward the second floor. The walls were white and bare, devoid of art or portraits. Judging by its appearance, the owner of this house appears to be focused on saving energy or money. Only three light bulbs were turned on inside the home: one at the front door, another in the kitchen area downstairs, and the third from the dimmed chandelier. It was so dim that it barely provided enough light to navigate the house without any significant issues.

Once we reached the second floor, Winston took a few more steps and stopped at the first door on our left.

The lights were also off there.

I saw a dark, shadowy figure standing in front of a wide window, gazing outside. The lack of light in the room made it hard to see her, but it was clear that she was wearing something resembling a housecoat or robe.

"Madam Elena," Winston said. "Your guest has arrived."

"Yes, I am aware of that," she said, her back facing us. Then she advised him, "Take the rest of the night off, and I'll see you in the morning."

"Yes, ma'am." He smiled as he turned towards me.

I could have sworn he muttered a sarcastic remark under his breath when he stepped away. But I'm not sure about that. Whatever it was, he wasn't bold enough to say it loud enough for us to hear him. I turned back to the woman. She was still facing the window.

"I'm new at this," she claimed. "So come inside and close the door behind you. I want to get on with this." She then watched a car drive by.

I walked up behind her and slid her housecoat off her shoulders. She wore a bra and panties. I think she was wearing leopard print, or maybe a cougar design lingerie. Either way you look at it, it had the look of something from the '60s. She tilted her head to the side, exposing her neck to me. I read between the lines. I kissed her just below her ear before I began to suck on the back of her neck. It felt soft. There was no doubt about it; she was advanced in age. Probably around 65 years young, give or take. At that moment, I was appealing to women in this age group.

I wrapped my hand around her, suckling her breast. Then, with my other hand, I shoved it inside her panties, running my fingers all along her sliding doors. She was shaven bald down there and wet. I thought I had felt something was hard, so I returned to the same area to investigate it. I hit it again. I found it. I smiled. She had her lip pierced with a ring. I played with the ring for a moment before I pushed my middle finger in her to penetrate her entrance.

She moaned, placing her hands over mine. I guess she wanted the real thing. And she damn sure about to get it by the way she perked her ass back against my hard-on. I removed my other hand from her breast to unfasten my pants. My man's muscles had grown strong behind her. I whopped my dick out and rested it behind her. She pushed back. Her ass felt soft against me, and I could only imagine what her inside felt like. I quickly reached for her panties, tugging them down her thighs. She helped by lifting her left leg first, followed by her right leg. Her panties fell to the floor. I turned her around to face me, and I instantly froze.

I couldn't believe it.

She was the same older woman who had been harassing me along with her friend on South Beach since my arrival in Miami.

I stepped back, placing my hand on her chest to keep her from getting any closer. However, her hands were free, and she took advantage of the situation. She grabbed my dick, facing me, slowly stroking my throbbing muscle. Her hands were soft, both.

"Please...," she whispered. "Give it to me."

I felt weak after she yanked on my man tool again. I kissed her on the mouth, ignoring her wizened face.

She kissed me back, pushing forward. I fell flat on my back, legs off the bed. I thought she was going to climb around me but instead she buried the head of my dick in her mouth. She wobbled her head in a slow, technical method I hadn't experienced before, working her way further down on me. For sure, she was a professional here. She held onto my tool, slowly stroking it, while her mouth worked wonders. I watched her for a hot second before I shut my eyes. She was probably an elder, but young at heart. She knew what she was doing in this field. She seemed to be an experienced driver as she bobbed her head slightly in response to a gentle pull, all in slow motion. It felt too relaxing. I rested one hand on the back of her head, then my other hand too. I opened my eyes again to take another peek at her—my mouth agape. I couldn't believe what I had missed all these years.

She began slurping, creating those beautiful love songs with her mouth.

Just as I was about to close my eyes again, I thought I saw a shadow, a phantom-like figure, looming over my face. However, it wasn't a shadow when I zoomed in on the dim image. Instead, it was someone's leg.

I focused in and saws someone easing her pussy downwards, straight for my face. I mean literally, straight to my face.

I was positive that it was Elena's friend who constantly hang out with her on the beach, even though Elena paused for a hot moment, from sucking on my dick, to say, "Pam, we finally got him. Make sure he eats it well."

And as Pamula was about to sit on my face, I guided her to my mouth just before she missed the bullseye slightly more to the left.

Alright, she established contact.

I lapped my tongue across Pamula's opening, then stretched her labia lips apart from one another. I took another swipe between her legs and put my tongue to work.

She leaned forward, hovering herself like a beautiful butterfly, resting her breasts on the headboard of the bed. I slowed my flickering tongue down when her pussy juice oozed from her love hole like a melting ice cream. Vanilla flavor. I slurped on her clitoris bud for a few seconds before I threw my tongue back in full motion. I revved her pussy up on full blast. Her legs jerked, and then again. My tongue was too much for her.

She attempted to jump off my face!

I held her in position, cuffing my arms around her thighs so she couldn't run. Then, I shook my head beneath her, sticking my tongue deep in her, which nearly drove her crazy.

"Uh, fuck!" she grabbed my head, pulling it up toward her pussy, while pumping hard against my face. "Eat this pussy, motherfucker! Eat it!"

I did. I kept licking and sticking my tongue in her. Then, within a matter of seconds after I swiped my tongue across her asshole a few times, she exploded with a massive orgasm. I could have sworn she had squirted a bottle of mayonnaise in my mouth if I didn't know better. I felt her stomach and legs go into a convulsion. I held onto her. I nibbled and sucked on her clitoris bud for about three minutes straight to help stimulate it, senselessly while her friend Elena worked wonders on me down below. And it wasn't long after that when I felt a tingling sensation in my stomach. I cupped the back of Elena's head and started pumping my tool in her mouth.

She picked up speed.

"Oh, keep going!" I mumbled with Pamula's pussy in my mouth. "Keep going!" I held my hand on the back of Elena's head, hoping to control her head motion. She went faster. "Uh, fuck!" My oil rig erupted like a volcano.

If Elena's mouth weren't there to catch it, my nut would have shot straight in the air. She removed her mouth away from my man tool after a few seconds, taking half of my nut down her throat. I felt the rest of my cum dribble from the head of my dick. Then, within seconds—or should I say after a second? Elena started flicking her tongue over my shaft.

And it felt fucking good!

I wanted to kiss Elena for her superb job down there, but couldn't because Pamula was still on my face. So instead of kissing Elena in the mouth, I just stuck my tongue deep inside Pamula's pussy, twirling it around, as if I was tongue kissing Elena. But to my surprise, Elena stopped flicking her tongue against my man tool and left it stranded, just like that. I felt abandoned. I wanted to cry because, other than that, I was still hard; I wanted Elena to keep going. But then … *oh, my goodness* Elena inserted my fat tool inside her pussy, working her way down on it.

It was a perfect fit.

Elena's pussy hugged me. Her love tunnel was not only hot and creamy, but it had a Tempur-Pedic feel to it. With no disrespect to those who are close-minded, I felt like a motherfucking god inside of her! I swear, after she made her way down on my rod, she bounced only a few times before she started gushing cum all over me like a busted kitchen pipe. Seconds later—no, in fact, it was about two seconds later, at most, when her contractions went out of control. I guess she tried to subdue her contractions by pressing her pussy against my pelvis area, grunting and screaming like a porn star, while trying to cram my dick inside of her.

Her pussy still throbbed with strong twitches, as she slowly stated gyrating her hip in a way that made me wanting to question her real age. Although she seemed to be in her mid-to-late sixties, up close, her movements didn't reflect that age; instead, she started rocking on me again as if she were in her early thirties, looking forward to her second orgasm.

It wouldn't surprise me if she had a 5-Hour Energy drink before I arrived.

And what seemed like a good half an hour of pure fucking and sucking, they both maneuvered around and switched places with each other, taking turns on me.

Now, let's talk about feeling cheap. But it was definitely worth it. I have a different taste in my mouth now. Salty yet sweet. For the thrill of it, I soaked my finger with Pamula's pussy juice and run my finger around the rim of her anus, hoping to bring her to another orgasm. I munched on her pussy at the same time as if I was eating a corn on the cob.

By the look of it, Pamula got excited by the way I was slurping on her pussy because she started rocking her pussy on my face, begging me not to stop.

I didn't know if she was talking about my finger or my tongue, so for the hell of it, I kept both at work. Then she humped back a little more, perking her ass back on my finger. Then, on the next pump with a little arch in her back, my finger slid in her ass, then popped back out.

Smooth Casanova

She grunted and started humping back a little further, trying her best, I guess to catch my finger again. Or perhaps she wanted to chase after that tingling sensation she felt a short moment ago when her body shivered like an uncontrollable freak. I kept my finger still, and she located it immediately. She perked her ass back some more, sorta like wiggling her hips backward until her asshole swallowed my finger, hitting the bullseye.

I guess that's what she wanted, then. So, of course, I pumped my middle finger in her ass for a hot minute, trying my best to bring her to another orgasm. But then she plopped my finger out of her ass when she climbed off me, letting her passion ebbed.

That threw me off because she was the one who was getting the better thrill of it. I couldn't imagine why she would suddenly stop like that.

Then she made it known when she said, "I want you to stick your dick in my ass."

Wow! I smiled when she got on all four.

Take 35

Rebecca slipped out from under the bedcovers, trying not to wake Juan.

She sneaked out of the bedroom into the bathroom, locking her door behind her. She looked at the engagement ring that Juan had given her, then at a shoebox that she had placed on the sink countertop. Her eyes watered as she opened the box.

She once exchanged letters, photos, notes, postcards, poems, and ripped ticket vouchers with someone else.

Old memories haunted her.

She went for the marriage proposal poem she had discovered on the side of the nightstand while cleaning a few months ago. After reading the poem, she folded it back up. Tears rolled down her face as she reached for the stack of photos next. The images included both old and new pictures she had taken over the years, from her college days to about seven months ago. She carefully scanned through the photos one by one. Among them, she spotted an old graduation photo taken on the beach during the Couples' Night Out event.

She tried to smile when she saw how silly she and her friends looked, all bundled up around a bonfire, making faces, she thought, if her memory served her correctly, while David was trying to take a picture of them. Nevertheless, she ended up crying as she remembered her past.

She set the photo down and reached for the other stack of pictures. Likewise, she went through them, one by one, reminiscing. There were senior prom pictures, park pictures, beach pictures, birthday pictures, and old photos she had taken while on a cruise ship to the Bahamas with the Princess Cruise Line. She knew her new life would never be the same again. She was absolutely certain of that—one hundred percent positive.

After admitting this to herself, she ripped a photo and tossed it into the toilet. She flushed it and then moved on to the other images.

She started to cry as she tore the photos into pieces, ripping three to four pictures at a time. Just when she was about to shred the very last photo in her hand, she paused: it was a goofy photo that she had taken with her ex.

She cried.

Then, a knock echoed from the bathroom door.

It was Juan. "What the hell are you doing in there?!"

Take 36

You can call it whatever you want: a foot fetish, a sexual fixation, or an obsession with toes. But to me, it's none of those.

I just loved the way Ms. Ginsberg smiles when I massage her feet. She seemed so at peace with herself, and that's even without me having sex with her.

"Oh, yeah … Right there."

"Here?" I used both thumbs on the bottom of her foot.

"Yeah." She leaned her head back, falling into a world of relaxation. "Apply a little more pressure for me, darling."

I did; I started to rub deep in the center of her foot.

Her toes curled, then she wiggled them like they played a good piano. She lifted her head. "What is it?"

"What, is what?" I was confused. "What are you talking about?"

"You know exactly what I'm referring to: Why are you smiling like that? It must be a reason behind it."

"I'm just thinking about you." That was the truth.

"About what?"

I kept that same smile on my face, unsure of how to approach the situation and ask her if she would mind taking our friendship to the next level. In a way, Samuel was right: I would rather wake up beside a female in the morning than not wake up beside anyone at all.

"What is it?"

Of course, I refrained from telling her the truth because she had advised me several times that she wanted to keep our relationship as it was, without changing it.

"Are you going to tell me or what?" she asked, then tried to seduce me by playing her other foot between my crotch area. "C'mon, tell me sweetie," she said, while pretending to be innocent yet exposing that lechery side of her, as she massaged my flaccid muscle with her foot. Then she dragged, *"Please..."*

Okay, I broke a bit without fully explaining it: "I would like to take you out somewhere. On my account."

She seemed caught off guard yet excited. "Where?"

"Anywhere. To a nice restaurant? Movie? Or perhaps, take you out to a nice movie theater, so we could go hide somewhere in the back and do something naughty."

"When?"

"Whenever you want to." I immediately thought about my date with Cathy tonight at six o'clock. "We can go now or later tonight to catch a late-night movie."

"It can't be today," her smile slowly deteriorated, "because I must meet up with Snookum at the office later. I must go over a few things with her, because I don't like how my records look right now."

"Do you need me to stop by tonight to check in on you?"

"That would be wonderful. But no. I don't know how long it would take me to review my record with Snookum. Because, unlike before, I intend to go over everything with her this time. My entire file. And this could end up with her all night." She paused, then added, "Let's just meet back here on Tuesday when I get back."

"Tuesday?"

"Remember when I told you last week that I had to go on a business trip to California for a few days?"

"That's right." I have forgotten about that.

The room got quiet.

Then she broke our silence: "I wish I could just take you along."

"Shoo. Who says you can't? Aside from meeting up with some old friends this weekend, I don't have any other important plans. I could easily set this weekend aside to go out to California with you, if you want me to."

"No. Perhaps next time."

The room grew quiet again, only for a short moment.

It seemed like she had second thoughts about inviting me to California with her, but then she quickly shook her head to dismiss the idea. She was sticking to her original decision. To ease the tension, she broke the silence again, saying, "I have spoken to Eddie, the captain of my yacht, today, in which he had informed me that everything is on schedule for you and your friends tomorrow."

"Thanks."

"Oh! So that's how you thank me now?"

Without saying a word, I released her foot from my hands and stood in front of her. She kept her eyes on me. I began to unbutton my shirt. After pulling it off, I turned my attention to my pants. I knew the perfect way to thank her.

She smiled broadly, as if she were smiling at the camera.

Cheese!

Take 37

"Would you like to have a little more wine, ma'am?"

"Yes, I wouldn't mind just a little, please." Cathy watched the waiter pour *Cotes du Rhone* into her wine glass. "Thank you."

"You're welcome. And what about you, sir?"

"No, thanks." I just wanted him to leave so I could spend some time with Cathy, but he kept returning to our table! "If I need something to drink, I'll make sure to flag you for one. But right now, I'd like to continue my conversation" –I stammered for the right words to use– "with my lady friend here."

"Oh, I'm sorry."

"It was well received," I said, without ending it with *Get the fuck outta here!*

He walked away.

My entire facial expression changed when I looked back at Cathy. She wore a stunning, sleeveless white dinner dress that exuded an Olivia Wilde vibe. In other words, Cathy was simply beautiful. She was a sight to behold. I guess that's why the man with the round face at the neighboring table kept his eyes on her the whole time. I didn't want to seem rude or out of line when I cleared my throat with a fake cough to grab the jerk's attention, but I had to. He was crossing a line, with his chair turned toward Cathy, watching her every move.

I can only imagine she felt uncomfortable.

That was the only reason I said, "Excuse me!" this time to him, because clearing my throat didn't work. "Excuse me, sir?"

The porky-faced man looked at me.

"Do you mind?" I shot him a look that said, *C'mon, dude, you're going a little overboard with this shit now.*

He made a wry face, huffed, and then glanced back at Cathy.

137

This might be a test, I thought. Cathy kept her gaze fixed on me. I barely shook my head, knowing this made me look like a punk in front of her.

This felt like a mix of pride and embarrassment in a big cereal bowl, as I geared up for a Friday night fight on ESPN, trying my best to impress someone I liked. I couldn't help but shake my head with a snicker because if I jumped from the table and beat his fat ass over there, I would look like the bad guy since he seems to be in his sixties. Okay, maybe in his seventies, with an oxygen tube coming from his nose attached to that small container beside him.

"I'm sorry for this."

"Pardon me?" I turned back to Cathy because her statement threw me off.

"I'm sorry for the way I'm dressed tonight."

"No, don't be. I am happy you dress like this. No, I meant–" I cut it short because I don't think that was coming out right. At least not how I wanted it to. "What I meant to say is that you look beautiful as you are. So basically, it's not what you're wearing; it's who's wearing it. And, bottom line, you looked beautiful in it."

I don't know if it was blush or makeup, but other than that, she managed to say, with a whisper, "Thank you."

We looked at each other and fell into a deep silence.

"Would you like me to refill your glass?"

Cathy and I both looked up at the same time.

It was the waiter again.

You must be kidding me, I thought.

But before I could say anything, Cathy interjected and said to him, "No, thank you. However, we would like to have our check, please."

She must have read my mind; I wanted to smile as the waiter walked away.

Then, minutes later, we decided to stroll along the beach instead of going to the movies as planned. "So, tell me," I began to ask her when two couples walked past us with their arms wrapped around each other, "what are you looking for in a man?"

Cathy gave me a disoriented smile while concealing her high heels in her hand.

"Allow me to correct that." I tried to approach my question from a different angle. "If you decide to get involved with someone, what would be your most important criteria?"

"My standards?"

I nodded.

"You," that slipped out of her mouth like a whisper, then she twisted her head toward the ocean as we continued walking on the sand.

I was willing to give her all the time she needed.

But then she twisted back to me and said, "I wish I had my long list with me."

I smiled.

She emphasized, "First and foremost, I would like honesty. That's the focus on all relationships. Don't you agree?"

"Of course." I wanted her to continue.

She did: "When it comes down to other potentials, I would like to have a close companionship with someone that I can talk to and hold a decent conversation with, and he has to be humorous and funny, too." She laughed, but it was a brief, giggling laugh. Then she asked, "Do you have the time to hear all the qualifications I would like to see in a good relationship?"

"I have all the time in the world, just to hear what you say."

She playfully muttered a second under her breath as a sharp hum. "Well, since you insist, I like someone open-minded and able to think outside the box … Uhhh … Someone kind and generous." She quickly paused for a moment. Then she immediately added, "I most definitely like to be treated with respect and pampered at times … uhhh–"

"Are you for real?"

"Yes. I'm for real."

I knew she was playing with me now, so I joked back. "I see that you must have researched me, then?"

"I beg your pardon?" Her smile vanished abruptly, as if she had been thrust into the spotlight before a grand jury.

So, I clarified: "I see that you must have done your research about me. Because of the qualities you're describing about a man standing beside you."

Her facial expression relaxed, and she seemed much more at ease than before. She appeared at a loss for words. Slowly, she looked away and then, with bated breath, asked, "And what about you?" She turned back to me. "What sort of qualities interest you in a good relationship with someone?"

"Honestly?"

"Yeah."

I was afraid of that. I just hoped she would be more open-minded.

Take 38

I decided not to lie to Cathy when I told her, "I'm somewhere along the same lines as you. I'm a simple type of guy who would be satisfied with someone who can sometimes be a backbone."

"So, are you weak?" she tried to throw a joke at me.

"No. Not at all." Well, at least that's what I thought. "But what I mean by saying that I'm looking for a woman who can be a backbone at times, is that I need one who can encourage me in times of doubt. To give me that push I need to be strong and move forward into being a better man for the sake of a good relationship, without her backsliding on our commitments," my voice faded low. Then I picked back up: "That's all I'm looking for right now. Someone I can believe in, and she believes in me." I shut it down right there. I had old memories running through my mind, sickening me, as we kept walking.

Then Cathy said, "Thank goodness then."

I looked at her. "About what?"

"That I don't meet your qualifications for a woman."

"You know," with all jokes aside, even though I started smiling with her, I told her, "you are such an asshole."

She laughed. It was so authentic, and loud too.

It was the first time she had stepped out of her shell, exposing that other side of her personality before me, and I enjoyed it.

From there, we discussed everything that came to mind while leaving specific topics about our past relationships open. Since she shared about her previous relationship, I learned that she had been with a guy who, it turned out, was sleeping with their next-door neighbor, who had a situation very similar to mine. I opened up and told her everything about Rebecca. I mean, truly everything. I even shared how I first met Rebecca in college and walked her through my past relationship with her up until the point when she claimed to be working overtime. Later, I discovered that Rebecca had lied to me when I caught her with another man, especially on our anniversary—the very day I intended to propose to her with a diamond ring I had worked so hard for.

"I'm sorry to hear that."

"Don't be unless you were the cause of our breakup. But knowing who I have met along the way now, after our breakup, I wouldn't mind if you were the cause behind it."

"Why is that?"

I remembered to smile. "Because I would have never had a chance to have met someone as sweet as you, if you hadn't done so."

She smiled back and did that thing with her eyes, while making a funny facial expression to indicate doubt about my statement.

We walked further down the beach and found a nice spot to rest our legs. Then we discussed other topics: What do we enjoy doing in our leisure time? Cathy said she likes to relax at the spa or in the bathtub; I mentioned that I enjoy writing poems. Next, I talked about food. Have you ever tasted this or that before? Besides that, she named foods and drinks that I had never heard of before, and I mean that literally. I laughed hard when she admitted to having tasted every possible food that I had mentioned to her: fried chicken, Jamaican curry goat, roast lamb in sweet gravy, and then, of all scavengers in the world, I added and lied about eating jerk pork.

I laughed when she claimed to have tasted them all, even the jerk pork, despite it conflicting with our kosher diet. After all, I knew she was joking about the pork mess when she said her favorite dish was pig mountain oysters.

Then, somehow, we drifted off to discussing our differing political viewpoints on how the government was operating.

It's funny how we were both conservatives, but I'm now leaning more toward the liberal side since Donald Trump emerged and lost sight of the real message: There's too much government control, and they don't see us as their citizens but rather as their slaves.

"It appears that Congress tends to forget what ignited the flames for the Revolutionary War in America against Great Britain," Cathy said. "It was the high taxes on everything that the people had had enough of and decided to fight for their freedom, by the only means necessary to preserve a better life for their children's future. However, today's politics are stripping us of the same freedom our Founding Fathers established."

I slowly nodded my head.

Then we switched channels and both agreed that George W. Bush was a good, if not excellent, president. Still, he couldn't expand his executive power to get everything in order before leaving the Oval Office. He was more focused on the global war on terror around the world—and I agreed with Cathy on this, too—while he attempted to sell the stockpile of military equipment that the Pentagon had accumulated over the years to members of the United Nations.

We had to devise a strategy to position ourselves effectively in the Arabian Gulf's oil market and find a way to sell our old military stockpile to them, thereby introducing the new toys: the Air Drones.

However, when it came to our backyard, President Bush couldn't clean up the mess that former President Bill Clinton had created just before leaving office, having signed the Free Trade Agreement without any stipulations attached.

Good old Bill was confused and unable to think clearly after the Monica Lewinsky scandal, which ultimately contributed to the financial meltdown in America as President Bush was leaving office.

"Truthfully," I threw in my two cents now, "I don't understand why Bush would take the fall for Bill Clinton's mistakes and not tell the American people the truth."

"That is because it was all a diversion, of staying on course of their ultimate goal of the New World Order," she said. Then she shifted to a different topic: "So tell me, have you ever traveled outside the United States?"

"Other than the Bahamas and Haiti, no. Not really."

"You ought to visit other countries and explore a world beyond your horizon."

I bet there is. But then again, there's no other country like America. Only the bureaucrats in Washington, D.C., are ruining it for us.

After ten more minutes of our idle chat, a cool breeze blew, and she shivered.

"What time is it?" she asked.

"It's … It's seven minutes to midnight."

143

"Well," she began to say, getting up from a folded beach chair, "it's getting late, and I need to start heading home now."

Damn!

She added, "Are you going to walk me to the boulevard to catch a cab, or are you going to sit right there?"

I finally got it. "I can drive you home, if you like."

"No, I'd rather take a cab home instead."

"But I insist."

"I appreciate your offer, but I must refuse it now."

She keeps her location hidden behind a veil of secrecy.

"All right then." I walked her to Collins Ave. "We need to continue our conversation on another date."

"On another date?" she questioned with a smile.

"Yeah." I smiled back at her.

She quickly raised her hand to hail a cab, just as the driver was about to pass by. "Perhaps."

"Perhaps soon?"

"Maybe."

The cab driver made a U-turn and pulled over. She extended her hand toward the back passenger door, but I quickly beat her to the punch: I opened the door for her.

"Thank you."

"You're welcome. But honestly, I'd rather settle for a kiss instead."

She paused from getting into the cab and twisted back to me. I kept still. She reached in and kissed me on my cheek.

It was well received: A kiss is a kiss, I last remembered.

She got inside the cab.

And I made a desperate plea: "Call me."

"I will."

I closed the door and watched my potential future wife slowly drive away with that Hispanic cab driver.

My insecurity kicked in, but I smiled nonetheless: I remembered that episode when she joked about not meeting the qualifications I was looking for in a woman. I kept my eyes on the cab and smiled even when I thought about–

"Casanova?"

I twisted to the side.

It was Emma Wolf, along with two of her girlfriends. "I was just telling them about you."

"Was it good or bad?"

"It was good, of course." She wore a beguiling smile. "And that was one of the main reasons I was about to call you to see if you would like to hang out with a few lonely ladies tonight?"

I quickly glanced at the older woman on Emma's far right—she appeared to be at least in her sixties—because a perverted smile spread across her face.

"So, would you like to hang out with us for the night?"

I cut back to Emma and then looked at the other lady on her left—she appeared slightly younger than both of them, placing her in her late forties. She was thoughtfully nodding her head, offering me an open invitation.

"Why not, since y'all beautiful ladies look lovely tonight?"

The older lady on the right hooked her arm around mine. "I would feel much safer like this. Would this be a problem for you?"

"No. But of course not." I hooked my arm back on hers, smiling with her.

"Well, I need to feel safe too, then," the other female said, who was standing on the other side of Emma while taking my other arm.

I hooked my other arm around hers, too.

"Oh, my..." Emma could have won an Academy Award for her excellent performance when she started to pat her pockets.

I fell for it. "Have you lost something?"

"No. Not really," she said. "I have accidentally left my billfold inside the hotel room." She smiled at her friends, then back at me. "Do you mind walking us to our room so I may retrieve it?"

Even though I had just realized she had been lying to me, I said, "Sure, why not?" with a smile on my face.

She led the way with a nice swagger.

I'm gonna have fun tonight, I thought. I had a fresh pack of condoms in my pocket: Lifestyle, ultra-thin.

Take 39

"I tried to get over here as fast as I could," Linda said to Rebecca from outside the driver's window as she pulled into Powell's Gym parking lot. "So, pop the hood of your car."

Rebecca did.

Linda parked her small Toyota Camry facing Rebecca's car, which had the hood up and the engine running. She got out of the vehicle with jumper cables in her hand.

"I don't know what happened to it," Rebecca claimed, stepping out of her car. "It just shut off on me. I might have left the door open, and it killed the battery."

"Well, hopefully this would work."

Rebecca helped Linda connect the jumper cables to both car batteries, then returned to their cars.

As Linda reached for her car door, she said, "I need you to try to crank it up when I tell you to!"

Rebecca pretended to be following her instructions.

Linda revved the car engine. "Try to start it."

Nothing.

Then Linda said, "Try it again!"

Nothing.

"Are you turning the ignition?!"

"I guess!"

Linda relaxed her car engine and stepped out. She walked over to Rebecca. "Try it again."

Nothing.

Rebecca regarded her with a blank expression, not even trying to start the car engine.

"You must at least turn the key in the ignition if you wanna start it up."

Again, no attempt.

Then Linda asked, "There's nothing wrong with your car, is it?"

Rebecca shook her head slowly, then turned her left hand palm down to reveal the engagement ring to Linda. She appeared more perplexed than enthusiastic.

"Oh my god, let me see it!"

Rebecca stepped out of the car so Linda could get a better look at her ring.

"It's beautiful." Linda kept her eyes on the ring, then looked at her. "So, who gave it to you?"

"Juan. He proposed to me the other day at work, asking me in front of my class: Would I marry him?"

"What did you say? Yes, right?"

"Yeah, but ...," her voice trailed off. Then she said, "I don't know."

"What don't you know about?"

Rebecca's eyes watered. "About everything," she said. "It seems so different."

It didn't need a rocket scientist to figure out what she was talking about.

That was the only reason Linda told her, "I love Cassidy with all my heart, and I love you, too. But you must let Cassidy go. He's gone. He went on with his life, which I think you should focus on yours now. I will still be here for you, whether I approve or disapprove of the choices you made or will make in the future." She paused. Then she added, "I'm your friend, Rebecca. And I'm here for you."

Rebecca wrapped her arms around Linda and shed a few tears. "I love you."

"I love you, too." Linda was the first to pull away. "If you're happy with this guy, Juan, marry him. Only if you believe it's worth it."

Rebecca slowly gnawed on her bottom lip.

"So, tell me," Linda began, "does he make you happy?"

"Yeah," Rebecca stammered.

"And he hasn't put his hands on you again, since then, right?"

"No. He hasn't," Rebecca lied, unknowingly gripping her arm. "He only hit me before when he was under the influence of alcohol, and he hasn't gotten drunk like that since the last time."

"Well," Linda smiled as she dragged her words, then added, "go for it. But you could only marry him under one condition."

"Which is?"

"Can I be a part of your wedding?"

"Of course." Rebecca finally smiled, wrapping her arms around Linda again.

At that precise moment, Linda's cell phone began to ring. She looked at the caller's ID.

It was from Ronald.

She took the call.

Take 40

"Here goes another joke," David said, as Ronald, Brad, and I walked down the marina dock with two cases of beer. "A guy from Vicksburg, Mississippi, wanted to travel the states to observe undeveloped areas. But when he reached a small rural town in West Virginia, he was suddenly caught off guard by a terrible thunderstorm and needed shelter for the night, at least until the storm calmed down. By the grace of God, there was a lodging house nearby, and he ran inside, soaking wet, demanding to speak to the hotel manager because the clerk at the front desk told him that there weren't any vacant rooms available for the night.

When the manager heard the traveler's sullen story, he told the traveler, *This is what I can do for you. There's a shed out back with a bed inside. For twenty dollars, you can have it for the night, so you can stay dry and perhaps get a good night's sleep.*

The traveler agreed. He went out and fell asleep in the shed. But then about three o'clock in the morning he was suddenly woke up by a double barrel shotgun to his head, with a fat hillbilly redneck shouting at him, demanding to know why the fuck the traveler was sleeping in his bed! So here the traveler stated crying, telling this fat redneck that the manager up front rented the shed to him for the night. However, the redneck didn't wanna hear that shit from him, showing little or no compassion at all for the traveler's unfortunate situation, but instead strongly advising the traveler that if he didn't suck his dick, he was gonna blow the fucking traveler's head off with the shotgun.

So, about twenty minutes later, the traveler came running into the front office, demanding to see the manager again. And when the manager came out, the traveler asked him what kinda sick fucking motel you're running here?

The manager asked him, *What happened?*

And the traveler told him that he as woke from his sleep with a shotgun to his head, with a fat fucking hillbilly demanding that the traveler suck his dick or else he was going to kill him in there.

So, the manager asked the traveler, *What did you do?*

The traveler replied, What the hell do you think I did? I'm here telling you the friggin' story as to what happen a short moment ago! That mean I had to suck his dick in there to live, you fucking asshole …! I want my twenty dollars back!"

We burst out laughing.

"Okay, okay, okay." David stumbled over his words: "Here's another joke."

We all continued walking toward the back end of the marina.

Then David asked us, "How much do you think it costs to have a good time on Friday night?"

Ronald retorted, "I don't know, how much?"

"I don't know either. But for all its worth, I think Brad's mom overcharged me a few extra dollars for a shot of her ass last night after she got me drunk with tequila sunrise over at her place."

Brad popped David on the head; he played back.

When we approached Ms. Ginsberg's yacht, I said, "Here we go."

David stopped horsing around and got excited: "Get outta here!"

It was almost exactly that moment when two guys who had piloted the yacht before, when I came out here with Ms. Ginsberg last month, were now excited about the vessel. "You're Cassidy, right?" the man on my right asked me.

"Yeah."

"Well, I'm Eddie. You and your friends can hop aboard so we can unfasten the lines for you."

"You're coming along with us, right?" I asked because Ms. Ginsberg informed me that he was.

"No," the other pilot said. "You have another captain on board the boat, and everything has been taken care of already. You all would sail down to the keys, then make ways toward Haiti; then back."

"Great." I twisted to the side when I saw David and Brad go abroad on the yacht, playing. Ronald got on board next, and I followed behind him.

Eddie and the other guy unhooked the boat's latches and waved their hands to another pilot behind the tented window, signaling that we were ready.

The horn sounded, and then the yacht gradually drifted away in shallow water.

David and Brad wrestled a bit for the corner seat. Brad won. Then David started clowning on him, making jesters that Brad be dancing for queers and transvestites at some colored people nightclubs for dollars.

"Yeah," Brad joked back, "and I saw your dad, too. He was wearing your mom's housedress, backing that ass up for one of the guys in there. But you should have seen him in the restroom stall afterward."

"Fuck you, dude!"

We all laughed as we headed out to the open water. Then we joked about how David had fought Joey a few times over comments he supposedly made about me behind my back.

But, hey! I don't care about the sarcasm that jerk wanted to spread about me in hopes of tarnishing my name and reputation, because Joey could never be me. Then we changed the topic to how David and a new guy named Marcus were neck and neck in hooking up with the women at my old job at Powell's Roofing. David claimed that he had beaten Marcus, but Ronald disputed David's claims by discussing a different point. Still, even with the information I had gathered so far, David had ended up with practically every girl I knew, including that Muslim girl, Fatima Nazanin Ahmed.

Unbelievable.

Fatima wasn't just any Muslim girl: she was an adorable Palestinian beauty, no doubt, with a nice figure reminiscent of Jennifer Aniston's. And from what I gather, Fatima enjoys it when someone takes her from behind.

Just sign me up.

"And you won't believe who's getting married soon?" David asked me, shifting the topic again.

"Who?"

But Ronald told David, "Don't do that."

"Why?"

"Because…," that's all Ronald said to him.

I glanced at David, then at Ronald. I returned my gaze to David. "What?" I asked, feeling both confused and excluded, although I wore a curious smile. "What's happening?" Nothing. I turned back to Ronald. "Why don't you want him to tell me?"

Brad said, "I think we ought to tell him," speaking more to Ronald than to us.

Ronald kept quiet.

"To hell with this!" David said, refusing to hold back from telling me. "Rebecca is supposed to marry that Hispanic guy, Juan, next month. Everything was already set. But Linda, on the other hand, is against the marriage because this guy, Juan, is beating Rebecca's ass regularly." He made a face. "As if you should care."

"Yeah, you're right: I don't care who she intends to marry." I meant that, "I have a new life now. So, she can marry whoever she pleases and get her ass whooped by him, too."

David turned to Ronald. "See, I told you so. My homeboy doesn't give a fuck about that shit!"

I turned to Ronald and asked, "You didn't tell Linda that I'm back in contact with you?"

"No," he barely shook his head.

"Well, don't. At least, not yet."

"Sure."

However, the look he gave me made me uncertain.

We all sank into a deep tranquility. Then David broke the silence, saying, "We should go fishing over there." He kept his eyes transfixed on a few other steadfast boats to our left. "Why don't you try to get the captain of this boat to go over there?"

Brad grabbed his fishing pole, and David did as well.

I attempted to get the captain's attention by swaying my hand and then both hands. However, the yacht continued to cruise further out.

"Give me a sec," I told them. "I'm going to try to have him go back there with those other boats, so we can go fishing with them."

They agreed.

I approached the captain's tinted window and knocked.

No answer.

I went to the door. The window on the door was also tinted. I knocked.

Again, no answer.

I knocked again. Nothing. I cupped my hands to my eyes to peer through the dark-tinted window for a clearer view inside the cabin. I saw a hand beckoning me to come in. I attempted to unlatch the door.

"It's locked!"

Then I heard a clicking noise.

I approached the door once more and opened it. "Hey, do you think we can sail back to where those other boats were so we can go fishing with them?"

"Why?"

I found it rude, if not impolite, to respond with another question. But when the pilot's chair turned around, to my surprise, it was Ms. Ginsberg wearing a captain's hat.

"Hey, there!" She smiled

I smiled back and closed the door behind me.

Take 41

I approached Ms. Ginsberg with a big smile on my face since she was at the yacht helm. "Whatever happened to your business trip to California that you had mentioned?"

"I rescheduled it for next week."

"Why didn't you tell me about this last night when we were together? I could have made some arrangements for us tonight."

"I wanted to surprise you instead," she said. Then she asked: "So are you surprised?"

"Yes." My smile was still painted on my face. "But of course."

She shut off the boat engine. I looked out the tinted window and saw Ronald and David casting their fishing lines into the ocean. Brad popped open a beer bottle.

"Come here."

I twisted back to Ms. Ginsberg and followed her instructions.

She took her hat off, leaned back in the chair, and raised her skirt a little. "I'm not wearing any panties for you."

I looked. I was amazed.

Then she said, "I want you to eat it for me."

I glanced at the tinted window again, trying to keep an eye on everyone out there, then back at her. "Right here? Right now?"

"Yes." She wore a serious expression this time. "I want you to do the same thing you did for me last night."

I stepped toward her, glancing back at the tinted window.

"Don't worry about them," she said. "I'll keep an eye out for us."

Say no more. I licked my lips, slowly taking a knee to the floor, then my other knee. She rested her hand on my head, guiding me toward her stash spot. I parted her labia lips and started feasting.

I began to work wonders on her, in an ungodly way, shivering and shaking my tongue against her clitoris for about ten minutes straight, while my middle finger played on her G-spot. I had her screaming in tongues, begging me not to stop. I'm not sure how many times she got off on me, but I am positive that she came twice when she squirted in my mouth, demanding that I swallow it. And I did. I kept beating my tongue against her clitoris bud until her legs stopped quivering. Then I heard a pleasant voice that brought music to my ears.

"I want you to stick your dick inside me now."

That's all I needed to hear. I got up. She helped me unzip my shorts. I looked at the tinted window again to see what my friends were doing. They were still fishing. Then, before I could prevent Ms. Ginsberg from taking over our little sexual encounter, she stroked my manhood a few times and then buried the head of it inside her mouth. My dick grew stronger by the second every time she bobbed her head over it.

I combed her hair aside with my fingers to get a look at her. It looked beautiful how her mouth stretched open for me. It was sort of like a remake of a Kardashian's sex flick. Ms. Ginsberg looked up, giving me that same sensational stare, all eye contact, serious facial expression, no smile, while doing her thing down there on me. She made sweet sounds with her mouth. Then she tightened her lips around me and firmly pulled away from my dick that almost made me fainted right there on the spot.

"Okay, it's ready now," she said.

You damn right, it was! I thought.

My man tool was more complex than a rock.

I reached in and kissed her on the mouth while helping her back up. When she stood before me, I twisted her around to position her from behind. I raised her skirt –just high enough to rest it over her back– and groped the head of my tool along the opening of her entrance. I slid my manhood into her. Her love nest blanketed me with devotion, and I showed appreciation by working the hell out of her for about five minutes straight before she came again. She slumped over the dashboard. I kept pumping in her, but very slowly, though, while feeling her inside muscles spasmed around me. I felt love. And only when her contractions stopped, I pull my tool out of her and rubbed it over her ass cheeks. I didn't want to cum yet. At least not for now. That was the main reason why I played with her, sliding my man tool along the crack of her ass, shooting it back and forth as if I was inside of her.

She gyrated her hips in small, circular motions. I pivoted right along with her until a naughty thought came to mind. I went for it:

I started pocking my man tool at her back door, barely grinding on it.

"No. Don't stop," I whispered, trying to work my way into her. "Keep moving for me."

She did. She started pumping her ass back toward me. Only a little though. "Don't go so hard. Take your time, sweetie."

"I am." I felt her sphincter open up for me, but then spat me back out. "Just relax a little."

No comments.

I pried the head of my dick back in her, slowly grinding in her back door. "That's it," I told her, after her asshole loosen up a little more. "Just keep moving like that for me."

"Like this?"

"Yeah." Her sphincter felt like a tight elastic rubber band around my dick when I pierced another inch inside her, then two more inches.

"Not all of it. Okay?"

"Uh-huh." I thought she was crazy for telling me that. I only had about four inches in her. I kept grinding in her hole in hope to get a little more on my tool inside of her, because, truthfully, I didn't want to hear that bullshit from her. Her love tunnel was feeling too good to only stick half of my dick inside of her.

She told me to slow down some more. I did. I dropped my pace a notch, trying to pry my tool further in her. That was a must. I had a little over half of my tool inside her when she started humping back on me. I went a little deeper into her. Another inch deeper. I grabbed hold of her hips and started picking up my pace again. Another inch more. It didn't take long for me to stick my whole dick inside her. She gasped with ecstasy when she felt my nuts slapping against her ass, moaning begging me not to stop.

I didn't. I kept pounding at her, with a straightaway motion, with no interruption. I brought her to an orgasm so powerful that she started trembling. Her body felt like it was going into convulsions. She shouted something in Yiddish, I think: She said it too fast, with a blurt. But I could tell you this: whatever she said got me so excited that I started pounding in her faster.

Then she said something else that I would probably never forget: "I want you to cum for me."

In her ass?

Smooth Casanova

You had heard it yourself. She said it in plain English. The old American way: "Cum for me." Then she said it repeatedly, but with a little twist, screaming. "Cum in me!"

I threw an arch in my back, ramming my tool deep in her. I kept going. I went into overdrive. I couldn't stop, not even if I wanted to. I felt a twitch in my stomach, then it tightened up. I tried to hold on to that feeling for as long as I could, but like I said, I couldn't. When she begged me again to cum in her, saying that she wanted me to fill her ass up with my semen, while rocking back and forth, I let go of it. All of it, shooting a heavy nut inside her ass. I collapsed right there on top of her.

I felt my dick pulsed, as she milked me with that same rocking motion. Then she pressed back against me to shove my whole tool even further inside of her. Sweat poured from us.

"Hey, Cassidy!"

I attempted to look through the tinted window and accidentally pressed a button. A siren blared, and red flashing lights circled around.

Ronald, Brad, and David looked up toward the tinted window.

Ms. Ginsberg quickly flipped a switch, and then everything— the flashing lights and siren—turned off. But it was still too late: David began walking toward the captain's station.

I quickly pulled up my shorts and dashed out the door. I attempted to joke by pushing David into the water, but I missed him. Instead, I slipped off the yacht and fell straight into the ocean.

David laughed and jumped right into the water with me.

Then I saw Brad walk up to the edge of the boat. "Come in!" I said with a little wave. "It feels great in here!"

David grabbed me, trying to pull me under the water.

I pushed him away, then glanced back to see where Brad had gone. He wasn't there anymore. I steered the yacht from where I was floating, swaying my arms back and forth. Then I saw him step inside the captain's station.

I panicked; then David grabbed me again, pulling me underwater this time.

Take 42

"Please don't look at me like that," Rebecca said to Ms. Nelson, sitting across the kitchen table. "I just need your support on this."

"But I don't think you should rush into this marriage too quickly. You need to allow more time to work on it, to see it through."

"To see what through?"

"Everything you're willing to sacrifice for him," Ms. Nelson said. "Today, you might be in love with Juan, wishing a marriage with him will seal the deal between you two. But tomorrow, you might get into a fight with him, regretting that you had married him."

"Tomorrow?" Rebecca asked, looking as if Ms. Nelson were going a little overboard with this.

"Yes, tomorrow. And if it's not tomorrow, what about the following week? Or even the following year? Five years? Ten years? Or even twenty years from now, realizing he's not the one you want to grow old with, looking no more than a divorce from him. Knowing he wasn't the one for you, all these years have been wasted for you. But then again, have you considered possibly having children? And what if this marriage doesn't work out between you two, because you are so quick to jump into this marriage?"

"I have thought about that."

"Oh, have you?" Ms. Nelson shot Rebecca a look of doubt instead of seeking reassurance from her. Then she walked away.

"You just confuse me at times." Rebecca waited for Ms. Nelson to stop and look at her before she continued: "Because just the other week you told me that I should settle with someone that I can call my own, without me growing old like—" she quickly paused, realizing what almost slipped out of her mouth.

But it was too late. Ms. Nelson's expression fell.

Rebecca said, "I'm sorry. I didn't mean that."

The room grew silent.

Ms. Nelson briefly held her gaze on Rebecca, then glanced at their hands. Rebecca's hand overlapped with hers. She shifted her attention back to Rebecca. She knew Rebecca was speaking the truth: Ms. Nelson was aging without a significant other. The mere thought of it brought back memories from the past. Ms. Nelson recalled when she was like Rebecca, making impulsive decisions without a second thought. However, Ms. Nelson's most critical decision was when she jumped into a relationship without considering her options, putting everything she knew on the line to see it through, despite warnings from people around her that the man she was dating had a history of dating many women before. But like every woman trapped in a world of delusion, Ms. Nelson dismissed her friends' sharp criticisms about the man she loved; her partner's past came back to haunt him, just as they all predicted, forcing her to flee from her embarrassment.

And like Rebecca's situation, Ms. Nelson recognized she was much like Rebecca at her age, being naïve and stubborn. She put up a defense mechanism in the form of an invisible shield to protect her self-image by remaining committed to her life choices. She was unwilling to compromise, like any other determined woman in the world, hoping to prove to everyone that they were wrong about her decisions and the choices she made as a result.

But Ms. Nelson didn't want Rebecca to travel down the same dirty road she had experienced before, forcing Rebecca to raise that same invisible shield against herself to hide from the naked truth.

The ice cubes crackled, shattering the silence between them.

Ms. Nelson looked toward the frigid, then back at Rebecca. Then she asked, "Do you love him?"

"Yeah, I guess."

"You guess?"

"Yes," Rebecca knew that if she didn't say the right words, Ms. Nelson would disapprove of the marriage. "Yes, I love him."

On that note, Ms. Nelson attempted to smile. "I'd be there at your wedding," she said, "only if you could honestly tell me that you love him to the point that you would lay your life down for his, if it comes to a choice to save his life?"

Rebecca slowly closed her eyes, her head tilted downward.

"Can you answer that?"

Rebecca opened her eyes once more.

Take 43

"**That's what I** like most about you," I told Cathy as we sat across from each other in Café Regazz during the afternoon lunch hour. "It seems like I have known you forever. I'm serious. And it's for this same reason that I would like—"

She smiled, shaking her head.

"What?"

She made a short scoffing sound and said, "Nothing."

"What's so funny then?"

She just smiled at me.

"C'mon. Tell me."

She hesitated for just a second or two before saying, "You stated that one of the reasons why you like me most is because it seems as if you have known me forever."

"Yeah, and your point?" I took another bite of my turkey sub.

"That's my point exactly," she said. "Other than the past two and a half weeks that we have been spending time together, during my lunch hour, how can you honestly say it seems like you have known me forever? C'mon, do you know anything about me other than the conversation we had with each other? For all you know, I could be a serial killer, luring you in to be my next victim."

"You see," I laughed. That's what I like about you. You don't hold back from expressing your thoughts and views; if a question needs to be answered, you will pursue it until you find the answer. You can be a great investigator."

She stopped smiling and looked away—only for a few seconds—then cut back to me. "And this is the only reason why you like me?"

"Of course not." I took another bite of my sandwich and washed it down with my iced tea. "You have other characteristics that I like about you."

"Like, what?"

"Like everything." I took another swing of my iced tea and continued, "How could you hold on to a decent conversation on any topic? The way you blush when I look at you." I paused again and added, "But importantly, it's how you carry yourself in public—your whole persona of being ladylike."

She smiled. "You need to slow down before you choke on that."

"Oh, I'm sorry." I tried to chew the rest of my sandwich before I took another swallow. "So, tell me–" I stopped right there when she reached for my face.

She wiped off a small portion of mayonnaise I had on the side of my mouth with her thumbs.

"Thanks."

No response. She just smiled while eyeing my mouth.

Then I broke our silence: "Why are you doing this to me? Better yet, to us?"

"Doing what?"

"This" —I fluttered my hand back and forth between us, then stopped— "what we have here." I paused so that what I said to her could marinate. Then I added, "We go out occasionally and enjoy each other's company, so why not take what we have with each other to the next level?" I paused again, waiting for a response. Something. Anything. But there was nothing. So, I continued, "I would like to get to know you better."

"You will, in due time. I promise you."

"But when?"

She smiled. "Let's take this nice and slow before someone gets hurt."

"You think I would hurt you?"

"I didn't say that."

"So, are you implying that I might get hurt by you?"

"No." She laughed. "I didn't say that either."

I remained silent for a moment, contemplating. My suspicion began to form. Then I asked, "Are you married?"

"No!" She laughed this time. Hard. "Not!"

"Are you seeing someone else at this time?"

"No."

I relaxed, then it hit me! "Are you—"

"What?"

I shot her that look. I just couldn't say it. I simply couldn't.

Then she spat it out: "A transgender or hermaphrodite?"

161

I kept my peace because she hit it right on the nail.

Then she eased my worry and said, "I am neither of those."

I smiled.

When she leaned forward over the table between us, I met her halfway. Then we kissed, lingering there for a moment.

She pulled away from my lips and said, "If what we have here was meant to be, let's take it slow so that we can enjoy every moment of it."

I smiled. She was right. We have all the time in the world to get to know each other.

I reached over the table again for another kiss, and she welcomed it.

"Why don't you two get a room?"

Cathy pulled away first, followed by me. We both glanced at the snobby old man who threw us an ugly stare as he walked by.

I grabbed my iced tea. "C'mon, let's get out of here."

"To where?" she procrastinated, then looked at her wristwatch. "It's a quarter to one. Our lunch break is almost over."

"We're just going for a little walk on the beach."

She exited her seat and trashed the rest of her unfinished meal.

As we crossed the street, headed for the beach area, my cell phone began to ring. I looked at the front screen. It was from Ms. Ginsberg. "Do you mind if I take this call?" I asked Cathy. "It's one of my clients."

"Sure."

I picked up my phone on the third or perhaps the fourth ring.

Ms. Ginsberg quickly asked in a slight tone, "Are you busy right now?"

"No. Not really, why?"

She overlooked my question to pose her own: "So did it take you so long to answer your phone?"

"I apologize for that. I was a bit tied up for a moment, but I'm free now."

"Oh," she appeared to have cooled down a bit.

"But what is it? Do you need to see me?"

"No. Not quite. At least not at this moment, probably tonight when you stop by, because I need your help to rub this cramp out of my neck again. It came back after you left this morning."

"Oh," I tried to sound like a professional masseur in front of Cathy while remaining discreet about what I wanted to say to Ms. Ginsberg. "Now you know I have the perfect remedy for that."

"What?"

I laughed since I couldn't say it in front of Cathy.

But then Ms. Ginsberg answered it for me anyway: "With what? Your dick?

I laughed again, looked at Cathy, then said into the cell phone, "Yes, but of course."

Ms. Ginsberg laughed back.

Cathy smiled, unaware of what I was talking about over the phone.

Then Ms. Ginsberg nearly shouted in my ear: "That's right!" then said. "I have just remembered why I called you."

"Why? What is it?"

She hesitated, then said, "I need you for a small project, for the upcoming weekend. So, try not to make any plans in the meantime."

"Sure. But what is it?"

"I would explain it to you when I see you tonight."

"Okay then."

She hung up.

I slid the cellphone back into my pocket and told Cathy, "That was one of my toughest clients ever."

"So, it seems."

Within seconds, my cellphone started ringing again. I checked it. It was Ms. Ginsberg once more. I then excused myself again. "Yeah, what's up?"

"Come over right away. You made me horny."

I cut back to Cathy.

Take 44

"Hey, Ronald!" Joey sprinted toward him in the parking lot after breaking away from his new buddies at work.

Ronald halted just before reaching his truck.

"Do you have a second?"

"Yeah, what's up?"

Joey looked apologetic, slowing his pace to a walk now. "I don't know whatever happened between us or why we stopped talking to one another, but you and I were like family."

Ronald didn't respond. He remained silent, wondering if there was an ulterior motive behind all of this.

Then Joey added, "I know David and I had our little differences between each other, but that shouldn't come between us. You and I have a history together. We have been friends since the ninth grade in Mr. Kipper's class." He paused for a moment. "Do you remember that?"

"How could I possibly forget that when you came to our English class, dressed like MC Hammer?"

Joey laughed, and so did Ronald.

Then they both sang together: "You can't touch this!"

They laughed a little longer, then fell silent, gazing at each other.

"Come here." Ronald broke weak, stretching his hand outward.

Joey stepped closer, and then they hugged.

"I'm sorry for being an asshole."

"The same here." Ronald pulled away first. Then he added, "We have to catch up for old times' sake and hang out sometime."

"Just us two, right?"

"Yeah," Ronald read between the lines, "of course."

"That sounds like a good plan," Joey said, then left his cell phone vibrating. He glanced at it before tucking the phone back in his pocket. "Well. I don't want to hold you up because I know you want to get home to Linda."

"Yeah, I need to head home to her because we made some arrangements for tonight. However, I'll probably be a bit late getting home to her because I have to wait for David to finish what he's doing first. He's in there talking to Marcus about something."

"The new guy, right?"

"Yeah."

"Alright then. I'd catch up with you later, because I don't wanna hold these guys up over there."

"Sure thing." Ronald looked over Joey's shoulder and saw six co-workers looking directly at them. One of them stepped away from the company's van, standing in clear view.

"So," Joey said, "call me sometime."

"I will."

"I'd keep you to your word on that." Jocy seemed about to walk away when he jolted his body slightly with a little twist, but then faced Ronald again. "May I ask you about something?"

"Yeah. Go ahead."

"Is that true what I heard about Rebecca: that she is getting married to that guy she's seeing?"

"Yeah." Ronald knew there had to be some motive behind Joey's visit to speak with him.

"Wow, that's crazy, huh?"

"What's so crazy about that?"

"She marrying another guy so quick, after shitting on Cassidy like that. It seems like she had it all planned out already. What do you think?"

"It's not what I think about that, because I don't care. It's none of my business what she does with her life. I wish her the best."

"So, have you been invited to go to the wedding?"

"I have been asked."

"Are you going?"

Ronald kept it honest with him: "I don't know. I haven't decided on that yet."

"Oh."

But Ronald had a question of his own to ask: "Now you tell me something?"

"What's that?"

"How did you find out about this?"

"About Rebecca getting married to that guy, Juan?"

"Yeah." Ronald was surprised that Joey knew Juan's name so well.

"My friend Scott over there mentioned to me." Joey quickly twisted his head around to look at Scott and Ronald again. "His wife Maggie is in one of Rebecca's aerobics classes, and she said that Rebecca told everybody in her class last week that she was getting married to her fiancé, Juan, soon."

"Oh."

"So, have you heard from Cassidy yet?"

"No." Ronald felt like lying to him. "But have you?"

"No. But it seems like he's under the radar or something. He probably even skipped out of town, you know?"

"Yeah, he probably has." Ronald kept a straight face. "Well, I don't wish to hold you up any longer than I must. It seems like David is finished already."

"Alright." Joey twisted around to see how far David was from them, then cut back to Ronald. "So, make sure that you call me."

"Sure."

Joey walked away, heading back to his new friends.

Ronald finally got in his truck.

About a minute later, David got in the truck, looking bothered about something. He tossed his jacket into the back seat.

"What happened?"

David said, "Nothing." Then he asked, "What the hell was Joey talking to you about?" He didn't wait for a response before he continued: "He wasn't talking about me again. Was he?"

"No."

"Oh, because I'd whoop his ass again, if he did."

"No, he just came here telling me how he would like us to hang out like old times, to catch up on a few things."

"What do you mean, both of us?!"

"No. Just me and him."

"Oh." The creases vanished from his forehead.

After a brief pause, Ronald said, "Then he mentioned Rebecca's wedding with that Hispanic guy she's dating."

"What the hell! You mentioned it to him."

"No. A friend of his told him about it."

"What a bunch of losers." David looked out the passenger window at Joey and the guys he was with. "They need to get a fucking life of their own and stop worrying about other people's affairs."

"Yeah, I know." Ronald cranked the car engine. "I wanted to tell him that, but he threw me off when he asked about Cassidy."

David turned back to Ronald. "He asked about Cassidy?"

"Yeah. Why?"

"Because," David snapped, reaching for the door latch, "I told that motherfucker never to mention Cassidy's name out of his mouth again!"

Ronald grabbed David's arm. "Look, chill out! You're hanging on a thin string here at this job. So please don't mess it up. Besides, Joey didn't say anything; he just asked if I had heard from him yet. That's all."

"Are you sure?"

"Yeah."

"Well," David stuck his foot out of the passenger door anyway, "I'm just going to remind him not to mention my homeboy's name out of his mouth again. I'm not going to do anything to him. I swear."

"David, don't start any shit out there!"

"I'm not. You have my word on that."

On that note, Ronald released David's arm, and David stepped out the door to confront Joey about his earlier warning. As David approached, he overheard Joey and the guys trash-talking Rebecca.

"I'm telling you, dude," Joey said. "I knew it wouldn't work out between them. She was too loose for him."

"How do you know?" one of the guys asked.

"Because she used to flirt with me whenever Cassidy wasn't around. I'm telling you, dude; I could have hooked up with her myself but—"

David pushed Joey from behind, making Joey cut his story short. "Why the fuck you over here, lying to them?!"

Joey caught his balance and quickly turned around. "What the hell is your problem?!"

The fellows stood between David and Joey, separating them.

David tried to break loose from their grips. "I've told you to keep Cassidy's name out of your mouth!"

"Fuck you and him! How do you like that out of my mouth!"

David made a mocking scoff. "It's funny how you can get so tough to talk shit when they're holding us apart."

"Man, fuck you! Who do you think you are, telling me what I can and cannot say? You and Cassidy can go fuck off and go to hell, for all I care! Because both of y'all are two lowlife bastards who can't hold onto a decent relationship to save y'all's lives. Even whores dump y'all! That's pathetic!"

David slowly bobbed his head.

Ronald quickly pulled up with his truck and slammed on the brakes. "David!" he shouted through the driver's window.

David and the rest of them looked at Ronald.

"Get the fuck in this truck!"

David cut back to Joey. "This shit isn't over with."

"Fuck you!"

David shrugged his shoulders, hoping to break free. "Man, get the fuck off of me!" he said to the guy behind him, who had David's arms pinned at the back. "It's over with! My homeboy's waiting on me."

The guy finally let David's arms go.

Ronald shouted: "Get in the fucking truck!"

David bobbed his head, twisting toward Ronald's truck. Then something must have clicked inside David's head because it happened so suddenly: he twisted back around and charged after Joey, giving him a right hook to his face.

Then, all hell broke loose.

Ronald jumped out of the truck.

Take 45

I kicked my legs off the bed and reached for my pants. "Okay, I will see you tomorrow." I leaned over the bed and kissed Ms. Ginsberg.

"Stay with me" –she tried pulling me back in bed with her– "for a little longer."

"Uh-uh." I broke free from her grip. "We can continue this tomorrow." Then I thought about what Samuel had told me a while back and decided to go with it. "Or, unless …," my voice faded: I changed my mind.

"Or unless, what?"

To hell with it! "Or unless you change your mind and allow me to spend the night with you regularly?"

She seemed to have considered it. "Okay then."

"Okay?" I felt a wave of joy shoot through me. I reached in for another kiss. "I knew you would eventually change your mind and ask me to stay here with you."

"No." She stopped me from entering the bed with her on the third kiss. "I meant, okay. I'd see you tomorrow."

"Tomorrow?"

"Yes."

"Alright then." I began to straighten myself up. "I'll see you tomorrow."

"Cassidy."

"Yeah." I looked at her as I zipped up my pants.

"Remember not to make any plans for Monday."

"I'm not. But what time do you expect me to arrive at your company party?"

"I prefer you to be there as soon as possible. Perhaps around six o'clock before everyone else arrives," she said. But then she had second thoughts. "No. I think it would be best for you to come to the party midway through it, while the party is winding down … you could be the center of attraction to bring some excitement back to the party with a new face." She paused again, then quickly added: "Yes, that's it! I think around eight o'clock would be perfect, so don't make any plans for eight o'clock on Monday night. No! Make that eight thirty instead, Monday night, downstairs in the ballroom."

"Sure. Eight thirty it is."

She threw a trivia question at me: "Where?"

"Downstairs in the ballroom."

She smiled. "I want you to put on your best performance ever. Because everybody who works for me should not only be there at the party, but I want everyone to enjoy themselves there as well."

"Okay."

"And remember, you are my private consultant. If anyone asks you any questions regarding your job description or about me, for that matter, tell them–"

I interjected, "I can't talk about company matters with anyone except Ms. Ginsberg. This is due to company policy and confidentiality."

She smiled harder. "That's why I love you, my darling."

I smiled back.

"Also," she added, "I would like you to go to Bal Harbour Mall tomorrow afternoon and see Aaron. I have prepared a little treat for you. He will tailor an Armani suit for you again because I want you to look your best for me on Monday night."

"But you don't have to. I already have plenty of suits at home. I could easily wear one of them instead."

"But I want you to feel at ease while wearing something new."

"But I have plenty of new attire I haven't even worn yet."

She gave me a reasonable stare, then said, "Okay, you won."

I smiled.

"But," she added, "I still need you to see Aaron tomorrow afternoon because I have already paid for a tailored suit."

"Alright." I gave her another kiss and grabbed my shirt off the floor. "I'll see you tomorrow then."

"Till then."

I took a few steps toward the bedroom doorway when it suddenly dawned on me, and I turned around. "Claire, do you plan to take your boat out on Saturday?"

"No. Why?"

"I was wondering if I could use it so the fellows and I could go out fishing again."

"Say no more, it's done. I will have Eddie get everything ready for you on Saturday. Now get out of here because you're making me horny. I'm afraid. I might change my mind and have you spend the night with me."

"Okay, tomorrow then."

No response. Ms. Ginsberg just watched me.

I headed back to the bedroom doorway. I stopped because my car key had slipped from my hand. I picked it up and then heard a soft voice behind me.

"Cassidy ... My darling."

I turned back toward Ms. Ginsberg because I was confident my strategy would work.

She held the bedspread open for me, revealing her nakedness beneath the cover.

I peeled my shirt off, smiling with her.

Take 46

Nothing is worse than an unwelcome surprise.

Rebecca was shocked to find Juan home early when she entered her apartment. However, her expression changed instantly upon noticing that he had company. It was the same guy she recalled from last time—the dark-complexioned Hispanic man. She thought his name started with Al; maybe Alberto, but she wasn't sure. A wave of unease washed over her as she noticed the way he looked at her, as if he were undressing her with his gaze. It felt as though he was scrutinizing every inch of her body. Yet, she reminded herself of the promise Juan had made to her about three weeks ago, swearing he wouldn't hurt her again, especially not with another man.

She believed him.

And besides, she thought they were getting married soon, so he wouldn't dare disrespect his potential future wife like that again.

She kissed Juan and then said, "Let me go take a shower so I can start preparing dinner for both of us," hoping he would read between the lines and send his friend away.

Juan seemed calm initially, but he soon continued his conversation with Alberto about a nightclub they had visited the week before.

Rebecca left the room and headed straight to the bathroom. She took a shower that was neither too long nor too short; it lasted a solid ten minutes. Once she finished, she stepped out of the bathroom with a towel wrapped around her, only to find Juan sitting on the edge of the bed in the dark. He had that mischievous look in his eyes, and she knew what that meant.

She glanced at the closed door to the room. Then, she turned back to him and whispered, "Where's your friend?"

"Out there, watching TV."

"Why don't we wait until he leaves?"

"But I want you now."

"But what if he hears us?"

"He won't."

"Are you sure?"

"Yeah." He scooted over to the center of the bed, taking his shirt off.

She closed the bathroom door behind her, making the bedroom completely dark.

She groped her hands out in front of her, taking a few steps forward until she felt Juan. He was taking his pants off; she helped him. His pants were tossed off the bed. She climbed aboard, resting her knees between his legs while grabbing hold of his dick. She stroked his flaccid muscle a few times before leaning against it. She wanted to get his dick hard while slowly pulling on it with her mouth every time she raised her head from it, then back down again.

And there it goes: Juan's muscles grew strong and stiff.

Rebecca sucked on his dick with a lot of spit in her mouth, started with a leisurely pace at first, with her ass jacked up in the air, while gradually picking up her speed. She bobbed her head up and down, making a slurping sound in the background.

Juan stretched his hand under her to fondle her love spot. She was wet. He stuck a finger in her. Then, two fingers immediately afterward, pumping in and out of her.

She moaned with a dick in her mouth.

"That's it, Rebecca." Juan felt her head bobbing up and down over his manhood, with a slow, wobbly motion. "That's it ... Don't stop ... That's right. Suck it for me."

"Juan," she mumbled while slurping on his dick, "I want you to stick it in me."

"Not right now," he kept pumping his fingers in her. "Keep doing what you are doing."

Rebecca was leaking juice all over his hand. She couldn't take it any longer. She maneuvered her body around into a 69-position, with her on top. She rested her pussy before Juan's face so he could eat it for her. He did. He lapped between her labia lips a few times before stretching her lips apart to get a better taste of her pussy. The moment he had her spread open, he shuddered his tongue nonstop between her split.

Rebecca started bobbing her head even faster now over Juan's dick. She couldn't hold out much longer: He was working wonders there. His tongue felt good. She tried to hold on to that good feeling for as long as she could. She felt like an addict, a chaser. A sex junky. A Miley Cyrus.

Rebecca didn't know how to hold onto those good feelings. She didn't want to let it go. She stopped bobbing her head over Juan's dick, hoping to control the sensational feelings he was sending through her body. But again, she couldn't control it. She felt that beautiful twitch below just before she rose on his face. Juan kept licking her split. It felt relaxing. After her body stopped trembling, she wanted to go for another blast, but this time, with him inside her.

So, she pleaded, "Please" –as she slowly stroking on his dick to keep it hard– "I want you to stick it in me."

He remained silent, feeling her hand move up and down on him.

Then Rebecca felt her labia lips splitting open again, and juice poured out of her. "Please," she begged with a whisper, "Stick it in me. I wanna feel you inside me." Then her body jolted, and she immediately dropped flat on Juan's body when she realized that it wasn't Juan's finger that he tried to pry inside her. It was much bigger, if not fatter. A manly tool. A strong pipe like. She panicked. She looked behind her and saw Alberto standing behind her with his dick in his hand.

It was at least seven inches long, uncircumcised.

"What the fuck's your problem?!" she shouted at him, feeling violated while trying to break loose from Juan's grip. "Let go of me!"

But Juan held on to her and said, "Do this for me, honey."

"But you promised me, Juan," she said, her voice trembling with the urge to cry. "You promised! You assured me you wouldn't repeat this."

"I know. But don't you want to make me happy?"

She stammered, "Yeah." Then she shouted, "But not like this!" She tried once more to break free from his grip.

He fought back. "So, make me happy then and do this for me."

"But Juan!" She stopped wrestling him. "I'm supposed to be your fucking wife soon!"

"And you will still be my wife soon." He kissed between her opening; then lapped it once, twice, three times, hoping to convince her otherwise before he continued: "Do it for me, my love. *Mi amor.*"

She felt confused. Lost.

Then Juan released his grip from around her, resting one hand on her back, guiding her back downward. With his other hand he grabbed Rebecca's wrist and placed her hand back on his dick. "For me, *mi amor.*" He lapped his tongue between her pussy lips again, but with a slow light drag. Then he did it again.

She wanted Juan in her life, but not like this. It just wasn't right. She had already lost one man, and she didn't want to lose another. She felt trapped, unsure of which direction to take, as if she were at a crossroads in rural Mississippi.

Her thoughts shot this way, that way. Up and down. Back and forth, twirling around in a circle.

Then Juan repeated himself when he said, "Do it for me, mi amor."

She didn't want to, but broke down in front of the man she wanted to marry. She declined her neck and put the head of Juan's dick back in her mouth. She pulled on it a bit, but his dick accidently plopped out of her mouth. She put it back in and repeated her steps, but this time she did not allow it to slip out of her mouth again. She worked her way down on him. Only half of it. His erection grew strong in her mouth. Then, within seconds, she felt Alberto grab her by the hips, pulling her back toward him. He maneuvered her to her knees again while standing over Juan's body. And immediately afterward, she felt Alberto groped his manhood between her pussy lips, sorta like swiping it across her entranceway to get it wet first, before he stuffed it inside of her.

She closed her eyes and cried, doing whatever it takes to make her fiancé happy.

Alberto picked up speed behind her, ramming her from the back, as if he were taking advantage of someone in the Gaza Strip's refugee camp.

She moaned for help.

Take 47

I made a right turn at a blinking light. They drove for a block up the boulevard to a small, gated community on the beach. The security guard cleared me through. I re-examined the navigation system to confirm that I was heading in the right direction.

I was.

I slowed down at the townhouse on my left, noticing the silver Escalade a few houses up the street. I smiled and checked the time on the dashboard; it read 11:09 pm. I had made it on time. After pulling into the driveway and parking beside the Escalade, I double-checked the house number to confirm it was the correct address. I exited the car and quickly approached the front door. Just as I was about to press the doorbell, the door swung open.

"What took you so long to get here?" Pamula asked as she stood in the doorway.

"We were waiting on you." But before I could respond, she grabbed me by the shirt and yanked me inside the house.

When I entered the house, I couldn't help but ask, "Where is your furniture? It's empty in here."

"It's up to you to decorate it however you like. It's yours after tonight."

"Mine?"

"Yeah." Pamula pulled my shirt out of my pants and began working on the buttons. "Elena and I found it on the market today. We got it for a great deal." She kissed my shoulder and added, "We decided to purchase it for you so we could meet up here instead to downplay any suspicion from our neighbors."

"So, where's Elena now?"

"Here I am!"

I twisted slightly to the left, looking up. I saw Elena on the second floor, coming down the stairs. Her blouse was unbuttoned, and she was wearing a black—maybe dark purple—bra.

She purred.

I smiled because last time I had her flat on her back, running deep inside her, she was mewing like a feral cat, while scarring my back with her nails.

"So, let's go on with it," Pamula said.

I turned back to her because she tried to snatch my shirt off me without unlatching the two bottom buttons. "Take your time." I helped her with my shirt before she ruined it. "We have all night to do whatever."

"But I can't wait."

Elena finally descended, stood behind me, and said, "I can't wait either." She crawled her hands around me.

I turned my head to the side to kiss her.

She kissed me back, then managed to get her hand into my pants. She held my growing muscle. "Are you going to give it to me tonight?"

"I wouldn't have it any other way."

She then grabbed me by the pants, leading the way. Pamula followed.

As we went upstairs, we headed to the second room on the right. The lights were dim. I spotted an air mattress in the corner of the room, with no bed sheets. Elena guided me straight to the mattress. She lay down first, crawling on her back to the center. I followed and lay directly on top of her, her legs spread and knees bent. I kissed her, then worked my way to her neck and then her chest. Her blouse was open.

I didn't have any time to unlatch her bra; I just flopped her titties out from under her bra. I sucked on her knockers for a moment, especially her nipples. They were stiff and swollen. I pulled them with my mouth.

"Ohhh, God." She moaned with a slight whisper, "that feels so fucking good. Suck on them a little harder for me."

I did. However, after a short while, I decided to work my way down on her, only stopping by her navel because her skirt prevented me from going down further. Her movements were so captivating that they demanded my full attention. I raised her skirt, rested it over her stomach, and then went for the panties. She helped me pull them off.

She relaxed again, lying flat on her back, gyrating her hips for me—or so I wanted to believe when I stuck a finger inside of her. She was wide open and wet. I went with two fingers now, hoping to do the trick while straddling her legs. Her knees were up in the air again and spread away from each other. I placed my mouth between her legs.

She ran her hands over my shoulders the moment I kissed her inner thigh, then moved to the back of my head. She combed her fingernails through my hair while guiding my head toward her cookie jar, even though I was already on my way there.

I licked her entrance, straight up the middle. Her body quivered, then relaxed. I parted her labia lips, pulling them upward. Her clitoris bud stuck out. It looked perky and beautiful. I kissed it. Then kissed it again before I started flicking my tongue against her *tender-roni.*

There's no other word to describe such a masterpiece.

She gripped the back of my head, and I kept working her. I went fast, then slow. Fast, then slow. I paused! Then I started up again—fast, then slow. After another pause, lasting two seconds longer than the first, I kicked back into motion.

She begged me to "Stop!" while trying to push my head away from her *nana*, but I was steadfast. I kept eating. It was like I had turned into Hannibal Lecter, not knowing how to control my hunger for the sake of humanity. I rattled and shook my head over her sweet mound, hard, then soft.

She pleaded with me to stop once more, but I ignored her. She then overwhelmed me with a heavy orgasm in my mouth. It tasted strange yet bittersweet. I kept going. Then she dropped another load on me, but this one wasn't as heavy as the last. I slurped and swallowed everything she gave me, while pushing my luck for more.

I felt Pamula was still having trouble with my pants. She had it halfway down my thighs. I eased up, leaning a little to my side to help her, as I kept my mouth on Elena. Then I felt my pants slide down, then off me. I kept eating. Seconds later, I felt something soft and wet, yet warm. It was Pamula's mouth over my intensified manhood.

I tried to stay focused on Elena, but I couldn't. Pamula kept bobbing her head over my man muscle for about four minutes straight before she brought me to the verge of a gigantic climax.

I thought of heaven when she told me to cum for her.

I did.

She swallowed my fountain of youth, and I couldn't wait to unload my next batch of semen elsewhere. But when she said, "Elena, it's my turn", I didn't have to be a rocket scientist to figure out what she meant by that.

I smiled when she switched places with Elena.

Rebecca walked into the bathroom and locked the door behind her, leaving Juan and Alberto together.

She turned on the shower faucet and stood under the water. She jolted, then bemoaned in a way she hadn't before. She crouched down into a fetal position.

The water cascaded over her.

She cried.

Take 48

Samuel turned off the yacht's engine and stepped onto the deck to join us. He sat next to David. They chatted about a little bit of everything, and the air was filled with laughter.

"Do y'all hear that shit!" David said to us, looking at Brad, and then at me. "That's the life I would like to live."

Ronald cut in: "Being single for the rest of your life?"

"Yeah. Why not?"

"You're an idiot."

"What? Sam's doing it. He's not an idiot. And look at him: he's not married and living a stress-free life, without someone nagging him every morning, telling him what he can and cannot do."

"Like, in your case, to go find a job?"

"Hey! Just remember, I had a job until that asshole friend of yours picked a fight with me in the parking lot and got me fired."

"How in the world did Joey get you fired when I told you not to start any shit with him?"

"Because that asshole shouldn't have said what he said to me out there then."

"But it was only words?"

"Words my ass! It's easy to say that because he didn't say it to you. He said it to me. And I'm not gonna allow that prick to talk shit about me and my homeboy. Telling us to go fuck off!" He then twisted to the right. "What would you have done under the same circumstances?"

I kept my mouth sealed, because I didn't want to get involved in their little argument.

But then David repeated himself: "What would you have done?"

I decided to shrug at the same time that I told him, "I don't know what I would have done," hoping that he would accept that as an answer.

But he didn't. "You fucking liar! You would have done the same shit to Joey as well and whoop his ass off there, too." He turned back to Ronald. "Cassidy just doesn't wanna hurt your feelings by telling you the truth."

I hoped Ronald didn't believe that.

"Well," David went on to say, "the truth remains the same: I want to live the rest of my life out like a bachelor, whether you like it or not."

"Yeah," Ronald retorted, "being unemployed. You would be a bachelor for the rest of your life."

"That's nonsense! If I want, I can easily find a good job by tomorrow."

"Yeah, with the economy in the way it's right now? I wish you luck."

"Wish me luck?!" David made a contorted expression to disagree. Then he added, "You don't have to wish me shit! Because my homeboys could find me some work in Miami. It appears that finding a job wasn't so hard for them. They're making it. Just look at them." He looked at me, then at Brad. "Nah, never mind you. Because I will never dance for a bunch of queers."

Brad laughed along with him. "Uh, fuck you!"

Then David turned back to me. "I know you can find me a decent job here in Miami."

I was lost for words. Unlike Brad, who was a male stripper, I was more like a gigolo. Lover-boy. Ladies' man. Philanderer. A cocksman, dick slinger. You can call it what you want, but I certainly wasn't going to reveal to David that I was a man-whore. So, I did what I knew best: kept my mouth shut and smiled.

Then David went to Samuel. "I know you could find me some sort of occupational job over here to hold me down for a while?"

"There's an opening at my job, washing—"

I cut in, telling Samuel, "He wouldn't want that sorta job!"

David asked, "Why?" Then he looked back at Samuel. "What type of work does it consist of?"

"Washing—"

I interrupted Samuel again to finish it for him when I told David, "Dishes! The job consists of you washing dishes."

David shot back at Samuel, "Oh, hell no! Thanks. But I must pass on that one."

Within a few minutes, the conversation shifted somehow to Rebecca. David initiated it by saying that he would love to run into Rebecca's fiancé one day to confront him. Even though I wasn't with Rebecca anymore, David still considered her an old friend of his.

Both Ronald and Brad agreed.

"Yo, for real," I cut them off, looking more at Samuel than at them because he seemed thrilled to see me upset every time I heard her name. "Let's not talk about Rebecca anymore. It's over between us. And besides, I'm seeing someone new right now."

"Yeah," Brad seemed surprised, "You're banging someone different already?"

"Yeah." As if that could be hard to believe.

David interrupted, asking, "So tell us about her?"

I glanced at Samuel, wishing he weren't here so I could deceive them.

They glanced at Samuel and then back at me.

Brad took over: "Tell us about her?"

Her? Which one was he referring to?

Then Ronald said, "C'mon. You act like you're trying to conceal a secret from us? We're curious to know about her."

I looked at Samuel again, hoping he would forgive me for what I was about to share with my friends. However, when Ronald and David's smiles faded, my curiosity intensified.

Silence hovered around us.

Then David, Brad, and Ronald slowly cut their eyes from me.

Samuel almost freaked out: "What the hell are y'all looking at me for?! I'm not a homo!"

They looked relieved.

But David, on the other hand, wasn't so convinced by Samuel's comments, which he then tried to insinuate: "You did say that you took my homeboy in your house, free of charge and expecting nothing back in return?"

Samuel ignored him, cutting back to me: "Goddam it! If you don't tell them, I will!"

I sighed, giving them the first female that came to mind: "I'm seeing a chick named Catherine Swartz."

"Is she Jewish?" Brad asked.

"Yeah." What the hell, she could be a Sunni Muslim for all I care. It wasn't like I was dating her.

Then David stated, "I don't believe you."

I pulled my cellphone from my pocket and tried to confront him: "What? You want me to call her to prove it to you?"

"Yeah. Call her."

Fuck! I tried to make another bluff. "I'll call right now. Do you think I'm lying?"

"I think you're lying. Now call her."

I hesitated before scrolling through a few incoming phone numbers on my cell phone because I couldn't quite put my finger on it. Cathy never gave me her number to call her; she always called me instead.

I wasn't entirely sure, but I was confident enough to think I found her number on my phone, the one she called me on last night. Or was it the new girl, Barbara, who called me shortly after?

Okay, I had my doubts. I wasn't sure anymore. I pressed the SEND button, hoping it wasn't from a pay phone. It rang. I looked back at David; he was shooting me with a suspicious, wry smile.

The ringing stopped!

Then a voice came over the phone: "Hello?"

"Oh, shit!" that one accidently slipped out by mistake: I was surprised. "Cathy?"

"Yes." She paused. Then asked, "Is this you, Cassidy?"

"Yeah, it's me." I couldn't stop smiling. "How are you doing?"

"Fine. But how did you obtain this cell number?"

"Umm, wouldn't you like to know?" I had to use the right words in front of my friends, especially in front of David, to prevent any misunderstanding. "But is it a problem?"

"No. Not at all."

I felt relieved. "So, sweetie," I wanted to give my best performance in front of everyone, except Samuel, of course. "What are you doing right now?"

There was a pause—a brief one. Then she asked, "Is everything all right with you?"

"Of course," I hope she will follow my lead. "I'm just hanging out with a few friends on the boat, fishing, and I thought about you." I paused. Then I tried to tense her with, "And ..."

"And what?"

David got up and tilted my cell phone to his ear to check if someone was on the line with me. He tried to eavesdrop.

She asked again, "And what?"

David got excited.

I attempted to push him away, but failed.

Then Cathy said, "Cassidy?"

"Huh?"

"I asked you, and what?"

"Well," I knew David would get a kick out of what I was about to tell Cathy, "I was thinking about something that you had mentioned to me the other night while we were together."

"And?"

"And I caught a chimera out here." I grabbed my dick through my pants, feeling bad for saying that to her. "Which I know you said you are willing to try anything out, but I'm certain you can't handle this tasty meal."

"But what's a chimera?"

David attempted to grab my phone from my hand when he shouted: "It's his Polyphemus!"

I pushed him away from me this time, chuckling to myself.

Cathy asked, "Who was that?"

"A crazy friend of mine." I punched David on the arm when he got close, around the same time I lied to her, "He's wrestling with a fish."

David then gradually made his way back to me, patiently waiting to finish listening to my phone conversation.

Cathy asked, "So what kind of fish is it?"

"I'm not sure, but I found it out here."

"And you have it right now?"

David nodded his head with excitement.

And I told her, "Yeah, I got it right here," while holding it.

"Is it big?"

"Oh, yeah. It's pretty big, alright."

"Well, if you have it, bring it to me. I'll eat the whole thing in front of you."

"The whole thing?"

"Yes," she joked back. "The whole thing."

I smiled. "I don't know about that. Because this kind of chimera that I have right now will probably make a female your size throw up on yourself."

"But not this female here."

I laughed, only if she had a clue as to what the hell I was gripping onto.

David whispered in my other ear: "Ask her if she has a friend for me?"

I whispered back to him, "She doesn't have one."

"That's bullshit!" he walked away and watched me from a short distance, taking a seat beside Ronald.

Cathy cut back in: "Who was that? Your friend, still?"

"Yeah. He had just lost his fish."

"Oh."

"Well," I guess that was enough to prove my case to my friends that I wasn't banging Samuel when I went on to tell Cathy, "I don't wanna hold you up, I was just checking in on you to see how you were doing."

"Okay, but hey! Before you go."

"Yeah. What's up?"

"I would like both of us to go out to eat again. I have a nice restaurant in mind."

"Sure. When?"

She stammered, "What's about next week, Friday? Is that good for you?"

"That's perfect for me."

"Okay, I will book a reservation for next week. But in the meantime, since you have my telephone number now, don't hesitate to call me whenever you like."

"Thanks." We both hung up after sharing our goodbyes.

Then David said the most idiotic, foolish thing I have ever heard: "That person you were just over the phone with, you know, there's a possibility that she's not a female, right? So, don't forget we're in Miami, dude. You might be banging a guy."

You know what: he was partially correct on something for a chance.

We were both in Miami. However, the scorching sun must be frying his brain out here, and I know the perfect remedy to cool him down.

I grabbed him and tried to push him overboard.

He fought back.

Take 49

To use the word *exhausted* in this context would be an understatement, because Rebecca felt completely worn out. She tried her best to stay focused in her aerobics class. Her Monday classes were always the worst for her, especially after a heavy weekend with Juan. He had her in overdrive, running another ménage à trois with two guys she didn't know, while Juan stood in the corner and watched.

That guy she was riding at first –the one with the hazelnut-colored eyes named Fernando– was alright with her. He had a regular size dick. Not too big, not too small. It was sorta like a perfect fit, but when that other guy, that stocky fucker who name was Raul, goes behind her and pushed her forward, forcing her to lay against Fernando's chest, he slapped his dick on her ass a few times. She thought nothing of it until he plunged his dick inside her. Her asshole stretched open. Wide open. It felt unnatural to her. Raul's dick was about eight inches, *no*, about nine inches long. Something like a heavy-duty flashlight from a hardware store. The one that takes at least three D-size batteries to operate correctly.

Rebecca couldn't take it. She tried to break free from Raul, but he held her down on top of Fernando's chest and dug her ass out as if she stole his bag of dope from him and he found a revengeful way to get back at her.

Rebecca tried to fight him off. She then bucked, kicking both legs backward in the hope of getting the hell away from him. But it didn't work. If anything, it backfired and gave Raul easy access to go deeper inside of her. He had her pinned down with his hands on her lower back, steadfast and locked in position –whatever you wanna call it– while ramming his dick in her ass without any lubrication. She tried her best to scream for help, but it didn't work.

Her head jerked back and forth, mouth agape, as she fought against the pain he inflicted on her.

Rebecca began to think about something else while still leading her aerobics class, focusing on a leg exercise. A troubling thought crossed her mind: what if that man had torn something or caused damage to her rectum? This added to her distress. However, what haunted her most was the confrontation with Raul, who had called her a "bitch" after he ejaculated inside her, and then appeared ready to slap her. She vividly remembered shouting out and quickly raising her hands to cover her face for protection. Juan, on the other hand, did nothing; he stood there and watched, as if he didn't even know her.

Rebecca's breathing grew heavy. She was angry but kept her feelings hidden. She continued kicking her knees upward, one at a time, so her aerobics participants could follow her lead. She glanced at her wristwatch; it read 5:41 pm. She had fourteen more minutes before the class ended. She kicked her right knee up, then raised her left knee and brought it down. Then she remembered Raul's threat when he said, "Bitch! Don't you ever raise your voice to me! I'd kill you in here!"

Rebecca looked at her wristwatch again. It read 5:42 p.m.

Time appeared to drag for no apparent reason. She looked at her participant again and saw a brief, blurred vision. Maybe she was dehydrated, or perhaps not. Her sight quickly cleared. Focusing back on her participants, she hoped they didn't notice her shaking her head to clear her vision. Suddenly, it happened again. A wave of exhaustion overtook her. She saw a flicker of light, but soon her legs gave way. Darkness surrounded her.

A few minutes later, which felt like seconds, Rebecca thought she had woken up in bed, unsure of how she got home. But then again, she didn't care. She felt at ease. In other words: relax. She looked up at the ceiling fan, enjoying the breeze blowing on her. It felt therapeutic. Just living free. What more could she ask for? She closed her eyes and lay there. Then she heard someone call her name. She opened her eyes and looked at the doorway of her bedroom, seeing Linda with a smile on her face, and then seconds later, Ronald. They were both smiling at her. Rebecca smiled back. Then she heard a familiar voice from a distance behind them.

Rebecca's smile widened, but once again, she felt hunted by guilt. She tried her best to ignore her past and pain because she just wanted to be happy again. She cried and closed her eyes.

Then she thought she heard Linda ask. "Are you alright?"

Rebecca nodded her head. She couldn't talk.

"Rebecca!"

She kept her eyes shut, and tears streamed down her face.

"Rebecca!"

Then it happened: the bedroom that Rebecca thought she was in began to spin around her, twirling in circles before fading into darkness.

"Rebecca!"

She barely lifted her eyelids, feeling woozy when she woke up in her aerobics class. She noticed a few friends surrounding her; Amy was fanning her with a sheet of paper.

"Are you alright?" Amy asked again.

Rebecca nodded. "Yeah. But what happened?"

"You were unconscious for a few minutes after passing out in front of your class."

"Did I?"

"Yeah," Amy said. She then quickly added, "No, no, no," preventing Rebecca from sitting up. "Lie back down until the physician comes back in here. You need to gain your strength back."

"I'm alright." Rebecca slowly sat up, tossing her legs off the couch. "I'm just gonna go home and get some rest."

"Let me take you."

"No, that's alright. I can make it on my own."

"Are you sure?"

"Yeah." Rebecca started gathering her belongings

"Well, don't forget this then."

"What is that?" Rebecca extended her hand towards Amy.

"It's a gift certificate for the El Rancho Grande Restaurant. A new class participant requested that you receive this information. It's supposed to be your pre-wedding gift, I think."

Any other time, Rebecca would have refused to accept such an offer from anyone, but since she was lightheaded, she put the gift certificate in her gym bag and left.

Under her rugged conditions, it took Rebecca roughly twenty minutes to drive home. She was nauseous, if not terribly weak, and worn out, too.

Smooth Casanova

Rebecca unlocked the door and entered the apartment, noticing Juan was hosting two friends. These guys were different from the ones the night before. She definitely remembered Carlos—how could she forget? Last time, he whispered "I love you" in her ear when Juan brought him into their bedroom. The other guy, however, was unfamiliar. He seemed a bit out of place, somewhat cocky, almost like a prison inmate, watching her intently.

Juan sprang from the couch and welcomed her with a kiss.

"I'm sorry," Rebecca began to tell him, "but I'm not gonna be able to make your dinner tonight. I'm not feeling good. I have a terrible headache. Could you and your friends please keep the noise down in here while I lie down? I need to rest."

"Yes. Sure."

Rebecca walked away and went to her bedroom to get ready for her shower.

Juan knocked on the door before pushing it open, despite Rebecca being undressed. She had her spandex pants pulled down to her knees and bent over, revealing her white G-string panties.

Carlos looked into the room and smiled.

Take 50

I arrived a little late at Ms. Ginsberg's party.

About a hundred people attended the event in the downstairs ballroom, give or take. Some clustered around a table with food and drinks, while others conversed in small groups.

I veered through the room, hoping to locate Ms. Ginsberg soon—no sign of her. Again, I quickly looked to my right, left, and straight ahead. Then I glanced to my left side again. I tried to perch among a small crowd of people doing—or at least attempting to do, I think—the shuffle on the dance floor. There were about seven of them. No, make it eight of them on the dance floor, if I must count that older gentleman doing the futuristic robot on the far side.

I smiled, then wove around a few other gentlemen on my right when I spotted Ms. Ginsberg talking to a small crowd ahead. Heads turned toward me as I walked past them. One face looked familiar, but I was unsure. As I approached Ms. Ginsberg from her blind side, three ladies and a gentleman standing in front of her quickly noticed me, looking over Ms. Ginsberg's shoulders, prompting her to twist around and look at me.

I smiled.

Ms. Ginsberg smiled back, meeting me halfway. "You finally arrived," she said with a drunken slur. "I'm happy to see you. Now, come. Allow me to introduce you to my friends." She grabbed my wrist and led me back to the small gathering where she had been standing. Then she said to them, "This is the young man whom I have been telling you all about."

"Oh, really," the lady on the right side said, then blushed deeply.

Smooth Casanova

Her name was Ms. Donna something. I didn't try to remember her last name; it didn't matter to me. It honestly didn't. Then I met Ted, followed by Norma, and then Shirley afterward.

They all appeared to be decent people until Donna asked me, "So, how long have you been working for Claire?"

I said one year; Ms. Ginsberg said two. Then, we both agreed that it was somewhere in between, even though we understood we were exaggerating.

Then, Donna asked me, "Regarding your occupation, how long have you been working in that field?"

"Well," –I remember what Ms. Ginsberg told me to say– "I have been a private consultant for about eight years. Ever since I graduated from college."

Donna twisted to Ms. Ginsberg. "But I thought you told us he was your private masseur?"

Shirley jumped in, saying, "Yeah, that's what I thought you said, too, Claire."

"Oh, did I?" Ms. Ginsberg seemed caught in a jam. Trapped, she needed a way out. She turned to a cocktail steward who was about to walk by and stopped him. "Scotch, please."

Norma shot Ms. Ginsberg with a suspicious look before turning to Shirley and then to Donna.

Then I came to the rescue and told them: "What Ms. Ginsberg probably meant, when she told you guys that, I used to work as a masseur to pay my way through college. But now, I'm a private consultant under my current profession."

Donna seemed uncertain. "To the contrary, I could have sworn she told us that you were her private masseur, who regularly gives her massages. In her own words, you give her the most beautiful massages that we could only imagine about—in our wildest dreams."

"Yeah, she probably has told you all that." I wanted to clean up Ms. Ginsberg's mess. "I guess I still know something about giving a good massage. I must admit, occasionally, I've given her a few massages here and there when I'm not occupied with her other assignments."

Donna seemed to believe my story now.

But what I told her about Ms. Ginsberg and me was true. I just omitted the good and naughty stuff.

Ms. Ginsberg smiled at me, then turned to her side when she saw that same cocktail steward about to walk by again. "I would like to have one of those, please." She snatched a glass off his tray before he noticed it coming. She gulped the Bordeaux down her throat in four swallows, then leaned in and whispered, "I have a nice treat for you tonight." She pulled away and winked.

I hoped they didn't see that.

Ms. Ginsberg was nearly drunk, just a sip away from peeling off her clothes in front of everyone and screaming, "Hey y'all, I bet you can't do that," while doing the chicken dance.

"So," Donna began to ask me with a beguiling smile, "do you offer any massage services on the side of your profession for extra money?"

Before I could answer, Ms. Ginsberg cut in and retorted, "What with all the damn questions?" Since Donna didn't say anything back and looked appalled, Ms. Ginsberg wrapped her arm around mine and advised me, "Let's go before she finds out about us."

There goes our little secret.

Ms. Ginsberg tugged me along. "Now, where can Snookum be?" She released my arm and moved through the room. After a moment, she exclaimed, "There she goes." Ms. Ginsberg grabbed my wrist again, as if I were a child, and we navigated the crowd with her guiding us. "I want to introduce you to her."

I kept quiet.

As we made our way to the table area where the competitors were gathered, Ms. Ginsberg excitedly called out, "Snookum!" Her enthusiasm was palpable as she shouted this person's pet name once more, filling the atmosphere with warmth.

A woman in a lovely evening gown —likely a Naeem Khan dress by the looks of it— turned toward us.

My wrist broke free from Ms. Ginsberg's grip as I stopped dead in my tracks, refusing to take another step forward, even though I was about six feet away. I couldn't breathe; it felt as though my chest caved in.

"Oh, my goodness!" Melissa seemed excited, smiling at me. "Where have you been all this time? Everyone's looking for you."

I glanced at Ms. Ginsberg and then back at Joey's wife.

Take 51

It's well known that pressure can cause pipes to burst.

And that's precisely how Rebecca felt when she had not two, but all three holes stretched open.

Juan had his manly tool in her vagina; Carlos had his rod in her rectum; and Pedro, *or was his name Pablo?* Rebecca couldn't remember his name. All she knew was that his name was pronounced with a "P" in the beginning and ended with an "o" sound. But anyway, this P-guy had his dick in her mouth. All three of them pumped their man tools in and out of her with a steady rhythm.

Rebecca became accustomed to how Juan was treating her now. What could she say? She began to develop a petulant attitude toward life and what others might think of her. She didn't want Juan to get upset with her like he did the other day when he choked her in the bathroom, threatening her to go out with him and some Hispanic girl who wore a pound of makeup on her face.

Rebecca didn't want to go through all the drama again, with Juan insisting that she wasn't good enough for him and that he could find someone better who could satisfy him both mentally and physically.

So, for now, Rebecca has challenged herself to keep Juan at all costs. She just wanted him to be happy and to accept her for all she could do for him. That even meant putting her feelings aside to please him sexually. She was determined to become his wife, to hold onto something that wasn't there. But she never imagined it would start like this. First, the emotional abuse; then came the physical abuse. Then, lies—many of them. Juan included Carlos again in their bedroom, despite having promised not to do so. But now, look: Not only did he bring Carlos into their bed, but he also brought another guy along with them who acted like he wanted to choke her every time he slammed her head down to his dick, gagging her every time. She wanted to cry, but lacked the strength to do so.

All Rebecca could do and say was "Uh-uh" while straddling Juan's body, with Carlos on her back, sandwiched between them. She just wished they could hurry up and get it over with.

For the sake of it, to speed things up, Rebecca squeezed her stomach muscles so that both of her holes –front and back– could feel tight for them, wishing that they would cum. She even faked an orgasm, hoping that would do the trick. But it seemed like it only worked for Carlos for the most part because when he picked up his pace behind her, slamming his family jewels against her ass cheeks, he suddenly plunged his dick so far in her rectum that she felt him squirted a monster load inside of her.

She thought that would be it for Carlos, but then he shouted over her back, "Hey, Pedro! Let's switch places so you can get a feel of her tight ass." Then immediately afterward, without any hesitation, he yanked his dick out of her and went straight for her mouth.

She finally gained the strength to cry now.

Take 52

"And I don't give a damn what they think!" Ms. Ginsberg slurred with an intoxicated voice before me and Melissa. "Because I know this is a kick-ass party!" Then she yelled, "Yeah!" while making a muscle with her right arm, elbow down at her wrist side.

I wanted to laugh, but I held it back—at least for now, since Melissa looked embarrassed.

Ms. Ginsberg took another swing of her Bordeaux. Then she said to me, "Drink with me, my darling," as she tried to tilt the wine glass to my mouth.

I remained still because I didn't want her to say anything foolish in front of Melissa. Some Bordeaux spilled on my shirt, but I laughed it off. There was no reason to get upset. Why should I? It was a shirt that Ms. Ginsberg bought for me anyway.

Melissa extended her hand toward Ms. Ginsberg's wine glass. "I think you had enough of this for one night." She pulled the glass away from her before Ms. Ginsberg made another mess. Then she added, "I need to take you to bed."

I agreed.

Ms. Ginsberg turned her head toward me and said, "Only if he can keep me company." She then placed her index finger in her mouth and hummed, *"Mmm-mmmmm"* while bobbing her head back and forth over it.

It was my turn to feel embarrassed: She was putting out business on Front Street, especially in front of Melissa.

"You have to forgive me for my aunt's manners," Melissa told me, then draped Ms. Ginsberg's arm around her shoulders, trying to guide her steps. "She doesn't usually act like this."

If only Melissa had known what happened behind closed doors, I've seen Ms. Ginsberg act worse than this before.

Melissa added, "Can you give me a hand with her?"

"Sure." I threw Ms. Ginsberg's other arm over my shoulder.

We entered the elevator and rode to the top floor. Upon reaching the penthouse, we escorted Ms. Ginsberg directly to her bedroom. Melissa moved the bedspread aside. I laid Ms. Ginsberg down. She attempted to pull me into bed with her, but I managed to break free. As I stepped back with a slight twist, I found myself directly in front of Melissa. I stood nearly seven to eight inches taller than her. We gazed into each other's eyes. This only lasted a few seconds before Ms. Ginsberg started to cry.

"I apologize for how I behaved downstairs."

Melissa walked away from me. "That's all right," she said, then went for Ms. Ginsberg's shoes. She pulled them off her. "Liquor could do that to people."

"I'm sorry," she cried without tears. "I didn't mean to ruin your night."

"That's all right." Melissa pulled the sheet up to Ms. Ginsberg's chest. "I was ready to go home anyway."

"Are you sure?"

"Yes. Now, sleep that liquor off for me."

"Okay." When Ms. Ginsberg shut her eyelids, she was out for the count.

"C'mon," Melissa turned toward me. "Let's see if we can get that stain out of your shirt."

I flipped the light switch on the wall and followed her lead straight to the kitchen sink. I swear, it felt strange standing in Melissa's presence.

"Take your shirt off for me," she said, removing her cardigan.

I hesitated at first, but then I began working on my buttons anyway. She helped me. When I pulled my shirt off, I said, "Thanks."

"Don't mention it." She looked surprised. "You must have worked out a lot."

"Yeah, sorta." I handed her my shirt. "Whenever I find the time to."

"Oh." She focused her gaze on my chest until I reached the kitchen island.

I took a kiwifruit from the fruit basket and turned to her. She scrubbed the wine stain with dish soap under the faucet.

"Melissa."

She glanced back at me, still scrubbing my shirt.

I froze.

"Yes."

I had no choice, so I gave it my best shot: "Can we keep this as our little secret?"

"Keep what as our little secret?"

I waited another second and then said, "That you saw me."

"Cassidy, whatever you decide to do with your life, that's on you." She seemed convincing. "You don't have to worry about me: My lips are sealed. If that makes you happy, I haven't seen you."

It seemed almost unbelievable. Although I have known Melissa for several years, I cannot say that I fully trust her. She is Joey's wife, which has always been my only concern. She will likely inform Joey that she saw me at Aunt Clare's company party when she returns home. I can imagine the scenario: before going to bed, she would tell him, "Would you believe whom I encountered earlier today at Aunt Clare's company event?" Upon his inquiry, she would respond, "Cassidy!" Consequently, a series of events would unfold.

That was the only reason I brought it up to her again: "Please keep this between us. I don't need the headache right now."

"Cassidy, stop it! I said that my lips are sealed already." She rinsed the soap from my shirt and then wrung out the excess water. "Let's go outside on the balcony to dry your shirt out there."

"Sure." I grabbed another kiwifruit and followed her closely.

She hung my shirt over the rail and gazed at the beach. I looked, too. It was nearly midnight, and there were a few people still out there enjoying themselves—about twenty of them. I smiled when I saw a guy chasing a girl down there, playing. I chuckled a little as I recalled days like that.

"What's so funny?"

I glanced at Melissa and told a lie. "It's nothing. It's just that it's beautiful out here."

She gazed back at the beach and then at the ocean.

I followed her lead.

Silence took over.

We watched the waves crash against the shore, one after another, for at least three minutes straight, desolating before our eyes.

Then Melissa finally broke the silence: "Let's go back inside because it's starting to get chilly out here. And you don't have a shirt on."

"We don't have to on my account." I guess I'm pretty much used to the tropical weather by now. "It feels fine out here to me."

"Who are you kidding?" She felt my arm. "You're cold!" She stepped in front of me, resting both hands on my arms, trying to warm me up again.

I hesitated for a moment, unsure why I acted that way—then, when she looked up at me, I kissed her. I pressed my lips to hers briefly and pulled back. I wasn't sure how she would react, but her expression showed she wasn't surprised at all. She looked more receptive than shocked, as if she had enjoyed it.

I leaned in for another kiss, and she met me halfway. Our lips touched, and her lips felt soft against mine. Gradually, I worked my tongue into her mouth as she began nibbling on my bottom lip. Suddenly, everything seemed to speed up. I unhooked the top button of her blouse, then the one just below it. She raised her arms in the air, and I pulled her shirt off, revealing a black bra. Her beautiful white skin had a nice glow. Then, everything slowed down.

I went straight to Melissa's neck and suck on it. She tilted her head to the side, allowing my tongue to explore. Her breathing grew strong. I unleashed her bra strap from the back and her titties hung freely. Peach colored areolae. Her nipples looked appealing. They were nice and hard. I reached in and sucked on her left nipple first, then on her right one.

"Cassidy," she panted, pressing my mouth against her breast. "We shouldn't be doing this … let's stop."

I didn't want to.

Then she kissed the side of my face and my lips after parting us by resting her hands on my chest.

I'm not going to lie here: she had my dick rock hard. It was trembling inside my pants like a live volcano that was about to erupt. I swallowed hard. I swear, I wanted her. Not later, but now. Right now! If only she knew, I could taste her in my mouth, and I haven't even gone down on her yet. I looked into her eyes, wrapping my arms around her. I tried to find the right words to persuade her so we could continue.

But when she asked, "What about Joey?", the first thing that came to my mind was, *Fuck him!* However, I kissed her, and she responded positively to it again.

She quickly reached for my belt buckle to unfasten it, and I assisted her.

Take 53

"You're a true don for real," Carlos said to Juan, then wiped the sweat from his forehead. "Your girl has some good pussy." He then sat down next to Juan and watched their friend Pedro on top of Rebecca, fucking the hell out of her.

Pedro had Rebecca's legs locked in his arms, trying to give her everything he had, while making ugly faces. She just lay there, watching him. Aside from his foul body odor, he wasn't hurting her. He had a small dick. He leaned in and tried to kiss her. She turned her head away and locked eyes with Juan.

Her head moved back and forth as she kept her hollow eyes fixed on him.

Then Pedro tried to thrust his dick as far as he could get in her. She just lay there, motionless. He kissed the side of her face. She didn't move. She felt like a blow-up doll in Charlie Sheen's closet. There was no emotion involved. No feelings. No actions. There was nothing, nothing at all. Not a damn thing! She was there, but then again, she wasn't. Or at least, that's what she wanted to believe. Then she felt Pedro's body twitch, giving a little jerk. She looked back at him. Sweat poured from him, dripping into her face and breasts, she knew he was on the verge of cumming when he picked up his speed, going even faster now.

She squeezed her pussy muscles, then relaxed them. She tried to keep up with his pace, hoping that he would hurry up to get it over with. She squeezed her muscles again, then again. Pedro took about four more pumps and collapsed right on top of her. He let go of her legs and she felt his erection spammed inside her. After he drained everything in her, he rolled off and lay on his back. He looked over at Juan and Carlos, then smiled.

They smiled back.

When Rebecca got off the bed, she didn't know which one of them grabbed her wrist, probably hoping to another round with her, but she snatched her arm away as cum dribbling down he legs.

Carlos slapped her on the ass as she walked by and said, "You go girl. What a performance."

She ignored him and headed straight to the bathroom. She locked the door behind her and turned on the water in the bathtub.

She felt filthy.

Minutes later, Juan knocked on the bathroom door. "Sweetie, I'm gonna drop my friends off. Try to have dinner ready for me by the time I return."

Rebecca never responded. She lay in the tub, resting the back of her head on the cushion, and then, slowly but surely, she dipped her head under the water, disliking who and what she had become.

Take 54

I felt a cool breeze on my face, around five thirty in the morning, while lying on one of Ms. Ginsberg's sunbathing recliners on the balcony.

"Now," Melissa said, resting her head on my chest, a blanket covering us, "that's a beautiful sight."

I looked toward the sunrise. "It is. Isn't it?" I kissed her on the forehead.

She smiled at me.

I reached in for a kiss while running my hand over her naked body under the cover.

She closed her eyes, welcoming me, while stretching her knee over my leg so I could fondle her front entrance from the back. She pulled her mouth away from mine, but tantalizingly, wanting me to chase after her.

"Cassidy," she moaned, her eyes closed, "let's stop before we do something again."

I paused.

She opened her eyes and gazed at me.

I reached in and kissed her. It was a little better than before. She kissed me back. So, on that note, I grabbed her left knee, which was resting on my pelvis area, and gently pulled it over me until she was centered entirely on top of my growing muscle. She gyrated her hips, then grabbed my manly tool. She groped it between her legs.

She was still wet down there. Without any hesitation, the head of my dick slithered in her; then gradually worked itself inside her when she sat up and rode me with a leisurely, slow pace. She moved with an unending rhythm, and we looked into each other's eyes. I could only imagine what thoughts were crossing her mind as she slowly moved over me. Then, leaning down, she kissed me before sitting back up to continue her movements. She swayed back and forth with a slight bounce, almost as if she were on a gentle ride. It didn't take long before she started to move with more confidence and intensity, her hands on my chest, taking all of me in. She slowed for a moment, then twisted her hips with a graceful twirl.

I can express that feeling with one word: Zion.

I nearly shed a tear. I had finally discovered a shortcut to Tina Fey's pink paradise.

"Oh, Cassidy….," Melissa whispered with a drag. Then she said, "You feel so good in me … I haven't felt like this in such a long time." She gnawed on her bottom lip, then added, "Don't stop … Please don't."

I opened my eyes, closed them, and then opened them back up when I felt a water drop clashing against my neck. I looked up. She had tears in her eyes again, but it was nothing like what I saw a couple of hours ago. I pulled her down toward me and kissed her to help console her.

She sat back up and started pumping me a little faster. "Ohh, Cassidy! Don't stop. I'm about to cum … I'm about to cum again."

I kept along what I was doing –nothing more, nothing less– at my same pace, while barely humping inside her: I didn't want to add or subtract: I wanted her to cum for me.

"Ohhh, Cassidy! Cassidy! I'm about to—" she started to say, picking up her pace, but immediately dropped flat on my chest. "Shit!" she tried to whispered. "My aunt just went into the kitchen."

Melissa tried to slide off me. But I stopped her. "No. Keep it in you."

"But my aunt is up from her sleep."

"So what?" I picked up from where she left off. "Just keep going for me."

"But what if she catches us out here together?"

"She's not." I tried to assure her. "Don't worry about it right now." I started pumping inside her like before. "I want you to cum for me first."

She stammered, panting, "Okay." Then she eased back up on top of me. She started pumping me back with the same pace that I was giving her, while keeping her eyes fixed through the balcony window. She wanted to keep a close eye on Ms. Ginsberg.

I didn't know about Melissa, but the thought of me sneaking around like this brought a thrill to me. I kept my eyes on Tina

Fey's, I meant. I kept my eyes on Melissa Welch's beautiful facial expression.

"Ohhh, Cassidy...." She took stronger pumps. "I'm about to cum. I'm about to cum."

"So go ahead and cum for me."

She swallowed heavily, then said, "I want you to cum with me." She panted, bouncing faster now, while taking her eyes off the window. She looked at me. "Cum with me, Cassidy." She reached in and kissed me. "I want you to cum with me."

"Okay," I said just for the heck of it, but I knew I wasn't ready yet.

"Cum with me."

"Okay." I just kept pumping into her.

"Ahh, fuck! Here it comes...," she slumped over me with her titties on my face, her eyes squeezed shut tight, going through a convulsion. "I'm cumming..." Her body twitched, then immediately twitched again and again. Then she collapsed right on top of me.

I felt her vagina muscles contracted. I kissed her forehead and kept pumping in her. I wanted to cum too.

"Wait a second." She caught on. "Let me lie on my back."

I didn't object to that.

Just as we were about to switch places, she nearly shouted: "Oh, shit! My aunt is heading our way."

I helped Melissa get off me.

She grabbed the blanket, wrapping it around her shoulders. She leaned in and kissed me, adding a little tongue. Then she joked, "We have to continue this at a later time." She kissed me again, then dashed into the penthouse.

To hell with my underwear; I slipped on my pants instead. I grabbed my shoes and peeked through the window. I saw Melissa talking to Ms. Ginsberg. Then they headed toward the kitchen. Without looking back at me, Melissa beckoned behind her as if she knew I would be watching her.

I suppose that was my cue.

I got up and quickly slipped through the doorway. I scraped my shoulder against the glass door. As soon as I stepped into the living room to escape, Ms. Ginsberg tottered back inside with her hand on her head.

I immediately dove to the floor. Seconds later, she did what I dreaded most: she settled onto the couch, her back turned to me.

Take 55

A knock sounded at the front door, followed by another.

"Who is it?" Ms. Nelson asked, but there was no response.

Then, less than a second later, there was another knock.

"Who is it?"

Again, no answer.

Ms. Nelson peered through the peephole and then opened the door.

It was Rebecca with tears in her eyes. "He hasn't come home last night."

"Come in. Have a cup of coffee with me."

A moment later, Rebecca sat at the table, in her usual spot, when they entered the kitchen.

Ms. Nelson called Sally's Gym while the coffee brewed and informed the receptionist that Rebecca would be unable to come to work due to the flu. After hanging up, she looked at Rebecca.

"So, what did she say?"

"She said she hopes you get better soon because she just got over the same flu. So, she can only imagine what you're going through right now."

Under normal circumstances, Rebecca would have smiled, but in this instance, missing a day of work doesn't cover the bills at home.

Ms. Nelson understood the situation and poured a cup of Maxwell House coffee for Rebecca. Taking a seat at the table, she aimed to convey an important message. "You can't settle for a man who has little to no ambition beyond wanting to exert physical control over you," she said. "The issue with many women today is that you seem confused about what you want in life."

"But I know what I want out of life."

"Oh, do you?"

Smooth Casanova

Rebecca gave a slight nod.

"When was the last time you had a good man in your life? A year ago? Two years ago?" Ms. Nelson paused as she saw Rebecca's eyes filling with tears. After a moment, she continued: "You girls buy into this nonsense that a woman needs a bad boy. You end up chasing after these delinquents, mimicking what you see in movies and music videos, thinking that's the way to live. Consequently, you let these uneducated men come in and ruin happy homes, all while treating women like dirt."

A teardrop fell from Rebecca's eye, then another one.

It wasn't that Ms. Nelson didn't care about Rebecca's feelings; she did. But Ms. Nelson wanted Rebecca to hear the truth. "And now that you have noticed the lack of respect a bad boy could have for you, as a female, you wish you had never met that pathetic excuse of a man and brought him into your life. Because when you look back on it and the gamble you took by being with him, you'd only realize that you should have never had that immature bastard in your life, with that bad boy image, in exchange for the good man you originally had.

A good, loving man who works a nine-to-five and would treasure the ground you walk on. But no. You didn't want that; you exchanged a good man for that bum who cares less about you and comes and goes as he damn-well pleases. And only God knows what else."

Rebecca stayed still, aware of the unspoken truths known only to God, as tears flowed down her face.

Ms. Nelson said, "I can't tell you what to do, but what I can share with you is some insight. As a lady like yourself, we are emotional creatures, and men are the conscious element of our existence. Without us, there wouldn't be any of them! Just remember that. They lack emotion; we are their sole provider who can balance their lives for them. You shouldn't forget that.

We shape their future. They rely on us as much as we depend on them. On a conscious level, a man only offers what he thinks we should expect. If you seek the *bad boy* persona, don't be surprised by his behavior and disrespect, as it may be all he knows. The reality is that he might not fully grasp what it means to be a true man. You shouldn't have to endure hardship or teach him masculinity. Why? Because it should be a man's greatest wish to bring happiness to his partner throughout her life."

"So, what do you think I should do about my current relationship?"

"You need to take a stand for yourself and let Juan know what you expect from him in the relationship. If he doesn't make any sacrifices for you in the hope of making your relationship work, not only does he not love you, but I think you should let him go. You deserve much better than him."

That was a tough pill to swallow, but Rebecca understood Ms. Nelson was right.

The room grew silent.

Then Ms. Nelson asked, "Do you miss him?"

Rebecca nodded, recognizing that Ms. Nelson wasn't referring to Juan, as tears began to well up in her eyes once more.

"I know."

"I miss him so much," Rebecca said in a broken voice, then let it all out and cried.

Take 56

I turned to my side and answered my cell phone on the fifth ring.

"Hello," my voice sounded slightly hoarse.

It was Ms. Ginsberg: "Did I wake you from your sleep?"

"No. Not really. I was lying here."

"Oh."

"Do you need to see me?"

"No. Not right now: I am quite busy at the moment," she said. "But I would like to see you later tonight."

"At what time?"

"Uhhh … let's make it around eight o'clock."

"Okay." I didn't seem rude to her, but I wanted to cut our conversation short. I was tired and wanted to go back to sleep. "Would that be all?"

"No. Not quite."

"So, what can I help you with?"

"Well," she was straightforward to the point, "this morning when I went out on the balcony, I noticed a shirt hanging over the rail."

That's where I left it!

"And," she continued. "Snookum informed me that it belongs to you."

"Who?"

"Snookum."

"Who's that?"

"My niece Melissa."

"Oh." I had almost forgotten.

"Well, she stated that it belongs to you."

"Yeah," I began to admit, taking cautionary steps along the way, "it's mine. But I never intended to leave it over there."

"Yes. Snookum told me that. She said I accidentally spilled wine on your shirt last night in the elevator, and she washed it out

207

for you before the stain became terrible. But you didn't wait for it to dry because you were too rushed to leave."

"Oh, she did?" I felt safe yet relieved that Melissa would come up with a story for me. Even better, for us. I smiled. "Well, I'll pick it up when I come by tonight."

"You can't."

"Why?"

"Because she has it."

"She has it?"

"Yes. I hope you don't mind my passing your telephone number to her, as she was insistent on giving your shirt back to you herself, personally."

I smiled. "Was she?"

"Yes. So, I hope you don't mind?"

I waited, then said, "For you. Of course not. It's okay."

"Good. So, I'll see you tonight."

"Okay."

She hung up.

Just as I was about to put my cell phone on the nightstand, it rang again. I answered it on the second ring without checking the caller's ID. "Hey. What's up?"

"Hello, sweetie."

"Who is this?"

"Melissa."

"Oh, hey!" I was glad to hear from her so soon.

"When can we finish what we have started?"

I snickered a bit. "Whenever you want to?"

"Well, what about now?"

I glanced at my wristwatch. It read 1:45 pm. "Are you sure about right now?"

"Yeah."

"Where would you like to meet me?"

"My house."

Did I hear that correctly: "At your house?"

"Yeah," she sounded serious. Then she continued, "Joey's at work and he won't be back until five, five-thirty."

I didn't trust it.

Then I reconsidered my doubts when she added, "I love what you did for me last night with the kiwifruit."

"Oh, did you?"

"Uh-huh." It sounded like she was trying to hold back a giggle. "And when I went grocery shopping this morning, I picked up a few kiwifruits and immediately thought about you. And ..."

"And, what?"

"And I wish you could make me feel like that again," she paused, then added, "I have a bottle of Burgundy on the shelf."

My smile widened. "Put it on some ice. I'd be over in half an hour."

Take 57

Rebecca sat quietly on the sofa, one leg crossed over the other, pondering how to confront Juan about the thoughtless and dramatic emotional roller coaster he consistently subjected her to. This experience left her feeling a mix of emotions: confusion, hurt, and, oddly enough, a sense of love. It reminded her of Jodi Arias's ordeal with her former boyfriend, who over time inflicted severe mental and physical torment, ultimately breaking her sanity. Sometimes, Rebecca felt as if she was losing her grip on reality, feeling lost, disoriented, and isolated. The prospect of being betrayed by someone who had exploited and mistreated her, someone who professed to love her, was both terrifying and unsettling. It was beyond comprehension.

To sum it all up, Rebecca had had enough of the second-guessing. She needed to know the truth. If Juan claimed he loved her, as he did many times after getting along with her, he must start getting his act together. Because if he truly loved her, he should be able to make certain sacrifices that Ms. Nelson advised her about to be with her. Rebecca also had a list of things to discuss with him.

She patiently waited, gazing at the front door while sitting on the sofa, with one leg still crossed over the other.

She had no option but to wait for him.

Then, about four hours later, around nine o'clock in the evening, just as her left leg was about to go numb, she heard a key rattle in the lock. Immediately afterward, the door opened.

It was Juan, and he brought visitors with him. She knew Carlos—a face she clearly recognized from a distance and probably wouldn't forget—but this black chick threw her off. She didn't know her. The word *cheap* is too kind a description for her. She wore a purple miniskirt and white leather heels, and with her belly ring exposed, she looked like someone Juan and Carlos had picked up from a hoe stroll in Miami.

Rebecca turned back to Juan just as she started to stand up. "We need to talk."

"Later."

"No, we need to talk now!"

He hesitated before saying, "Let's go in the back room to talk."

"No!" She was too familiar with his tone and understood what he meant by it. "We don't need to go back there! Tell your friends to leave so we can discuss it here."

"My friends are right here with me! They don't need to go anywhere!"

"Alright then. I need to ask you and your friends to leave my apartment before I contact the police."

"Just go ahead and do it, if you think you're fucking bad! Because I'm not going anywhere and neither are they!"

Rebecca hesitated as she noticed him moving closer. This was her first warning. She wasn't naive; fear surged through her veins. She didn't want Juan to confront her in front of them. "Fine then! I'll leave!" she declared, stepping away just before he could reach her. Heading to the bedroom, she quickly grabbed her duffel bag and packed enough essentials to last a few days, planning to return later for the rest of her belongings.

While exiting the room with her bag, Juan asked her, "Where do you think you're going?"

"I'm leaving, Juan." She clutched her belongings in case he tried to grab the bag from her. She made her way to the door.

But Juan stopped her. "Just wait a second!" he barked, gripping her arm tightly. Then he turned to Carlos. "Why don't you and Niki go in the car and wait there for a while?" He then stuck his other hand inside his pocket and pulled out his keys. He handed them to him. "I'll call y'all when I'm finished here."

"Alright." Carlos left with Niki.

Juan cut back to Rebecca. "Now. What's your fucking problem?!"

"Juan," her voice cracked with fear as her eyes began to fall, "Why are you doing this to me?"

He squeezed her arm even harder this time. "You're the one who's acting fucking stupid here!"

"You're killing me, Juan." She started crying. "You're killing me…"

He finally let go of her arm. "How?"

She didn't know where to start, but she gave it her best shot: "You don't suppose to be hurting me, if you claim that you love me. You're supposed to make me feel happy and safe."

"But don't I make you feel happy?"

"Not anymore," she admitted. "It's not like before when you made me feel like I was loved. But now I feel threatened whenever I'm around you. All we do is argue. And the only time we don't argue or get into a fistfight is when we are having sex. Our relationship shouldn't be based solely on sex. If that's the case, I need out, and we should go our separate ways. Because it doesn't provide a foundation for me to understand what I'm looking for in a relationship. I need love, companionship, and someone who knows how to treat me as a woman.

I want someone who loves me for who I am and treats me well, not like some street prostitute! At the end of the day, when I'm supposed to come home to my partner, I need comfort, cuddles, and happiness," she said, her voice beginning to tremble again. "I want to feel secure and fulfilled, knowing that you love me and only me, without sharing me with anyone else." She paused, hoping her words would resonate with him. After a moment, she continued, "But when I find myself questioning whether you love me, it's only because that love seems to be gone," she cried.

"But do you love me?"

"Naturally, you would say that. The reason being, it's either something you know I want to hear or something you want me to accept." She shook her head slowly, displaying confusion. "But no matter how I see it, I don't feel the way I once did with you." Her voice faltered again. She continued, "Consider this: When you got that new car, you proudly drove it around and showed it off to your friends. You haven't let me or any of your friends take it for a spin because you cherish it. Yet, I don't get it: Am I not more valuable than that damn car of yours?!" She paused, hoping he would reply.

But Juan didn't move. He just stood there, his mouth shut.

So, she went on instead: "I'm supposed to be treated like that car out there as if I were your precious prize, for you and you only! Someone … someone special who's not to be shared amongst your friends!" Her chest hyperventilated, while she cried hard now. "But I still put up with your bullshit! Because I wanna make you happy." She paused again, trying to catch her breath. "Let me ask you this." Tears ran down her face. "When was the last time you took me out somewhere, so I can feel special?!" she cried. "When?!"

Nothing but a stare.

Rebecca shouted, "Answer me! When?!"

After a long pause, Juan finally said, "But I was planning for us to go somewhere."

"When?!" she shouted again, tears streaming down her face.

"I just haven't gotten to it yet." He pulled her close to him. "I'm sorry. I'm gonna work on something for us soon. I promise. But I didn't know you felt like this."

"But I do." She tried to push him off her, using her forearms. "I have always felt like this."

"I'm sorry." He hugged her and kissed her forehead. "Things will change now. I promise."

"You said that last time!"

"I truly mean it this time. I promise. I'll dedicate more time to you and take you out, as well. Does that sound good?"

She could only wish for the unimaginable.

He kissed her forehead again. Then he asked, "Didn't you make plans for us at some restaurant this upcoming Friday?"

"Yeah." She slowly bobbed her head.

"So, I promise from now on, things will change between us. Okay?"

She nodded her head again.

Juan reached in and kissed her. She returned the kiss, wrapping her arms around his shoulders. He lifted her, her legs straddling his hips, as he carried her to the bedroom.

Take 58

"And I shouldn't have to tell you what happened next," I said to Cathy over the phone as I stepped outside to continue our conversation, leaving Samuel alone inside the house.

"Please, tell me."

"After I found out she was having an affair with someone else, I decided to drink heavily and ended up passed out for two whole days." I leaned against the rail, observing others as they strolled by on the beach. "I felt completely lost, unsure of how to start fresh on my own, leaving everything behind. So, that's the story."

"I'm sorry to hear that."

"Don't be. As I told you before, we would never have met if I hadn't gone through that with her."

"Yeah, I suppose you're right then."

I laughed. "You didn't have to say it like that, you little punk!" I tried to joke, flipping everything back on her. "You sound a bit delighted that I caught my ex cheating on me, because it led us to meet each other."

"Absolutely!" she chuckled. "You don't want me to be dishonest, do you?"

"No." I laughed with her.

Then our phone line grew silent, retreating into a hollow corner.

After a brief pause, she was the first to speak. "Cassidy?" her voice was soft yet low.

"Yeah."

She hesitated: "You're too sweet for anyone to cheat on you."

"How do you know? Have you tasted me before?"

"No," she dragged with a cackle.

"So would you like to taste me then?"

"No," she dragged again, but this time with a hearty, robust laugh.

"Oh, I was just wondering. Because if you wanna taste me, I wouldn't mind you know?" I waved at three females who were smiling at me as they walked by. "There's this particular part I want you to try first."

Cathy laughed on the phone, saying, "You're so nasty!"

"Nasty!" I continued to play with her. "My crusted toenails aren't nasty. It might sound disgusting, but not nasty. You don't know what you're missing out on. But on the contrary, nasty is what I did to myself in the shower last night when I got off the phone with you."

She laughed.

"What?" I paused for a second. "Aren't you gonna ask me what I did in the shower?"

She was still laughing when she dragged with another, "No."

"Are you sure?"

"Yes, I'm sure!"

I remained silent, listening to her laughter. Once she finished, I asked, "All jokes aside. When will I see you again?"

"Soon. Very soon."

"When? Because I'd like to take you somewhere."

"Where?" she tried to joke. "To your bedroom? I think not."

"No, you pervert!" It was my time to turn the tables on her. "So, get your mind out of the gutter. But seriously, I'd like to take you to a lovely park where I've seen elderly people enjoying each other's company."

"Why there?"

"Because it may encourage you not to experience aging alone, but instead, to age alongside someone like me, if I have that opportunity with you."

She never commented on that.

"Cathy?"

"Yes."

"Are you alright?"

She sighed, then said, "Yeah."

"So when can I take you to this park I told you about?"

"Well," she began with a hint of uncertainty, "I'm currently involved in a project. However, I promise we will meet on Friday to have dinner. And if you get past third base, you can take me to the park you mentioned."

"Make it pass third base, huh?" That wouldn't be a problem for me. "Well, just to tell you something, I'm gonna smack that imaginary ball right out of the baseball field, hitting a home run on you. So, it's on now."

"Sure." Her voice had changed. "Only time will tell."

"And it will be my time to shine."

"I hope so," she said. "But Cassidy…"

"Yeah…"

"Never mind. Let me go. It's getting late. I have something to do before I go to bed."

"Okay. I'll speak to you tomorrow."

"Sure." She hung up after we exchanged our goodbyes.

I stayed outside for a few more minutes, thinking about her. I liked Cathy as a person, even more so as a potential girlfriend. But she had a wall up against me. She wasn't letting me in for a reason. Hopefully, things will change when I hit that home run with her on Friday.

I walked back into the house and went to bed.

My cellphone rang.

It was Melissa. She sneaked out of the house and asked if I wanted to visit her at the Marriott or on LeJeune Road.

Of course. "I'll be there in twenty minutes."

"And Cassidy."

"Yeah."

"Bring some extra clothes with you."

"Why?" I asked, smiling. "Are you taking me on a field trip?"

"No. Not really. It's just that Joey and I got into a fight. And I would like for you to spend the night with me."

"Say no more. I'm on my way."

Take 59

"Ohh, you feel so good."

Rebecca woke up, hearing Juan moaning behind her, while feeling her labia lips stretch open for a hard erection. It was making its way up inside of her. She eased her leg over a little to get in a better position. Getting spooned from the back was one of her favorite sexual positions. Her breathing grew strong. She grabbed her breasts, caressing it, while feeling that fearless dick slowly sliding in and out of her.

But she wanted more of it.

As Rebecca maneuvered herself on all fours so she could take it from the back, she panicked when she saw Juan on the other side of the bed, getting his dick sucked by that colored girl who came over at the apartment earlier.

"What the fuck!" Rebecca quickly lay flat on her stomach and then rolled over to see who the intruder was behind her.

It was Carlos with his dick in his hand. It glistened.

Rebecca grabbed the pillow and covered herself. Then she cut back to the man who had broken another promise to her.

Juan locked eyes on her with an ugly, contorted, gratifying, love-making expression on his face. That black trix was sucking the hell out of his dick. You could probably hear the slurping sound from across the room.

Rebecca couldn't believe she was seeing it with her own eyes.

Juan leaned in and tried to kiss her. Without moving, Rebecca remained still, staring at him in shock. He had promised he wouldn't do this; that was all she could think about. Her eyes quickly filled with tears, and then her lips started to quiver. Juan tilted his head and kissed Rebecca's lips again while Niki continued to work on him below.

As tears streamed down Rebecca's face, Juan told her, "I love you."

Nothing in return. But don't get it twisted: she wasn't giving him the silent treatment on purpose. She didn't know what to say.

He kissed her again, but this time he pressed his tongue into her mouth. Then he broke free from her lips to say, "I love you. This is nothing. It's you that I love, Rebecca. I love you." He pushed his tongue back inside her mouth. "I love you."

She shut her eyes and cried quietly.

"I love you," he said again, kissing her once more.

She stretched her neck toward him slightly and kissed him back.

Just moments later, she felt the pillow shift beneath her as Carlos climbed on top of her. She paused kissing Juan and lay flat on her back, her knees raised to prepare for Carlos. At that moment, she felt torn and conflicted emotionally. Her head tilted back as Carlos entered her. He had a fat dick; it was at least six and half inches long. She opened her eyes to look at him, then closed them back. Carlos plunged into her again, then reached in to kiss her.

Rebecca didn't understand why she broke weak, but she kissed him back, thinking about the man from her past when she moaned, "Oh, Cassidy…"

Her tears runneth over.

Take 60

I find it utterly ridiculous, if not dangerous, that I have fallen for Joey's wife in such a way.

What I can say is that I started to harbor feelings for Melissa. That's understandable.

Initially, all I wanted to do with Melissa was to grudge-fuck her to have somewhat like a personal vendetta against Joey, but over time, things began to change. I no longer viewed Melissa as his wife but rather as my girlfriend on the side. She was down-to-earth, someone I could relate to, and someone with whom I could envision a good relationship in the future. Yes, she was the one I could eventually wake up to every morning. Yet, I was still aware that this beautiful person was married to that creep Joey.

If you've realized it by now, I was somewhat jealous of Joey, to be honest, but also confused about the direction I wanted to take in life. Was it with Melissa or someone else who could fill my emptiness? I didn't know. I was uncertain about which way to go— left, right, or straight ahead.

I felt like a desperate traveler during a crucial moment, stranded in the middle of a three-way crossroad, unsure which direction to take: this way or that way. If I go left, there's Cathy. She is elegant, well-mannered, and sophisticated to the highest degree. She is a potential wife. I know we could have a beautiful family together: two boys and a girl, or vice versa. It wouldn't matter to me which sex my children are, as long as I have them with her. But the only downside I see is Cathy. She is too secretive. She holds everything back, not wanting to let me in. I suppose it's a trust issue she has with me right now until I'm able to gain her confidence. I don't know what it is, but only time will tell.

Now, if I bear to the right, there's Melissa. She radiates class and intelligence. Unlike Cathy, Melissa also possesses a delightful sense of humor that makes her company truly enjoyable. Just thinking about Melissa brings a big smile to my face. I can't help but feel a strong affection for her—she's genuinely one of a kind. The only hiccup I see with Melissa, aside from her being married to that unfortunate guy, is that she prefers to hang out indoors, wanting to keep our time together just between us. Thus, movie theaters, restaurants, hair salons, shopping malls, and parks are all out of the question for now, so to speak. I must wait until she files for divorce from that chump, then perhaps I could step up to the plate.

Now, if I go straight ahead, there's Ms. Ginsberg. Where should I start with her? She's cool as hell. She's well-established financially and great in bed. Her blowjob is magnificent; not to mention her asshole, too. She's well-rounded in all areas that Cathy and Melissa can't match. Ms. Ginsberg and I go places together as if we were dating: the movie theaters, restaurants, shopping malls, you name it. I'm talking about everything couples do. However, the only issue I had with her, besides feeling like her gofer at times and her bedroom playmate at others, was that she was content with our current standing in our relationship.

A bridge to nowhere, as I perceived it.

Ms. Ginsberg had no intentions of advancing our relationship to a more serious level, nor did she express any desire to do so. As she has repeatedly stated, "Let's not spoil what we have here." Additionally, she encouraged me to pursue relationships outside of ours, as long as I exercised caution and used protection, specifically recommending Trojan condoms. She was concerned about the potential risk of contracting a sexually transmitted infection and accidentally transmitting it to her. This concern is reasonable, especially considering that we engage in unprotected sexual activity. She preferred our encounters to be intimate and passionate, and I felt the same way about her. She enjoyed it rough, particularly from behind, and I'm not just referring to doggy-style. I'm talking about anal fucking, with her lying flat on her back, her legs straight up in the air.

It's a beautiful sight to see her eyeballs rolled toward the back of her head, as if she were having an epileptic seizure with her mouth open, speaking in tongues, when she's about to cum from her ass.

Even with these three wonderful women in my life, I still felt a sense of emptiness. I longed to be with just one of them, to wake up beside her every morning as if she were my main squeeze— my girl, my boo, my future partner. I envisioned someone I could share intimate moments with in the early hours of the morning when I woke up with desire.

During this crucial phase in my life, I aim to put my best foot forward on dates, but I still feel a sense of disconnection from true happiness. I hope one of my significant others can offer the comfort and security I desire. Therefore, I'm wearing my favorite cream-colored Versace linen pants tonight, which have a loose fit around my legs. Just as I grabbed my dress shirt from the bed, my cell phone rang.

"Hello?"

It was Cathy: "Sweetie, do you mind if I send a chauffeur over to pick you up?"

"No. Not really." I didn't mind. "But why?"

"Because I believe it'd be best to have a chauffeur as part of our arrangement tonight, I'd prefer that we sit back and relax to enjoy the night out together."

"If you say it that way, it would be a great idea."

"Fine. He'll be over shortly."

"He?" I was a bit puzzled. "Aren't you driving with him?"

"No, I'm more of a conservative type: I believe traditionally. A man is supposed to pick his date up."

"So," I smiled, because it was about time, "you're finally going to tell me where you live?"

"Live? No. Not quite. I'm currently staying at the Sheraton Hotel until my project is over."

"Your project?"

"Yes."

I'd prefer not to ask her about it. I stayed silent.

Then she continued, "Let me go. I need to get dressed."

"So, you aren't dressed yet?"

"No, I'm in the process of getting dressed."

"*Soooo,*" I slowly dragged out in a suggestive tone, "are you naked then?"

"Yes," she said, but cut it short right there. Then, between laughs, she added, "Cassidy, you need a cold shower before we go out tonight. You're a nutcase. I don't think I could control you tonight."

"Yeah, whatever. So, are you?"

"Am I what?"

"Are you naked?"

She laughed even harder this time. "I'll see you when you get here."

"No-no-no! Don't hang up yet! I wanna know if you're naked or not?"

"Bye-eeeee, Cassidy," her voice trailed off.

"I wanna know."

She hung up.

I smiled. I couldn't wait to get to second base with her. She was promising; she had so much more to offer when she let down her guard and trusted me. I believed I could make it work between us. We were somewhat compatible. We were both young and free, and I was willing to adjust. I'm open-minded, I thought. I wouldn't mind giving it a try, at least.

I buttoned my shirt and headed back to the bathroom to look at myself in the mirror. For all it's worth, I looked friggin' handsome!

I heard the doorbell ring.

Then, after a brief moment, Samuel yelled: "Hey, Cassidy! It's for you!"

"Tell him I'll be right there! I need a second!" I glanced at my reflection in the mirror.

"It's not him! It's a young lady asking to see you. And I think you ought to come quickly!"

Take 61

Juan held Rebecca's hand as he drove down I-95 South, listening to reggaeton with the volume low. He glanced at her, then back to the road.

She looked at him, appearing innocent. Her eyes were locked on him as he raised her hand and kissed it. His lips felt soft against hers, and she admired his occasional gentlemanly behavior. Her conversation with him a few days ago seemed to have made a difference. He had made some adjustments for her—nothing major, but something is better than nothing at all. She appreciated his effort to make it work and didn't feel as threatened by him as she had before, since he had stopped yelling at her. She glanced back at the windshield, hoping this moment could last forever.

"Rebecca."

She glanced back at him.

He brushed his lips against her hand again. "I love you."

She just stared at him, lost for words, as if she had long waited to hear that from him.

"And after we get married next month," he continued today, "I would like to start being a father soon."

"A father?"

"Yeah, I want us to have a family together: a boy for me and a girl for you."

Her smile slowly faded. Tears began to form. She looked away.

"What's the matter?"

She looked back at him and said, "Nothing."

"You sure?"

She nodded her head while lying.

"But don't you wanna have a family?"

"Yes," she admitted. A teardrop slipped from her eye.

He caught it for her. "And I know you would be a great mother."

"Thanks. And what about you as a father?" she asked, seeming curious. "Are you ready to be a father?"

"But of course. I know what it takes to be one." He glanced ahead quickly, then returned his gaze to her. "That's easy."

"So, what does it take?"

"What are you talking about?"

"What does it take to be a father? "

"You know," he started, his gaze shifting from her back to the road, "the regular staff," he paused, gathering his thoughts. Just when he seemed to lose his words, his cellphone rang. He answered quickly, saying, "Hello." After a brief silence, he continued, "Nah, with Rebecca … I'm not lying … Yeah … Uh-huh … Nah. We're going to a restaurant. … I don't know, probably an hour or two … Oh, yeah." He cast a glance at Rebecca before resuming his conversation. "Is, you know … Yeah, with you right now?" he paused again, this time sounding excited about something. Then he elaborated, "No. But what about the other one…? Yeah ... Okay ... I'll call you when I need you all to come over … Yeah, definitely … Okay ... Okay ... Later." He ended the call and turned to look at Rebecca.

"Who was that?" she asked.

"Oh, that was Carlos."

Take 62

I felt like a mannequin in the JCPenney store, with a fixed smile on my face. Honestly, I was love-struck.

When the chauffeur pulled up in front of the Sheraton Hotel, Cathy stepped out from under the porte-cochère, looking stunningly beautiful. She wore a red evening dress, matched with matching pumps and a handbag. I didn't blink. I guess I didn't want to. Her appearance alone was captivating, mesmerizing, if I may be technical about it. Cathy wasn't just any ordinary woman out here tonight; she was the lady in red.

"Please," I told the chauffeur, "Let me get the door for her." I immediately jumped out of the limo and approached Cathy. I couldn't resist telling her, "You look beautiful." I took both her hands in mine.

"Thank you." She smiled. "You look quite handsome yourself."

Her compliment did not register with me immediately, as I was fully engrossed in appreciating her overall beauty. I felt confined within my thoughts, reluctant to allow any external interruption. It is worth noting that, before her transformation—if one chooses to describe it as such—she was already a naturally attractive individual who rarely required additional effort to enhance her appearance. Nevertheless, she took considerable time to assemble an outfit of this caliber.

It felt like I was standing in front of Sandra Bullock, looking at her with desire. Cathy is beautiful, and I pray to God that she could be my soul mate—someone with whom I could grow old until death do us part. Because, let's be honest, she embodies that virtuous status as a woman.

"Cassidy…"

And if I wanted to build my future with her, I needed to step up tonight and convince her to take our friendship to the next level. Because I swear, I wouldn't mind working on her to be my–

"Cassidy?"

"Huh?" Her beautiful smile interrupted my train of thought.

"We're going to be late for our dinner engagement."

I pulled her hands close to my chest, wishing she could feel my heartbeat. "Let's forget about dinner tonight," I joked, "and go straight to Vegas instead."

"For what?"

"To get married over there, I can have you as my wife. To have you as someone I look forward to seeing every day, waking up beside."

She cackled, then leaned in and kissed me on the cheek. "You're so sweet. But I don't want us to break our engagement for tonight."

"So, what about tomorrow?"

She smiled, "For what? Marriage?"

"Hell, yeah! Why not?" I smiled back, jokingly. "I can give you the time of your life."

She laughed as she broke free from my hands. "Let's take this one day at a time." She then headed for the back door of the limo.

"Please, allow me." I rushed to the back door of the limo like a hotel flunky and opened it for her.

"Thank you." She ducked inside.

I was astonished, honestly taken aback. Her scent was enchanting. I hurried to the other side of the car and climbed in. We shared a few words but then fell into a comfortable silence, stealing glances at each other. I hesitated to speak, not wanting to ruin the moment. For me, this represented a fresh start—a new beginning for everything. I believed that with Cathy at the center, my perspective on life, relationships, and all else could shift positively. I envisioned it all: hand in hand on the beach, enjoying picnics at the park, and snuggling on the couch while watching movies together. I genuinely wanted everything to flow smoothly for us. I held onto that hope.

When we came to a complete stop, our doors opened. I was the first to get out, followed by her. We walked to the restaurant entrance, where I held the door open for her.

"Thank you," she almost whispered.

"No. Thank you," I kept it honest with her, "for giving me the honor of having you as my date tonight."

She smiled at me as we walked toward the reception area, where a young lady was standing.

"Welcome to El Rancho Grande Restaurant," the host said. "My name is Alexis. Do you have a reservation, or would you like a table?"

"Yes," Cassidy had a brisk, businesslike tone. "We reserved a table for two, under Catherine Swartz."

"Oh, yes. Here it is. Ms. Swartz. Your table awaits you. Can you please follow me?"

When we stepped into the dining area, the atmosphere was breathtaking. There were about twenty—or maybe thirty—tables in a large, open space, most of which were occupied by customers, primarily affluent older individuals with wizened faces. I was surprised by the quietness as we were led to our table. Perhaps the calmness stemmed from the tinkling sounds mingling with the soft instrumental music played by a small orchestra in the center of the room. There were five musicians, excluding the pianist, who was conversing with an older gentleman on the side. Moreover, the musical tone created a cozy, relaxing feeling when we reached our table.

There's no doubt about that.

I had the honor of pulling out the chair for Cathy and then sliding it back in after she sat down. Just as I was about to take my seat directly across from hers, an elderly couple who seemed genuinely happy exchanged smiles with me. I returned their smile, and they turned back to one another. By the way he held her hand, I could only guess it was his wife.

"Perhaps," I whispered to Cathy across the table, "that could be us one day?"

"Perhaps."

I watched her blush and felt like I was in heaven. It couldn't get any better than this. I sat back and relaxed, hoping to enjoy the moment. As the waitress walked by, my eyes shifted to the other side of the room—the left side—and then sort of in front of me. I froze. No. It can't be. I focused on being sure, but then my countenance dropped immediately.

I couldn't believe it!

The joy I had just a moment ago abruptly ended when I noticed the couple sitting in front of me, about two tables away from our table. Yes, the table was directly behind Cathy's seat. I felt uncomfortable.

"What's the matter?" Cathy asked.

I glanced back at Cathy, uncertain how to respond to her question.

She turned around to see what had captured my attention back there.

I cut my gaze back to that same table behind her and wondered why this bitch was staring at us, particularly at me.

Cathy twisted back to me and asked, "Who's that?"

"That's my ex: Rebecca."

Take 63

Call it fate, coincidence, or sheer bad luck!

But Rebecca was the last person I expected to see in this restaurant while I was on a date. Of course, there's no denying it; I have always known that once someone ends a relationship, it usually takes a year or two before they hear any news about their ex. They might be in another relationship, married, have children, be doing well, or be struggling. However, in this case, Rebecca and I saw each other for the first time in nine months without anyone giving us the actual scoop about each other.

Yes, I would occasionally get tidbits about Rebecca from David whenever he accidentally let something slip before Ronald interrupted him. However, the few details from David hardly amounted to a scoop. I mean the real scoop—the complete story laid out so you wouldn't be left wondering about anything else.

And from the look of it, Rebecca just sat there, staring at me with that Miranda Lambert look in her eyes, as if she wanted me to acknowledge her with either a smile, a nod, or a slight wave of my hand. However, I did the opposite: I ignored her, as if I didn't know her, turning my gaze back to Cathy. That should do the job. Besides the fact that I didn't like sitting just two tables away from Rebecca –not to mention while she was with her friggin' new fiancé– we were facing each other, aligned in the same direction. It felt like we were intentionally positioned to look at each other.

"Does her presence bother you?" Cathy asked me, looking a little uncomfortable. "Because if anything, we could request to be moved to another table?"

I scanned the room for another available table, but I couldn't find any. "Should we consider going to a different restaurant?"

She remained silent. It seemed that my question had unsettled her.

So, I quickly added, "I'm sorry. I apologize for that. We shouldn't have to leave because of her. Let's not spoil our night together."

Cathy's eyes seemed to glow again, but they looked fake.

I reached over and took her hand, her right hand. I kissed her fingers—once, twice, three times—with a lingering kiss. And I hope that bitch was watching me over there because, honestly, I wanted her to know I was a survivor. Yeah, she probably tore my heart to pieces, but not my soul. That was the root of my recovery, my survival kit, my Ace bandage and Band-Aid. *So, what did you think?* I thought, *I couldn't make it without her.*

You're a joke! Samuel played a Gloria Gaynor CD at least twice a week: "I Will Survive."

Cathy and I quickly began discussing various topics. During our conversation, I occasionally caught a glimpse of Rebecca unintentionally. This was not deliberate, so it should not be misunderstood. My glances were more of a distraction, often looking over Cathy's shoulder. Although Rebecca and I briefly made eye contact, it only lasted a moment before I turned my attention back to Cathy to continue our discussion about life.

Shortly after, a waitress approached our table and asked if we were ready to place our order.

I looked at Cathy and then back at the waitress. "I'm going to allow my beautiful girlfriend here," I said, turning back to Cathy, "to order our meal for both of us."

Cathy, displaying a slight blush, proceeded to order two beef tenderloin entrées accompanied by a cucumber-mango salad.

The waitress walked away with our order.

"Like I was saying," I told Cathy, "Life has so much to offer. The beauty that it holds and the remarkable treasure that it provides. But it's a tragedy that we only have a short time to enjoy all this."

"So," she began to ask, "what do you want out of life?"

I smiled. "You."

"I'm serious."

"Seriously, I just wanna live in pure happiness."

"What sort of happiness are you referring to?"

"The joy of living free without any misery and pain"

"But isn't that a part of our growth process? The process of experiencing certain turmoil in life, and the joy of overcoming it?"

"Perhaps."

"Perhaps?!" she laughed at me.

"Yeah, perhaps." I stood my ground, even though she made a valid point there.

"Explain."

"I will. But where would you like for me to start?"

"Anywhere. Amuse me."

"Okay," I started easily so that she could think outside the box. " Have you ever been at a certain point in your life that you didn't need anything else?"

"I don't believe I can say yes or no to that, because reality speaks for itself: the more we have, the more we want."

"Okay. Since you would like to take it there, please allow me to elaborate on this then."

"Sure, go ahead. I would like to hear how you explain this to me."

"Okay," I began with a little cackle before giving her something from my personal belief. "You see, the Torah teaches me that in the beginning, when God created Adam, he created Adam from the soil. And symbolically, some of us can interpret soil to represent the lower stage of man's life since the closest thing to the ground: Dirt! Do you agree?"

She tilted her head to the side. "If you say so."

"Whatever!" I ignored her sarcasm and went on to make my point. "When God created Adam, He said something like, 'It's not good for man to live alone.' For that reason, He created animals and gave them to Adam, hoping that Adam could enjoy the comfort of life. But this wasn't the case here because God knew all that He had made for Adam, and it still didn't meet Adam's needs for that happiness. So, what then? I waited for a response from her.

Cathy barely gestured to the side to indicate she didn't know.

So, I continued: "Did God give up on Adam? Of course not. To Torah went on to say that God knew what Adam needed in life— a helpmate. Someone is happy and complete. But God didn't create Adam a guy friend to hang out with, to help Adam along the way. No. It was nothing like that. God created Adam a significant other. A woman. A woman by the name of Eve. Adam's better half is to make him happy. As the Torah goes on to support this happiness, not only for Adam but for all people, it states that when a man leaves his father and mother and marries a woman, the two of them become one flesh."

"But," she cut in, "I still don't see how this has to do with you living pure happiness?"

I cackled a bit. "You don't get it, do you?"

"Obviously not." She laughed back. It was fake.

"Well, just look at it like this then," I said. "It was only after God created Eve that Adam found his happiness. He did not need to want anything more" –I tried to mock her back by making quotation symbols with my fingers– "as you said, because he had a woman at his side. Adam didn't need the riches of this world or anything else to make him happy. And you can see it for yourself inside the Torah that not only did God stop creating things for Adam, but it goes on to say that although Adam and his wife Eve were both naked, they were not ashamed." I paused, hoping that it could resonate with her before I continued. "Meaning, that Adam and Eve didn't have much. They didn't need anything else because they were both symbolically naked: Stripped of everything. Naked. They did not need the materialistic things of this world, and they weren't ashamed of it either." I paused again, then asked: "Would you like to know why? Why weren't they ashamed?"

"Yes. Why?"

"Because they were happy and content with one another. That's the same happiness I want in my life: To have a woman at my side to make me complete as well."

"Are you some sort of religious fanatic?"

"Hell no!" Never that. I laughed a little. "I just like some of the fundamental principles that the Torah expresses about females."

"Oh...," she wore a smile now. "So, what do you dislike about the Torah, then?"

"What do I dislike about the Torah?" Wow! I found it a bit odd to ask someone Jewish.

"Yeah."

I smiled with a slight hesitation before I said, "I don't like the fact that the Garden of Eden was started with Adam and Eve."

"Why?"

"Because I'd rather it started with you and me instead. Because I know you would have been my happiness, as Eve was to Adam."

She didn't respond. She just stared at me.

"What's the matter?"

"Nothing," she said in a whisper. "I just find you to be a sweet person."

"So, I have heard." I grabbed garlic bread from the appetizer plate and took a bite.

Silence hovered over us.

Then she asked. "May I ask you a question?"

"Sure." I was about to take another bite of the garlic bread, but I didn't. I just kept my eyes on her.

"You don't have to answer it if you don't want to."

That's cute. I almost laughed. "What is it?" I was curious to know now.

"Have you ever expressed this same view to her?" She barely shook her head to the side a bit. "When you two were together?"

"With Rebecca?"

Of course I have, I thought. She used to be my girl, my Eve, my first love—the one person I thought was my better half. Rebecca was my happiness back then. That happiness that made me feel complete, of not wanting anything else in this world other than making her happy. And there's no doubt about that. I shared my thoughts with Rebecca when we were together.

"So, have you?"

I allowed an extra second before I told Cathy the truth: "Yeah." I guess I didn't want to lie to her if I genuinely wanted to build a good relationship with her.

"Do you mind if I ask you this then?"

"Go ahead." I had nothing to hide here.

"Can you honestly say that you let her go?"

Take 64

Cathy's question felt worse than a slap.

A bitch slap at that!

It didn't make any sense. The relationship I had with Rebecca was completely over when she cheated on me—that was a closed chapter in my book. She was done in my eyes, out of my life. But then my thoughts shifted to something else: Why would Cathy ask me: Can I honestly admit I let Rebecca go?

I found Cathy's question odd while we were at the same restaurant with Rebecca. We sat just two tables away from hers, directly in front of me.

Then, either by chance or perhaps unintentionally, I glanced over Cathy's shoulder again and saw Rebecca. She was still sitting with her date, fiancé, or whatever he was to her, appearing upset. As far as I could tell, Rebecca hadn't touched her entrée yet. She sat there, avoiding eye contact with her plate and him.

I didn't have to be a rocket scientist or a genius to know Rebecca was upset about something.

Just trust me on this.

I lived with her for eight years. Yeah, that's eight years of my life. So, who would know her better than I do?

Not a single soul. Just me.

I knew everything about Rebecca: her likes and dislikes. Her choices were yes, no, or maybe. It's funny how a mind can drift off sometimes. I remember an incident from a few years ago when Rebecca and I went to a movie theater in Fort Lauderdale together, and she gave me the silent treatment. The reason was that—without any exaggeration—Rebecca and I had planned to watch The Anti-Christ about two weeks earlier, before deciding to go to the theater together. But when we arrived, she noticed that Blackout was playing and suddenly changed her mind, wanting us to watch her movie instead.

Believe me, I would have gone along with Rebecca's preference to watch "Blackout" with her, but all the guys at work gave me great reviews about "The Antichrist." I just had to see it for myself. It was an action-packed movie.

So, to make a long story short, when Rebecca and I entered the theater together, we grabbed our seats. She looked away from the screen, just as she was doing now in the restaurant, to her food and the guy she was with, telling me that she didn't want to watch The Anti-Christ with me.

Yeah, at first, I didn't care. But about fifteen minutes later, when that movie intensified with hand-to-hand combat and explosions around them, I wanted Rebecca to enjoy the film with me, but she refused, looking upset. So, to play her little game, I wrapped my arms around her shoulders when it seemed like she was about to get up and leave.

The thought of that moment brought a smile to my face.

Rebecca was acting like a little brat that day. I fondly called her my little red-haired brat as I pulled her closer to kiss her neck. She never resisted. Instead, she turned her head to the side, allowing me to continue kissing her. After a moment, she turned her head toward me and playfully stuck her tongue in my mouth. We kissed, and for a while, I completely forgot about the movie. Before long, I felt her hand slipping inside my pants. I kept my eyes closed, and I don't need to go into detail about what happened next in the theater that night.

It was obvious.

But I could tell you this: When I woke up toward the end of the movie, with Rebecca in my arms, she told me that I had missed the best part. But overall, I didn't care because at that moment, I was living the best part of my life when she was near. So, in a way, not only did I mold her this way, but I also spoiled her into being who she is now—that little red-headed brat who always got her way, especially with me.

Yet it surprised me that Rebecca still hadn't gotten up by now and—

There she goes: she grabbed her purse and pushed her chair back.

Then, in just a few seconds—perhaps two—I lost my composure when I saw Juan grab Rebecca's arm to stop her from leaving the table. I'm unsure if he was squeezing her arm, but she

235

showed a wince and said something to him. He responded, and she then closed her mouth, saying nothing further.

"So can you?"

"Huh?" I looked back at Cathy.

"So, can you honestly say you let her go?"

"Yeah." I didn't bother looking back at Rebecca. But then again, why should I? "I let her go the moment she stopped loving me when she opened her legs for that guy she's with."

Cathy paused and looked at me with intrigue, seeming satisfied with my response but eager to continue.

So, I said, "Enough about her, our food is coming. Let's dine and enjoy our night together without mentioning anything more about her."

"Sure." She agreed with me.

The waitress approached our table with our entrees: beef tenderloin, slightly smothered in mushroom gravy. I couldn't wait to dig into my plate.

A short moment later, when we began to eat, I couldn't take my eyes off Cathy. In addition to her exquisite beauty, her table manners were striking. She sat up straight, with impeccable posture. Her table manners were flawless. It was all so new to me, but I knew I could get used to it. I smiled as I watched her cut her steak into bite-sized pieces, her arms resting on the table.

"This is delicious," she said, then placed another steak with her fork, smearing it in the gravy.

I remained silent, savoring the moment.

She raised her eyes and noticed my focus on her. "Here." She smiled warmly as she offered her fork toward my mouth. "Try it. It's delicious."

I felt awkward. But then again, I didn't want her to feel embarrassed by rejecting her offer. So, I did what any other man would do in the same situation: I opened my mouth, and she fed me.

"Now, doesn't it taste good?"

But just before I could respond to her, I heard a slight commotion in front of me. I looked over Cathy's shoulder and saw Juan using one hand to pick up a wine glass that had somehow tilted over on the table, while his other hand gripped Rebecca's arm. I guessed he was squeezing her arm tightly this time, judging by the way she was slumped to the side, leaning toward the same direction where he held her.

Rebecca winced; she was clearly in pain, as her facial expression revealed.

My first reaction when I saw her in pain was, like, That's good for her stupid ass! She chose him over me. So that's what she gets! She made her choice, so let her deal with that now!

But then Rebecca did something I didn't expect: she raised her head slightly, as if she could read my thoughts when she looked at me. I swear, I wanted to look away, but I couldn't. I didn't have the strength to do so. Her eyes were filled with tears; then she dropped her head to hide her face from me. Then I saw it: her upper body jolted slightly. She was definitely crying now.

I'm not going to lie—how do I describe this? It felt like a grand ripper had slowly thrust his hand into my chest and seized my heart, trying to stop it from beating. My breathing became heavy; I needed air. I started to breathe through my nose like a raging bull.

Then something happened: I had a flashback to something Samuel had told me a few months ago.

"You can tell if you've lost your love for someone, the one person with whom you've built a history with, when you see that person in pain and just walk away without helping her in a time of need."

I thought about Samuel's statement for a second there, then shook it away. I was sure that I no longer loved Rebecca.

On that note, I thought it would be best for me to mind my own business. Rebecca wasn't my girlfriend anymore, and besides, this wasn't my fight; it was hers. Yet, I couldn't understand why she didn't fight back like Jodi Arias did and stab him with something. She could have grabbed a fork, knife, or just about anything else, but she didn't. She didn't even try to defend herself. She just sat there and endured whatever pain he inflicted on her, as if she were completely helpless!

I resolved to stay out of it since it wasn't my fight. However, when Rebecca glanced at me again, I felt that it was indeed my concern: I unknowingly clenched my hand into a fist and gripped a section of the tablecloth.

"Are you okay?"

"Huh?" I shifted my focus from Rebecca to Cathy. "Did you say something?"

"I asked if you're alright?"

"Yeah. But of course." I released my grip on the tablecloth. "Why do you ask?"

She disregarded my question, turning to see what was distracting me behind her. She paused.

When she turned back to face me, I interrupted her before she could say anything else: "Please excuse me for a moment." I stood up from my seat. "I need to use the restroom."

"Sure." She placed her utensils on the table and gave me a disheartened look.

I left and went straight to the men's room. When I entered, I was greeted by a Black man who had various items available. He offered things like chewing gum, mints, candy, dental floss, a selection of colognes, and other essentials for freshening up. However, I wasn't in the mood for anything except to clear my mind for a moment. I paced back and forth in the restroom until I finally approached the sink to splash some water on my face. I needed to pull myself together. As I looked into the mirror, I ran my fingers through my hair.

I had to remind myself that *Rebecca wasn't my girl.*

I guess I didn't like seeing someone I know, or any other woman for that matter, broken down like that in front of me, especially by a coward trying to take advantage of a defenseless woman who couldn't defend herself like a man.

What a punk!

The restroom door swung open as I leaned my head under the faucet again to rinse my face with water.

Then I heard that same-colored guy, who had just asked me a moment ago if I wanted to buy any accessories from him, say to someone else, "Oh, man! What'd happened to your shirt?"

"A fucking dumb bitch out there spilled my drink on me!" the angry man barked with a Hispanic accent. Then he asked, "Do you have anything I can use to take this stain out?!"

"Well, let me see if I can find something for you."

Something compelled me to turn my head for a glimpse of them. I was shocked to see it was Juan! He stood next to that colored guy who had been in the restroom with me. My heart raced once more. My breathing intensified. My legs quivered, and soon my left arm started to shake uncontrollably.

I need to get out of here! I grabbed a paper towel to dry my face. Then I reached for another because the first one wasn't enough. My arm shook uncontrollably, followed quickly by the other. Both trembled fiercely. I threw the towel into the trash and headed for the door.

Just as I reached for the door handle, that colored guy told Juan, "I don't think you're gonna be able to get this stain out of your shirt."

I froze when Juan said, "Just wait till I get that bitch home! She's gonna fucking regret it, for messing my shirt up!"

I wanted to leave the men's room, but I couldn't. Instead, I removed my hand from the door handle.

Take 65

I **swear, and** God is my witness to this, too, that I tried to stay out of Juan's affair before I turned back around.

But, as you already know, I couldn't: I just had to tell him, "It's only a friggin' shirt dude. Unlike a woman's feelings, that shirt could easily be replaced with another one." I stuck my hand in my pocket and pulled out my wallet. "Here! Take this!" I tried to give him all the money I had there. It was probably around $400, if not $500, in cash.

Juan declined to accept it. "I don't want your money!" he pushed my hand aside. "I have my own shit! I'm going to teach her a lesson so she learns not to disrespect me when I ask her to do something!"

"Well, if you feel like you have to teach a woman by beating on her," I started to say without considering the consequences of my words, "you're not a man at all."

"What?"

I guess he didn't hear me, so I said again: "You're not a man at all, if you feel like you have to beat a female to make a statement to her. That's only a cowardly move, dude."

"Cowardly move?" Juan mocked me with a deadly glare, then barked in my face: "Who the fuck you think you are anyway to be dipping into my conversation?" He glanced at that colored guy, then back to me: "It's none of your business what I do to her. You're nobody. I don't have to explain anything to you … Get the hell outta my face!"

Whew! I really hated that!

He waved his hand dismissively at me, like I was just a pesky fly buzzing around a meal. Honestly, that gesture felt incredibly disrespectful in Hispanic culture, similar to a hog spit in someone's face. Both actions convey the same message: a belittlement of a man's dignity. Perhaps that's why I threw the first punch as he turned to confront me. I hit him on the right side of his face, close to his ear.

He turned towards me with surprising precision, as if he knew just where I was, and landed a powerful left hook on my jaw. The impact made my legs wobble a bit. Following that, he delivered a body blow to my ribs, this time with a right hook. He struck again with another right hook. The pain was quite intense, causing me to double over slightly. I suspect he might have fractured a rib.

I felt the wind get knocked out of me. I couldn't breathe. I tried to gasp for air. Then, before I saw it coming, he shoved me with the sole of his shoe.

I flew back into the stall door, landing directly on a toilet stool. He then rushed at me and hit me with a right punch to the side of my temple. I saw a flash of light when I turned my head. For a moment, I thought I had gone blind. I swear, I couldn't see anything in front of me.

Then I heard that colored guy shout, "That's enough! He had had enough! You're gonna kill him!"

But that thoughtless bastard didn't care. He hit me with a left hook to the other side of my temple. Once more, I saw a flash of light. Then he threw another punch. I thought it was all over: he intended to kill me in there.

I tried to cover up when I told him, "I'm sorry!"

He kept swinging his fists, and just as I grabbed him, he struck me hard on the back of the head. I saw a flash of light that lasted longer than the previous ones. I wrapped my arms around his waist, doing my best to twist him around and get out of there. That didn't work. In a moment of desperation, I tried to push him forward, hoping to create enough space to escape the toilet stall. Instead, he countered by slamming me against the stall wall before I could let go and run.

I felt myself being tossed from side to side. For the love of God, I couldn't let him go now. I wanted to survive! I thought about Ms. Ginsberg, Linda, Elena, and Pamula. Of all things, I began to wonder why I had chosen to visit this restaurant today, considering all the regrettable experiences I had encountered on South Beach. I swore I didn't want to die like this—at least not at my age. I was still young and had many more years ahead of me.

I held onto him tighter; my life depended on it. I didn't regret this morning. Then, this thoughtless bastard tried to do something

I dreaded most: he attempted to peel my head and shoulder away from his side.

"No!" I gripped my arms tighter around him. "Why don't you chill out, dude? I already said I'm sorry!"

"¡Tu puta, madi con!" he shouted in his native tongue about the same time he socked me in the ribs again.

I lost my strength.

I wanted to scream for help, but that colored guy finally did it for me when he ran out of the restroom yelling, "Call the police! Call the police! Hurry! A man is being attacked inside the men's room!"

Juan then delivered a sharp and forceful elbow strike to my back.

For goodness' sake, it felt like a friggin' sledgehammer! I swear, I had no choice but to bite him.

I tried to pierce my teeth into his skin, applying pressure.

He yelled something distasteful again. But at this point, who cares? I didn't give a damn! He finally yanked me off him, throwing me to the floor. I landed on my back, looking up at this madman. He looked possessed by the devil—Lucifer himself. Juan's eyes burned with fire. He glanced from me to his ribs. His face grimaced, then he immediately looked back at me. Vengeance mixed with a hint of psychopathy was written all over his face.

I thought it was all over when Juan charged at me. I closed my eyes and curled up in fear. I'm not sure what happened next, but I think he might have slipped on something because all I know is that his groin slammed into my left knee. I felt it. He collapsed right there, holding onto himself and moaning in pain. I pushed him off me, and he rolled over onto his side, still groaning and clearly in discomfort.

I quickly tried to get up, but I slipped, landing on one hand and one knee on the floor. I steadied myself. "You sick mutherfucker!" I punched Juan in the face.

He didn't even attempt to cover up.

So, I punched him again.

That crazy bastard just tried to kill me!

I hit him in the face once more and got to my feet. "You sick bastard!" I kicked him in the ribs. "What's your damn problem?!" I kicked him again. "Were you trying to kill me?!"

He curled up into a fetal position.

I kicked him again, and a few more times after that.

I felt a slight sting on my lower lip. I checked it with my shirt sleeve.

Damm it!

That bastard split my lip! So, I went for his face. And yes, I tried to kick his fucking head off, as if my life depended on it.

"You sick motherfucker!" I kicked him in the face again. "How does that feel to you?" I kicked him again. "Huh!" Again, I kicked him. "You sick bastard!" I spat on him. "You like beating up on girls?!" I kicked him in the stomach since he left that area open. "You friggin' punk!"

The door swung open behind me as I continued to kick Juan in the stomach repeatedly.

I didn't care who it was, a police officer or a patron. I didn't give a damn about that at this point. "You friggin' asshole!" I spat on Juan again. "You like beating up on girls?! How do you like this!" I kicked him again.

"Hey! That's about enough!" someone shouted behind me. "The police are on their way. You need to stop. You've made your point to him!"

Damn, if I did! Then I remembered that time when Brad went to jail for a year and a day for that assault.

Given Brad's situation, it was not justified. He assaulted his ex-girlfriend over a misunderstanding, even though she had done nothing wrong. However, my scenario was distinct. The womanizer lying in front of me was worth any prison sentence. So, I kicked that worthless scumbag again.

"If you ever put your fucking hands on Rebecca again," I began to tell Juan as I kicked him once more, "I will kill your fucking ass! Do you fucking hear me, you sick mutherfucker?!" I managed to take one more kick at him before two guys grabbed me from behind.

"That's enough," one of the guys said.

I broke free from both of them and charged after Juan. I stomped on his head as if he were a roach on the floor. "You sick fucker!"

They caught me again just as I was about to take another kick.

So instead, I hog spat on Juan and told him, "I swear to God, I'll kill your fucking ass if you ever put your hands on her again! Do you hear me, you sick asshole?"

Juan didn't respond.

"Okay," both guys who were holding me said. "He had enough."

"Alright!" I tried to shake my arms free of them. "Let me go!"

They did so only when they turned me toward the doorway.

I froze

A small crowd of spectators stood there, watching me. Rebecca was among them, her eyes watery, and a forlorn expression on her face. I think she heard me. They heard me. I felt awkward. I shifted my gaze from Rebecca to Cathy, who also stood at the doorway. I walked past Rebecca, and a few people stepped aside.

I approached Cathy. "Do you mind if we leave?" I wiped blood from my lip.

"Sure." Cathy glanced away from me to Rebecca, then back to me. "I need to gather my belongings first."

Take 66

Cathy and I stood silently in front of El Rancho Restaurant as we waited for our chauffeur to arrive with the car.

I was speechless and unsure how to reply to her. I behaved poorly in that situation and stepped out of my usual self. It's uncharacteristic for me to show my frustration regarding the breakup with Rebecca.

Cathy glanced at me, and I returned her gaze. She turned away, wearing a serious, contemplative expression. It appeared she was deep in thought.

Seconds later, Rebecca stepped out of the restaurant, glanced at us, and then walked away. She dabbed her eyes with a tissue before continuing up the street.

Cathy pulled away from me. When I turned to her, she had already looked away again. She appeared to be deep in thought about something.

The limousine arrived.

"Let me get that for you." I opened the rear passenger door for her.

She acted as if she were about to get in, but she froze instead. Suddenly, she turned toward me, and we stood face to face. She leaned in for a kiss, and I felt relieved as my burden lifted. I tried to wrap my arms around her to kiss her, but she pushed me away, her hands resting on my chest.

"Gosh," Cathy began in a whisper, "I thought she was exaggerating about you. But it's true." Her eyes watered, and she tried to stop crying. "I wish we had met under different circumstances."

"What are you talking about?"

She didn't answer me; her mind was occupied with something else. Then, she placed her hands on both sides of my face and leaned in for another kiss, her eyes closed. Once more, she pulled away when I tried to hold her.

"No." She had one hand on my chest this time. "Don't."

"But you have to tell me something."

She slowly shook her head. "I can't do this to you. To us, Cassidy. It wouldn't be right."

"Please don't say that." I rested my hands on top of hers. She pulled her hands away from mine. Then, I practically begged, "We can work through this."

"We can't. I've already violated my rules."

"What rules?"

Nothing. She simply kept her eyes on me.

"Cathy, please talk to me."

"I went too far," she said, as if she were talking to herself. "I shouldn't have." She closed her eyes and opened them.

"Cathy, stop this."

"No!" she exclaimed, her voice trembling with emotion. "Please, stop it!" A few tears escaped from her eyes.

I tried to hold her, but she pushed me away. Again, I stayed where I was, maintaining that small distance, just an arm's length apart from each other.

"Go," she said in a soft voice. "Just go."

"Cathy."

"Just go!"

I stepped closer, wanting to console her.

"Stop!" She fought back. Tears ran down her face. "You need to find your happiness. So go!" She cut her eyes to the right, looking up the walkway.

I glanced back as well. She must have been referring to Rebecca. I turned toward her again. "But I've discovered my happiness," I started to explain to Cathy, reaching out my hands toward her, "and that's with–"

"Stop!" She gently placed her index finger on my lips, silencing me. "Please, don't." Then she removed her finger with a soft sigh. "You would only make it harder for me... I've already crossed too many lines here when I shouldn't have. I'm really sorry."

"Don't be."

"Cassidy, no." After a thoughtful pause, she gently continued, "Rebecca is your happiness. Please don't lie to me or yourself about that." After another brief moment, she added, "At first, I was in denial, not wanting to believe it from her when she said you are still in love with her. But it's true. You both are still so in love with each other."

"What are you talking about? Not wanting to believe it from her? Better yet. Who's her?" I pulled my hands away from her. "What are you talking about?"

Cathy just looked at me as if she had accidentally let that one slip out of the bag.

It is now too late. "Tell me!" I have grown weary of the cat-and-mouse game. "What on earth are you referring to? Have you been communicating with Rebecca?"

Cathy finally answered me, "No." She paused and then said, "I was hired for a project."

There goes that word again. "What sort of project?"

She stammered. "To look for you."

Did I hear that correctly? "To look for me?"

"Yes." She nodded slowly, her bottom lip beginning to tremble. "I'm, I'm truly sorry, Cassidy. You have to believe me."

I felt confused and trapped. I shut my eyes, hoping to clear my mind for that moment. Then I opened my eyes to look at her. "So, what are you? Some friggin' Private Investigator or something?"

She kept quiet.

I must have been spot on. "Who hired you?" I was treated like a fool. "Tell me."

Nothing.

"I want you to tell me!" I didn't mean to raise my voice at her, but I did. "I have a right to know."

She closed her eyes, and tears poured down her face.

"I'm sorry." I broke down; I pulled her close to comfort her. "I would like to know. That's all. Who hired you to find me?"

She opened her eyes and looked at me.

I wiped her tears away with my thumb. "Please, I need to know."

She finally broke: "It was Ms. Nelson. She hired me."

"Ms. Nelson?" I felt lost. "Who's that?"

Take 67

Cathy confessed to me, "Ms. Nelson was your next-door neighbor when you lived in Fort Lauderdale."

No, that's impossible. "Ms. Nelson, Nelson?" I stuttered. "From the apartment across from me?"

"Yes."

"But why?"

"She was worried about you when you ran off. So, she hired me to help find you. But …"

"But, what?"

"But when I found you, I fell for you." Cathy started to cry again. "I'm sorry."

Okay, she answered a question I didn't need to ask since she had already said she had fallen for me. "So," I proceeded in the same direction by asking, "why are you fighting against something that we both feel about each other?"

Her eyes filled with tears again. "Because you will never love me, as long as you're still in love with her."

"But I don't love her." I wiped her tears away again.

"Yes, you do. So, please stop."

"You're wrong, Cathy. I want you." I reached in and kissed her. Then she pulled away from my lips. "I can't do this."

"At least let us try."

"No. We can't; you still wouldn't love me fully."

"Yes, I can." I reached for another kiss, but she stopped me.

"If that's true, seek closure from her first."

"I have done that already."

"No. You haven't," Cathy's voice sounded low. "You need to speak to her to find that closure." She paused and then added, "Please, do it for me. And if you still love her, reclaim your happiness. Because I can't live with the thought of your heart belonging to someone else if I open up to you."

"But—"

"Please," she interrupted me again. "This is what's best for both of us. If you truly need closure from her… talk to her. And if you choose to stay, I'll understand. I'll only wish you the best. However, if you find closure, you'll know how to reach me."

"But I will be happy with you."

"But I won't," she began to say, "if your heart still lies with her."

"But—"

She placed her finger back on my lips and asked, "Do you remember that time on the beach when you were writing that poem, What if?"

"Yeah." I nodded my head.

"It was the most heartbreaking poem I had ever heard. Although I realized it was about a woman who broke your heart, I could see that you were also in love with her. Later, you opened up about Rebecca, the one who wrote the poem. I admired the love you once had with her ... Any woman would. It inspired me to want to learn more about you through Rebecca ... I wanted to meet her."

Why would Cathy want to do that? I wondered.

"I had to meet the person who captured your heart and whom I was competing with," she confessed. "When I joined Rebecca's aerobics class, I discovered that she was still in love with you as well."

"Enough!" I've had it with this nonsense! "You have no idea what you're saying! Haven't you heard? She intended to marry someone soon."

"Who?" Cathy made a face. "To that guy in the restroom?"

"Yeah!" I was confident about that. "They're supposed to get married next month."

"Don't be naïve," she said. "I remembered when he came into our class and proposed to her. I saw the expression on her face that day. And from the looks of it, she wasn't happy at all about his marriage proposal. Just remember, I'm a female, too. She only agreed to his proposal because she was under the spotlight in her class."

"But that still doesn't mean anything!"

"Perhaps it doesn't, or perhaps it does."

Then, I became curious about the truth: "Did you set this up for us to be here inside the restaurant together?"

"Yes." A guilty expression crossed her face. "I bought her a gift certificate for two, pretending it was a small gesture of appreciation since she was my aerobics instructor. However, on the day I intended to give it to her, she fainted in front of everyone. So, I entrusted one of the other instructors to hand the gift certificate to her on my behalf."

"But why?"

"When you aimed to advance our relationship, I simply wanted to confirm."

"To make sure of what?"

"You wanted to be with me with no strings attached here."

I kept quiet. I didn't want to say anything wrong—anything Cathy could take offense at. Up to that point, it seemed clear that she knew I wouldn't make it to third base with her, instead just fouling her.

Cathy continued, "As difficult as it is for me to admit, Rebecca needs you. Since that guy proposed, I've seen her energy drain during class; she's not herself anymore, and everyone has noticed. Maybe there are aspects of you that have shifted during your time apart. Only you can decide if what I'm saying resonates. However, what I do know," she said, jabbing my chest with her finger, "is that deep down, you want to uncover the truth behind all of this."

"But at this point, it wouldn't matter."

"Yes, it would." Cathy tried to smile as she stuck one leg inside the limo. "It's only one way to find out." She slowly pushed me away from her. "Go … Go to her … Find your closure or that happiness you once had." She then took the backseat, sticking her other leg inside the car. "Go for her before she gets away."

I stepped aside as Cathy moved to close the door. Seconds later, I found myself gazing at a reflection of a confused man in a tinted window I stood before. I remained there, watching myself for a brief moment until the limo slowly drove away. I felt stranded as I watched the limo head up Collins Ave before making that first left turn at the light. Only then did I notice Rebecca up the block, standing at the corner, ready to cross the intersection.

I felt both disgusted and weak.

One half of me wished the worst for Rebecca, given all the pain and embarrassment she had inflicted on me, while the other half felt a bit concerned for her because she seemed disoriented and gloomy. She didn't appear to be in the right state of mind, wandering the streets alone. A car full of guys honked the horn at her, slowing down as they approached. She ignored them and walked back across the street, looking vulnerable and exposed to any potential mishap that could occur.

If that's the case, she ought to understand what she put me through.

To hell with her!

I walked away from her, but after a few steps, doubt struck me. Maybe Cathy was right, and I just needed closure from Rebecca. I turned to look for Rebecca, but she was no longer there.

Shit!

I panicked! What if those guys made a U-turn and snatched her up in their car? My heart pounded. I raced up the street, two blocks. Just as I was about to run up another block, I stopped when I saw Rebecca across the street. She was safe and sound, heading toward a pay phone.

My shoes felt heavy, like cinder blocks. Walking across the intersection wasn't easy, but I managed to do it.

"Rebecca," my voice was low. I guessed she didn't hear me, so I repeated, "Rebecca!"

She spun around, her eyes watery and her expression frightened, when she saw me standing behind her.

I was at a loss for words. A few seconds passed, feeling like endless hours. My throat grew dry and felt constricted. I could only stare at her.

She then bowed her head and shut her eyes. "Cassidy, I'm sorry," she said, perhaps out of shame or for what she had put me through, as tears streamed down her face. "I'm sorry for what I've done to you … to us!" Her voice broke with a sob. "I'm sorry!"

It felt as if I couldn't escape the pain in my throat. It was like a terrible knot, burning in my soul. My heart. I couldn't breathe. I leaned back, then forward. At least that's what I wanted to believe. I never thought I would see Rebecca again, yet here she was, wrapped in my arms.

I suppose I was just glad to have my Rebecca back.

Three months later

Take 68

What else can I ask for?

I had found peace with myself.

As I stood indoors, admiring the new scenery from my bedroom window, I couldn't help but appreciate the luxury of living in Surfside. It was characterized by astonishing beauty. Along with the shrubbery and small palm trees planted in front of the condos, life thrived within this gated community. Everyone was friendly.

I glanced to my right and saw two squirrels running across the street and up a giant tree. I smiled.

"Now tell me the truth," Brad began to ask me when David walked away to go into the other room to hang out with Samuel, "and don't lie to me either."

"I won't."

He then inquired, "If you could go back and change what occurred with you and Rebecca a year ago, what would be your first step to improve the situation?"

I smiled and looked out the window again.

"What is it?"

I turned back to him. No words.

"So, what would you change or fix?" he asked.

I broke my silence and shook my head. "Absolutely nothing."

"Yeah?" he appeared surprised by my response. "But why?"

"Because I have gained so much more since then: First, I have my lady back. She appreciates every moment we share, in a way that's even better than before. She loves me for who I am, not for who I pretend to be ... I have met some interesting people, many of whom are my friends now ... I have my friend back." I flipped my hand out toward him. "And your punk-ass better teach me the stock market, too, since Ms. Ginsberg had purchased me a few shares."

He smiled—one of those sarcastic smiles he always gives me whenever I mention Ms. Ginsberg's name.

And I would prefer not to ask him why either. "To answer your question, I wouldn't change anything." I looked out the window again.

Brad placed his arm around my shoulder. "I feel the same way here," he said. "I wouldn't want to change anything about what happened with Monica either. Aside from not running a train on that bitch before I split!"

I laughed because I knew he was telling me the truth. Then I stopped chuckling when I saw the taxicab pull up in the driveway. "She's here." I smiled and turned back to Brad. "C'mon. Let me introduce you to her." I strode away and quickly ran down the stairs. By the time the front door opened, Ms. Nelson had already paid for her cab fare.

Ms. Nelson paused when she glanced my way and noticed me. She smiled back. The cabbie backed out of the driveway and drove away. Then she held up a small paper bag in front of her.

My smile widened as I approached her. "You shouldn't have." I genuinely meant that. "But what is it?" I extended my hand to take it.

She scrunched her nose with a half-smile and said, "It's an old sardine can that stinks badly! Can you trash it for me?"

"Come here!" I set down the bag and embraced her. Then I added, "Thank you," without elaborating because she understood exactly what I meant. "Thank you for everything."

"No. I appreciate you coming back to your senses." She released her grip on me. "Now let me go before that wild fiancée of yours comes after me with a knife, misconstruing our situation."

I laughed and let her go.

"And where is she, anyway?"

"She's in the house with the other guests, getting ready."

"That's good," Ms. Nelson barely shook her head in wonder, a fantastic smile on her face. "Now let me have a good look at you."

I took a step back, smiling, and spun around in a full circle in front of her with my arms spread wide.

"You look handsome. But you would look even better if you removed that ponytail and cut your hair back to its original length."

I didn't know about that, but then again, I stayed silent, gazing at the woman who helped shape me into who I am today.

"And you need a necktie to go along with that shirt. You have one, right?"

"Of course, it's inside the house." I grabbed her hand. "I would like to introduce you to everyone." I led her to the condo. Brad was standing by the front door. I introduced him to her first and then stepped inside the house. I saw Rabbi Emanuel Hirsch talking with John and Emma Wolf straight ahead.

Yes, the same Emma Wolf whom I taught the four Ts a few months ago: horseback riding, rodeo, hula hooping, and cow milking techniques.

To make a long story short, without going into detail about why Emma Wolf was at the house with us, I invited her over not only because I work for her at the Fine Arts Gallery in Miami Beach on the corner of Washington Ave about once or twice a week, whenever I'm available, but also because I see her as a close acquaintance. She's a lot of fun to have around. I'm not just saying that because she's enormous, being 327 pounds, which is considered overweight for someone who is five feet seven. But anyway, I introduced John and Emma to Ms. Nelson and then to Elena and Pamela, who were standing by the punch bowl in the next room.

"Rebecca's in that back room over there," I told Ms. Nelson. "But could you help me with my necktie before you see her?"

We ascended the stairs and entered the first room on the right. I glanced at the bed and then at the pillows. After that, I returned my gaze to the bed's edge. I could have sworn that was where I last spotted my necktie.

"So where is it?"

I glanced at her before exiting the room. I moved to the opposite side of the bed, paused to look around, and then made my way to the windowsill where I had been standing just before going downstairs.

"Why don't you just wear another tie instead?"

"No, I'd rather wear that necktie since Rebecca gave it to me on our first anniversary together," I replied with a smile. Then I called out toward the open doorway, "Hey Sam! Ronald! Have you guys seen my necktie?!"

It was Samuel, not Ronald, who yelled from his location: "I have it with me!"

"Let me have it!" I walked back toward the mirror wall on the left side of the bed to boost my confidence.

Ms. Nelson stood behind me. "You would do fine," she said, raising my shirt's collar. "And I'm proud of you, too."

"Thanks."

"Are you nervous?"

"Uh-huh. Sort of."

She smiled over my shoulder; I smiled back, looking at her reflection in the mirror.

Then David stepped into the room, his face lighting up with a big, bright smile. Ronald and Samuel followed closely behind him. However, Samuel abruptly stopped in his tracks when he noticed Ms. Nelson standing nearby.

I extended my hand to him. "Let me have the tie."

However, Samuel seemed oblivious to me, lost in his thoughts. His face remained expressionless, as if he were stunned, with only his eyes blinking occasionally. Finally, in a soft, apologetic whisper, he said, "Nette," before gradually stepping toward Ms. Nelson.

Her eyes filled with tears, and her bottom lip quivered.

"Nette," Samuel repeated, but his voice sounded much clearer than before. "I thought you were–"

I cut in by mistake, feeling confused, and spoke to no one in particular: "This Nette?" I paused for a few seconds to gather my thoughts. "Ms. Annette Nelson?"

She glanced at me, then back at Samuel. When he stepped toward her again, she ran.

"Nette!" Samuel ran after her.

Take 69

"Holy shit!" I tried to keep up with Samuel and Ms. Nelson, chasing after them.

Ronald, David, and Brad pursued the chase.

Ms. Nelson raced downstairs and then dashed down the hall to the back room, almost slamming the door in Samuel's face. However, Samuel caught the door just in time. He pushed his way into the room, forcing the door open against her. Ms. Nelson relented and hurried toward Rebecca, who was standing in front of the mirror with a couple of her friends gathered around her.

"Nette! We need to talk."

Ms. Nelson turned her back on Samuel. "Tell him to leave," she instructed Rebecca.

I felt captivated, enthralled, and intrigued. I became speechless when Rebecca turned around and saw us at the doorway.

"Cassidy! You shouldn't be here and see me before the wedding ceremony!" She swiftly turned back. "It brings bad luck!"

"No. It's not."

Ms. Nelson said, "I'm not talking about Cassidy! I'm talking about the one who is standing beside him. Samuel!"

"Who?" Rebecca turned around once more.

Samuel approached Ms. Nelson with measured steps. "Nette, I have waited almost eleven years for this moment. I cannot recall how many nights I have self-medicated to sleep, trying to dull the pain of uncertainty about your existence. I hold myself responsible for the anguish I've faced and will keep facing due to your absence." He gently rested his hand on her arm, trying to pivot her so he could meet her gaze.

But she fought back, holding onto Rebecca.

"Nette," Samuel said, "don't do this to us. We both deserve better than this. I know I still love you … What about you?"

"That was a long time ago, Sam," she told him. "Things have changed over the years."

"For whom?"

She hesitated. "For us."

"How?"

"Because we had grown apart from one another."

"That's impossible," Samuel exclaimed. "Ever since you left me in Chicago, and later learned that you had moved to South Florida, I packed all my belongings and came down here to find you … I didn't want to feel that abandonment of being away from you, even though I wasn't able to locate you."

"Why?"

"What do you mean by why?"

"Why can't you let me go?"

"Because I can't." Samuel forced her to look at him. Then he quickly added, "Because I still, and always will, love you."

She quickly turned away, presenting her back to him. "But I don't look the same anymore, Sam. I look much older now."

"And so do I," he admitted. "Which is a blessing to grow old at our age, knowing what we once shared. We could start where we left off and continue to share that same love for the rest of our days together. Because I don't know about you, but I would rather live my life with the one and only person I will love … and that is with you."

I pulled Rebecca away from them, wrapping my arms around her as we watched Samuel and Ms. Nelson stand face to face, staring at each other.

Ms. Nelson looked at Rebecca and then at me. I tried to smile, hoping she would smile back, but she didn't. Instead, she did the opposite: her eyes became watery, and then her bottom lip began to quiver again. She covered her mouth with her fingers. Samuel removed her hand. She lowered her head slightly to hide her face from him. But he lifted her chin just enough to catch a glimpse of her eyes again, and then he leaned in and kissed her.

"I missed you, Sam," Ms. Nelson exclaimed, embracing him tightly as if her life depended on it. "I miss you so much."

"I know you have." He cried with her.

Rebecca lifted her head from my shoulder and looked at me. Then she softly whispered, "I don't ever wanna separate from you again."

"You won't." I kissed her forehead before pressing my lips against hers.

Someone faked a cough.

We turned toward the bedroom doorway.

It was Rabbi Emanuel Hirsch. "I don't want to interrupt," he said, glancing at his wristwatch before returning his gaze to me. "But we need to conduct this wedding before sunset."

"Rabbi Hirsch," I asked him, "Do you mind if we hold our ceremonial right here?"

"In this room?"

"Yeah." I then looked at Rebecca. "Because I don't want to leave her side."

Rebecca tilted her head to kiss me, and I leaned in closer.

"Sure," Rabbi Hirsch said, stepping further into the room. He then asked, "Can someone retrieve the huppah so we can get on with this marriage?"

David dashed out of the room.

Rebecca and I moved closer to the back window to create space for the others to join us in the room. Approximately twenty-five of our friends and colleagues attended. I couldn't help but smile when Ms. Ginsberg began complaining to Melissa about being squeezed into the smallest room in the house, despite having invested a significant amount in decorating and furnishing plenty of seating outside for everyone to enjoy the wedding ceremony.

Melissa overlooked her as they both approached the corner. Melissa flashed me a beautiful smile, and I returned it with a smile.

A moment later, when David returned to the room with the huppah and placed it above Rebecca and me, everything was in order: Ronald stood by my side; Linda stood by Rebecca's side.

Rabbi Hirsch highlighted the importance of marriage, stressing its value in God's eyes and the essential unity between a man and a woman. He noted, "For it is written, 'Whoever finds a wife finds a good thing and obtains favor from the Lord our God.' It is also written, 'Therefore a man shall leave his father and mother and cling to his wife, and they shall become one flesh.'"

I couldn't believe it: it was finally happening. Ronald passed me the ring. Then, I repeated the ceremonial formula after Rabbi Hirsch: "Harei at mekudeshet li be-tabba'atm zu ka-dat Mosheh ve-Yisrael." I slid the ring onto Rebecca's finger.

Rebecca smiled as she watched. Then, it was her turn. She had a little difficulty speaking Hebrew, so Rabbi Hirsch asked her to say it in English. She did: "Be you consecrate unto me by this ring, by the laws of Moses and Israel."

I swear, I felt lightheaded; my adrenaline was racing. I wore my wedding ring.

Then Rabbi Hirsch told us, "Rebecca and Cassidy Zimmerman, I pronounce you husband and wife." He then gave me a good look and added, "You may kiss your bride."

That's precisely what I did.

People cheered.

Just as Rebecca and I were about to leave the room together, Ms. Ginsberg grabbed my wrist and said, "I must talk to you first before you go off to celebrate."

I looked at Rebecca as Ms. Ginsberg dragged me off to the hallway bathroom. Ms. Ginsberg then locked the door behind us.

The Aftermath

As the taxicab arrived at the condo, I glanced at Rebecca sitting next to me in the backseat, then looked out the window to see David rinsing the soap off my car with the hose. He appeared half-soaked. The cabbie halted in front of the driveway.

David seemed surprised when he saw us smiling.

The cabbie said, "That would be thirty-six dollars, please."

Rebecca covered his expenses.

He opened the car trunk, prompting me to rise and grab our bags.

David extended his hands, offering help. "Why didn't you call me so I could have picked you up?"

"Are you joking?"

"No, I'm serious."

"Well," I looked at the cab driver as he drove off, then turned back to David. I attempted to call you, but your cell phone was not working and indicated that your number was no longer in service."

"Damn, I forgot to give you my new number when I spoke to you last week."

"You changed it again?"

"Yeah, because this friggin' chick who I met the other week won't let me breathe after I picked her up in your ride."

I felt the urge to smile.

Rebecca interjected, greeted David, and then asked me for her small duffel bag: "I'll be inside, okay?"

"Okay." I kissed her and then turned my attention back to David as she walked away. "So did–" I paused, feeling thrown off. "Why are you smiling at me like that?"

"Did you all have a good time in Costa Rica?"

I stayed silent. I thought he could answer that himself.

"Yeah," he started bobbing his head with a broader smile on his face now. "Y'all must've had a good time down there since y'all didn't come back home when y'all were supposed to."

Okay, I smiled back. "That hotel we stayed at was beautiful. So, we decided to stay an extra week to catch up for old times' sake."

"That's good as long as she's happy."

"So," I changed the topic, "did you encounter any issues at the house?"

"No. Not really. Other than the two older ladies from the wedding, they were bugging the hell out of me, looking for you. They kept coming over here almost every day, even though I told them you were on your honeymoon."

"So, did you let them in?"

"Hell, no!"

Damn! My plan didn't work.

Then he asked, "But what's the deal with the little stubby one with brunette hair?"

"Who, Elena? Why? What about her?"

"What about her?" he tried to mock me. "Dude, she came by the other night around eleven, clearly having had a few drinks. She mentioned she was in the neighborhood and just wanted to say hello. A few minutes later, while we were chatting at the front door, she suddenly said she needed to use the restroom because she had a full bladder. Before I had the chance to invite her in, she pushed past me, shoving me aside. I could have sworn she brushed against me as she walked by. Then, five minutes later, still in the bathroom, she called for me to help with her stuck zipper, saying she didn't want to pee on herself."

"So, what did you do?"

"I entered and attempted to assist her. However, this annoying lady made a move for my zipper instead."

I laughed. "And what'd happened?"

"I tried to kick her outta the house, but she started crying, begging me not to send her out in the condition she was in. Then, she asked if she could sleep over on the couch until she sobered up by morning, so, after I agreed to it, about four o'clock in the morning, while I was sleeping in the back room, I woke up with a hard-on with this old-ass lady kissing on my chest, with my dick in her hand! And she was friggin' naked, dude! Can you imagine what I had to wake up to?" he paused. Then he added: "What? You think this shit is funny?"

"I'm sorry." I tried to control my laughter. "So, what do you do when you get up?"

"The before or after when she left?"

"Let me hear the before part, first."

He made a scoffing sound. "I told her to get the hell out of the house! Then she started begging to have a piece of me inside of her."

I couldn't help myself; I laughed harder this time.

"I was shocked that she would say some shit like that to me, dude. I swear on my mom, I friggin' lost it! I pulled my dick out in front of her, trying to intimidate her with it, telling her, 'I could kill you with this shit if I slid it inside you! And what the hell do you expect the State of Florida to do with me afterward: Charge me with a First-Degree Murder?' So, rather than she just running off when I shook my dick in front of her, she dared to ask me to let her touch it instead, making all those porno facial expressions, as if she was in friggin' heat or something … At this point I had enough of her bullshit, so I gathered up her stuff and kicked her out of the house, naked! I just didn't give a fuck if she was sobered or not."

"I'm sorry!" I couldn't stop laughing. "I have to give her a call to let her know that I'm back."

"You don't have to worry about giving her a call because you'll see her drive by in a few minutes," he said. "It's like ever since I showed her my dick, she has been stalking me. At first, I thought it was just a coincidence that we kept bumping into each other in some of the unusual places in Miami. Still, it became obvious when I caught her trailing behind me at three o'clock in the morning, after dropping Stacy home in Fort Lauderdale. But that ain't shit, because on four separate occasions since the other day, I received dozens of roses from her, still apologizing for the way she had acted when she was over here, asking me to let her make it up to me by taking me out to a restaurant." He shook his head. "So, I think it would be your best bet to find another realtor before she tries something on you next."

Only if he knew. "And what's that after part you had mentioned?"

"What after part?"

"You said there were before and after she left the house."

"Oh," he seemed to remember now. "That friggin' lady had my dick so hard that I had to jerk off in the shower. And the only visual I had in mind was her fondling on her titties, slowly sticking her tongue out at me."

I chuckled a bit. "Where's my phone so I can call her?"

"Oh, yeah, I had almost forgotten," he said as he stepped away to the car. He returned with my cell phone. "It seemed like everybody was trying to contact you last week when you were supposed to have come back."

"Yeah." I grabbed my cell phone and started scrolling through the missed calls. "So, did you ask what they wanted?"

"No. I just told them you weren't in yet and to call you when you get back."

Damn. What the hell did he think I left my cell phone with him for?

Then he added, "There was that one chick from the wedding, too. Ms. Ginsberg. She kept calling for you as well."

"Yeah." I was focused on all the new telephone numbers I wasn't familiar with.

"And you're a friggin' liar, too!"

"About what?"

I observed that Joey attempted to call you several times.

"When?" I didn't look at him. I continued scrolling through my missed calls.

"All last week, around the same time everyone else expected you to come back." He paused, then immediately added with sarcasm: "So you and Joey are buddies again, huh?"

"Absolutely not!" I continued scrolling through the numbers. "You know I don't communicate with him. But how do you know he tried to reach me? His cell number isn't on this list."

"Because he called you from his house phone, on a few occasions," he said. "And since I didn't answer his calls, he must have thought I was a friggin' idiot or something because about a half hour later, he tried to call you on Melissa's car phone, trying to disguise his number." He paused, then asked, "Why are you smiling?"

I looked at him briefly then turned my attention back to my cell phone.

"What's so funny?"

"That wasn't Joey," I murmured softly.

"You must think I'm stupid or something. So, who else could it have been?"

I looked at him, gave a smirk, and then went back to my cell phone.

After a few seconds—no more than three—he nearly yelled, "Get the hell out of here!" He smiled, glanced at the front door, then back at me. "Are you serious?"

I looked back to make sure Rebecca wasn't at the front door, then turned to him. "Melissa is such a sweet girl. It just happened one day. Ever since, we've been seeing each other regularly. It's unfortunate she's married to that jerk."

"Damn, she called last night! I should have answered your phone." He then snatched the cell phone from me. "I need to get her number."

"Stop playing!" I began to wrestle for the phone. "You might delete all my phone numbers, silly!"

He fought back, trying to bite my hands.

It was around that exact moment when my cell phone started to vibrate. David tried to answer the call, but I grabbed the phone from him.

"Hello."

It was Ms. Ginsberg: "Cassidy?"

"Yeah." I started laughing because David pressed his ear to the edge of the phone, trying his best to eavesdrop on my call. "How are you doing? I haven't heard from–"

She interrupted me: "Why weren't you answering your phone?"

"I just got back a moment ago."

"From your honeymoon?"

"Yeah."

"Oh." She took a moment, letting a few seconds pass before asking, "So, have you had a good time?"

"Yes, but of course. And thank you for taking care of everything for me."

"Don't mention it," she paused once more.

"Is something bothering you?"

"Yes." She sighed. "I'm so stressed out here in California."

"Oh, I didn't realize you were out of town."

"I've spent the last week in California. I wanted to see you before I left, but you didn't return my call. So now I'll have to deal with Carol's nonsense for the next two weeks until I return."

"Who's that?"

"Who's who?"

"Carol?"

"A business acquaintance of mine constantly voices complaints throughout the day. If she's not lamenting about her age, she's finding fault with various things. I think what she truly needs is to have something in her mouth, honestly, to silence her."

I chuckled.

The phone line grew quiet between us.

David interrupted me as he started gesturing at his chest, quietly asking me to connect him with her friend. I brushed him off, trying to focus more on my phone call.

Then Ms. Ginsberg said, "Alright, now you had your little break; I need you to come out here and tune me up a little."

"Now?"

"Yes, now! That's what I said." Then she went straight to the point: "I'm horny! I need you over here right now! You have a week's worth of catching up to do."

I checked my watch. "Well," –it was just after two in the afternoon– "I'll see if I can catch a flight out of here tonight. But what about your friend?"

"Who, Carol?"

"Yeah."

"I don't know. I would need to come up with a good strategy to get rid of her before you arrive, as she tends to want to hang around me all day. And as I see it, it's going to be hard to get rid of her since I'm staying at her cottage with her in Santa Barbara."

I looked at David and smiled as I told her, "I think I have a plan for those little problems of ours."

"How?"

"Just relax. I'll be in tonight with a friend of mine to keep her company."

"A friend?"

"Yeah, and that's all I'm telling you." I paused, then added, "I'll call you once I get there."

"But–"

I hung up on her and asked David, "Do you have any plans for the week?"

"No. Not really. Why?"

"I need you to go out to California with me."

"For what?"

I glanced at the front door of the condo, then back at him. "I need your help with a little mission."

"Doing what?"

"To keep someone company while I'm with someone else."

"The person you want me to keep company with is a woman, right?"

"Yeah."

He smiled. "What does she look like?"

"I don't know." I wanted to be honest with him. "But does it make a difference?"

"No. Not really. But how old is she?"

"She's legal. But why do you ask? Do you have a certain age bracket?"

"Age bracket?" he laughed at me, then threw his golden rule at me: "I'll fuck anything between eighteen to eighty; deaf, blind or crazy. If she has a split between her legs, sure enough, I'm playing in it."

I laughed back. "I hope that you stand by your word."

"But for real, though: How old is she?"

Just when I was about to tell him that I didn't know, my cell phone began to ring. I answered it.

It was Ms. Ginsberg again. "Are you sure you can bring him along with you?"

"Yeah. I had just asked him."

"Is he there with you now?"

"Yeah."

"Let me have a word with him."

"Hold on." I passed David the cell phone.

"Hello," he said with a smile, then paused. Then, after a short moment, he added: "Yeah. He just asked me a second ago … Yeah, I'll be there…" He laughed a little. "Oh, really … Yeah, I'm single … Uh-huh. I worked out here and there. Why? … Yeah … Hold on for a second, please." He then pressed the mute button on the cell phone and said to me, "Dude, your girl sounds sexy as hell!" He then released the mute button and got back on the phone with Ms. Ginsberg: "I'm sorry for that. Now, what are you saying again?" he paused, laughed. Then he added: "Well, I hope so too … Uh-huh … Sure … Yeah, tonight … Thank you … Uh-huh … Okay then … Oh, I'm sorry. My name is David … Yeah, I have a last name … What do you need that for? To Google me? … Well, your friend would have to wait until I give it to her, then." He laughed with a broader smile that time. "That's cute. I like that ... Okay. Until then ... Yeah, the same here ... Okay ..., I'll make sure that I'd do that ... Uh-huh ... Would you like to talk back to him ... Okay, then ... Later." He passed the phone back to me. "Dude, she said her friend Carol hasn't been touched in a very long time." He shot me with a greedy smile. "Yum, yum, I'm gonna get me some."

I laughed.

"So, what are you gonna tell Rebecca?"

"Ms. Ginsberg requires my presence in California for a few days for her business project."

He smiled back. "But dude, the chick I had just gotten off the phone with is a bit thrown off, though."

"Why do you say that?"

"Because he told me that I didn't need to pack any clothes with me. Just come as I am. To which she recommended that I wear a regular shirt, something like you wore and tore off in front of her."

I smiled.

He then added, "She asked about my last name, but I didn't provide it. She likely wanted to Google me to check my profile. What are your thoughts?"

"I don't know."

"Well, she went on to say that she didn't need it anyway because she has a nice name for me."

"Which is?"

He bobbed his head slowly, as if his mind were drifting off somewhere.

"So, what's the name she gave you?"

"Valentine," he said. "She named me David Valentine."

I booked our flights.

Cut

That's a wrap!
Till next time.
So, stay tuned for the sequel in
Casanova's Protégé : David Valentine

The Author's Notes and Thoughts

Similar to Rebecca from this novel, she faced abuse from her partner, Juan. We should not support or condone this behavior; instead, we must actively oppose it. Thus, I invite you to collaborate with me and organizations like the National Networks to End Domestic Violence (NNEDV) in promoting awareness for women's safety and striving to eliminate domestic violence against women.

It is the right thing to do.

For additional information on domestic violence and ways to assist, please go to www.NNEDV.com or call the National Domestic Violence Hotline at 1-800-799-SAFE (7233). Their team is available to listen and offer support.

Forever me,
Davis Zebrowski

Davis Zebrowski

Decorous Books
Presents

Davis Zebrowski's exhilarating new fantasy novel artfully intertwines romance and drama. It tells the story of Michael Cohen, a driven entrepreneur who undergoes a profound transformation during a crucial moment. With assistance from his obscured past, which he has yet to remember completely, he must face his history before it's too late. This fascinating tale guarantees to keep readers captivated.

Blackout

Available in December 2026
Please turn the page for a sneak preview.

Prologue

Act 1

August 17, 1873
Sioux stronghold, South Dakota

Chief Crazy Horse once shared with his eldest son, Teco, many years back that love is the most beautiful force, as it is crucial for overcoming life's seemingly insurmountable challenges.

As Crazy Horse stated, the passionate love stirred the hearts and spirits of his ancestors. This was one of the powerful forces that united the Sioux nation in their struggle against the White men, aiming to avert the destruction of their people. It was this same love that empowered him to endure another day and witness the dawn of his next generation.

Yet now, Crazy Horse dreaded the intolerable fate awaiting him.

Teco lay on a straw mat, drenched in cold sweat. His body temperature soared to 113 degrees. Despite burning with a severe fever, he shivered with coldness. It coursed through him, even with three blankets already piled on top; a fourth would offer no additional warmth. He knew this, and so did they. He closed his eyes and then reopened them, coughing as if his lungs would burst. Another chill swept through his body as he contemplated the disappointment he might cause his father's hopes for the ancestral line.

Teco's thoughts gradually returned to the time six years ago when his father first tried to arrange a marriage for him with a local girl named Olowan Sitting Bull. She came from a reputable lineage of hunters and warriors, and her father was a close family friend. The villagers expected, if not actively encouraged, this union. However, Teco had no interest in it—at least not at that time. Other candidates, such as the beautiful Tawanna Jumping Eagle, Mia Bright Star, and Sonja Red Cloud, were mentioned, but for Teco, seeking a wife to alleviate his presumed loneliness was far from his primary concern. Finding a partner was the least of his priorities, if he had any at all.

To Teco, the most essential thing in life was to create a sustainable living for his family and community. Tilling the land, showing perseverance, and working tirelessly were all in the hope that his people, the Sioux nation, would survive the hardships of the coming winter. As for marriage, that could wait; hunger and protection for the Sioux tribe were top priorities. Yet, there was nothing in this world that could convince him otherwise, even though death was lurking at his feet.

As Teco's seven siblings knelt beside him while a medicinal man chanted a ceremonial prayer for Teco's recovery, a young servant girl from another local tribe pulled the tepee curtain open and crouched inside. She paused at the entrance, afraid she would be punished for her actions, but she didn't care. Her eyes were gleaming with tears, bloodshot red. She lowered her head toward the ground and cried as they all looked at her.

Teco's younger sister returned to Teco and held his hand.

"Why do you weep, sister?" Teco asked her with the bit of energy he still possessed, his eyes barely open and his face drenched in sweat. "For we all have known this day should come to pass when I shall return to the soil of Mother Earth and be reunited with the Great One."

Beyond Teco's sister whispering, the young servant girl dropped to her knees in a kowtow position and bawled out: "Take me!" she cried, pouring handfuls of dirt over her head. "Please take me, O' Great One! Take me instead!"

Without hesitation, three of Teco's brothers looked at their father, Chief Crazy Horse, hoping for a decision to send the servant girl away from their private gathering. However, Crazy Horse nodded toward Teco instead, understanding that the young girl had loved his son deeply since she arrived on their land.

So, not three but two of Teco's brothers approached the young servant girl and assisted her to Teco's side.

"Teco," his youngest brother began to ask, "will the Great One heal you like He did for me?"

Teco attempted to smile. He started, "Yes, little brother–" but immediately began coughing up blood.

The tepee grew silent. Even the medicine man ceased his chanting of a prayer.

The servant girl tried to wipe the blood from Teco's mouth with her hand, but he jerked his face away. She felt hurt, heartbroken, and dejected. Lowering her head, she began to weep.

"Rest, my brother," one of the siblings told Teco. "You'll need your strength."

"No, for my strength lies right here–" Teco began to say just before he coughed up more blood. Then he returned from where he started: "My strength lies right here with you all … For my love and courage run through our blood."

As the tepee fell silent once more, a strong wind surged through a small opening near the entrance. The flame was extinguished within the firewood. It became as dark inside the tepee as a blindfolded night in the forest.

"Hurry!" Crazy Horse shouted. "Light back the fire!"

Someone did.

"The Great One has sent His message for–" Teco began to say before coughing up more blood again. "They have come for me."

The servant girl wiped the blood from Teco's mouth. This time, he accepted her help, leaning his face toward her with a growing smile. She smiled back. But then, suddenly, Teco took a deep breath and gasped for air. He took another wheeze—a much stronger one, though still only half a breath. He didn't have the strength.

The servant girl clung to his hand tightly. He squeezed first, but it was futile. In an instant, he exhaled all the life he had left, and then darkness enveloped him.

Teco's spirit floated up and away.

Act 2

Four months, seventeen days ago

Michael Cohen has had better days before.

He leaned over his office desk, resting his forehead on his arms. The room was dim, with only a faint light emitted from the lamp hovering over his computer as he sat in front of it. He was filled with uncertainty; his mind raced at a mile per minute. To make matters worse, it was late—eleven forty-six to be exact. He tried to stay focused, but couldn't. There was music playing beyond his office door. "Loyal" by Lorde, he thought. His colleagues were having a company party just six doors down the hall in the common area. He raised his head and looked across his spacious office, which was adorned with state-of-the-art appliances and furniture. Most items were imported from Italy, and he loved the European look. It gave him strength and empowerment. The beautiful oil painting of Albert Einstein, hanging on the right side of the wall, was especially inspiring.

As he ran his fingers through his hair, searching for a compelling web-based business concept with a fresh innovation that would challenge major companies like TikTok, Facebook, and YouTube, the office door swung open. The music was much louder now. He looked across his desk.

It was Richard Armstrong, the CEO of Decorous Enterprise, and a close friend of his.

"What are you still doing in here?" Richard asked him while standing between two women. No, correction: He was standing between two dime pieces. Straight 10s on a scale of 1 to 10, as if they were hand-picked from a beauty pageant. One was a brunette, the other a blonde. Sandy blonde hair, if we needed to be precise about it, with long curls. Both women looked beautiful, with slim and trim physiques, nicely toned shoulders and arms, and dressed in formal evening gowns. "The party's out there. We're all waiting on you."

Let's delve into some historical facts. In 1996, Richard Armstrong graduated from the University of Florida, known as the "Gators," at the age of twenty-two. Standing at 5'8" and with a once geeky and slender build, he earned an honors degree in computer science, ranking among the top three in his class. His classmates, Sarah Chapman and Kyle Morrison, landed jobs with major companies like Google and Amazon as fellow computer technicians. However, what set Richard apart from other graduates focused on Internet companies was his passion for advancing computer technology. For him, it wasn't about the financial rewards; instead, he saw the enhancement of cyber networking technology as a significant contribution to the global history of computer science in the digital age. This drive was similar to that of pioneers like Steve Jobs and Bill Gates, who have fundamentally shaped the world of online information sharing.

Yes, globally, that was historic for a cyber-geek like Richard.

Nonetheless, this was the sole reason Richard declined multiple job offers from major tech firms and chose to join a smaller company named I-Bic Computer System, located in Titusville, Florida, just west of Orlando.

Within just eight months, and with near-universal acclaim from I-Bic's executive officers, Richard earned the promotion to Chief Technology Officer. As CTO, he assumed a leadership role, receiving a larger office on the top floor next to fellow executives. His working hours were flexible, often stretching between 12 to 14 hours a day, including Sundays. For Richard, the effort was completely worthwhile. Unlike his counterparts, he enjoyed the unique privilege of attending board meetings and company negotiations dressed in a T-shirt, shorts, and sandals—those classic, inexpensive flip-flops commonly seen at the beach and bought from a discount store.

As Walt Thomas, one of the executives at I-Bic, once said, "There will always be a fundamental shift In technology that comes around every 3 to 5 years, and much of the same can be easily compared to the ideas that Richard stumbles upon so often."

It wasn't that Mr. Thomas was stroking Richard's ego; the compliment about Richard was genuine for many employees who encountered him in person. This guy, Richard Armstrong, just one year out of college, possessed the kind of wisdom not only as a computer technician to keep a company running and on track, but he was like an industry guru capable of running any Fortune 500 company, if given the chance. Give him 10– No! Better yet, give Richard five minutes to speak, and he will make anyone, including you (yes, you!), a true believer in his ideas and beliefs.

But like the end of a chapter in a James Patterson novel, Richard's misfortune came crashing down on him as he was sealing a negotiation deal for I-Bic in hopes of purchasing their projected competitor software company, SuWu Incorporated, which posed a significant threat to all companies, including I-Bic, poised for success in the competitive market.

You see, SuWu Incorporated was a computer software company that developed and built firewalls to protect against cyber-attacks and viruses from entering one's computer mainframe.

Well, after everyone at I-Bic had spoken and Richard was up next to seal the deal, with everyone holding ink pens and smiles on their faces, Alexander Crawford, the owner of SuWu Incorporated, gave Richard a tired, forlorn look that made him hesitate.

Then, rather than allowing Richard to speak freely, Mr. Crawford asked him, "If the company were yours, from all that you know about SuWu Incorporated, what would you do? Would you sell it?"

There was no doubt about it; for Richard, acknowledging the truth of the matter was indeed challenging. However, as he gazed upon the wizened features of the man who appeared to be in his late eighties and had now dematerialized, Richard noted his attire: a simple black blazer and pants. The elderly man's eyes were deep-set and dark brown, each partially obscured by thin wisps of brow. He bore a striking resemblance to a character akin to Gollum from The Lord of the Rings, almost like a grandfatherly figure without exaggeration.

Richard told Mr. Crawford, who sat three seats down and across the table from him, "To be honest, sir, if SuWu Incorporated were my company, I wouldn't sell it for twenty-five million dollars or anything close to that. That's my opinion of your company. Moreover, not only do I deeply despise the fact that larger companies try to acquire small companies' concepts at an enviable price, but I also resent that they often succeed in doing so. However, if I had designed that software from scratch, as you have, I would want to see my company succeed even more, without hesitation, pushing it to its highest potential." He paused to scan the old man's face, then continued. "And from what I know about your software program, you are just a few steps away from seeing your company flourish with a few technological tweaks. You might be sitting on a gold mine, but that's for you to decide, not me."

For some, the conference room fell silent on that gloomy day. At least for a long minute, you could hear a hard swallow from the other end of the table.

All eyes shifted from Richard to Mr. Crawford, then back to Richard, with no smiles—only a perplexed expression on their faces.

Here, Mr. Crawford rose from his seat, bracing himself with both hands on the table, and told everyone in the conference room that he needed a little more time to think their offer over. Then he left.

Based on the information gathered afterward, Mr. Thomas, one of the executives at I-Bic, contacted Mr. Crawford just three days later and asked him to return to the office in hopes of renegotiating a better offer that he wouldn't refuse. Mr. Crawford agreed, but when he later learned that Richard Armstrong was terminated not only as I-Bic's CTO but also completely from the company, he had second thoughts, because, in other words, Richard was fired – vamoosed, out of there; out on his ass – for expressing his honesty to Mr. Crawford about not selling SuWu Incorporated if it was his.

After discovering Richard's termination from I-Bic, Mr. Crawford declined the generous offer from the company to buy him out for $45 million. Instead, he sought Richard's whereabouts and found him two days later, thanks to information provided by the I-Bic front receptionist. When Mr. Crawford located Richard and asked if he could be his computer technician to reconstruct and make the necessary adjustments to his software, Richard readily agreed, not only to get back at those who had cost him his job at I-Bic, but also to take on that challenge.

Two and a half months later, SuWu Incorporated became the leading software company in the Western Hemisphere, developing a firewall that safeguarded against cyberattacks and viruses with a 99% success rate. Almost six months later, Mr. Crawford sold SuWu Incorporated to an undisclosed buyer in China for $825 million, who then outperformed other competitor companies, leaving little to no breathing room for I-Bic Computer System as well.

In turn, Mr. Crawford wanted to share ten percent of the profit from his company's sales with Richard. However, Richard politely declined to accept any money for his services. Instead, Mr. Crawford, as a philanthropist, offered to donate a lump sum of $43 million, to be exact, for the sole purpose of building a computer technology company that Richard would own and operate. This initiative aims to assist companies that are struggling in certain areas due to outdated technology, with the hope of getting them back on track.

Now, that was an offer that Richard could not refuse. Since then, Decorous Enterprise has been established in a small area of Miami, Florida, called Overtown, near the Miami Arena downtown.

In the first year, Richard understandably hired nine personnel to assist, ranging from receptionists to technicians. By the end of the second year, ten more employees were added as word spread about Decorous Enterprise. Generally speaking, both old and new companies came seeking help, often clinging to a thin lifeline before they collapsed. Some companies could be saved, while others couldn't. However, before Richard and his team decided to take on a task, they would thoroughly investigate the potential for the company's profit margin turnaround. If it wasn't deemed worth the time and effort, they would recommend that the owner of the company bail out immediately at a price they could estimate for them.

Then, let's not get it twisted here: the funds that came in from various companies saved by Decorous Enterprise or sold by their owners at a higher price prompted Richard to stop accepting donations after four years. This decision was not solely because his employee wanted a steady income, but rather because he took Decorous Enterprise public, enhancing its proficiency. Now, Decorous Enterprise not only helps refurbish both old and new companies, whether large or small, with a technology makeover for improvement, but also takes the initiative to assist entrepreneurs with a profit-sharing cut that could range from 15 to 35 percent in commission.

That was a deal no one would turn down. It was like the show Shark Tank on ABC, but better. Much better. You can check it out for yourself. Once you understand the unforeseen obstacles in the business world, manufacturing costs are constantly rising, and ideas and concepts keep evolving. The young entrepreneurs in today's society, right before our very eyes, witness this virtual idea that is continually advancing. Consider Pierre Omidyar, the founder of eBay, or Mark Zuckerberg of Facebook, for example; both started at a young age and are now multimillionaires.

For that same reason, Richard decided to visit the Miami-Dade Community College campus downtown, specifically in its outdoor leisure area, to speak with his person of interest and align with the ideological vision for the future of Decorous Enterprises. He focused on five candidates, then narrowed it down to three, and finally selected one hopeful candidate to fill the position at Decorous Enterprises, who sat two tables away from him amid a diverse crowd. He maintained good posture, looking almost groomed, seated with a group of five while discussing the economy. However, he didn't have a backpack, laptop, or even an iPad. He lacked any of the trendy gadgets that tech enthusiasts—or some might call them computer geeks—always carry. Instead, this dude had nothing noticeable—absolutely nothing but a basketball, which he rolled from side to side on the table in front of him.

But then, just like that, it was as if a Savior from the heavens had felt Richard's disappointment when he heard someone say, "If you were an entrepreneur in today's society, you might have a better chance of getting your dick sucked in the White House than seeing a small company grow to its virtual status."

Richard twisted to his right, glancing over his shoulder at the two guys sitting at a nearby table facing each other. Then, immediately afterward, the other guy, the one wearing the black rectangular eyewear, followed up with, "Well, I must agree with you on that. Due to the current entrepreneurial landscape, small business owners struggle to build successful, long-lasting companies, as larger firms often obstruct them, acting as corporate bullies to monopolize the competitive market. Here, check it out for yourself."

He then turned his iPad around to show his acquaintance something on the screen.

"I have my resources," he gestures as if typing on an invisible keyboard.

A light clicked: he was the one. At that point, Richard rose from his seat and approached this person of interest to ask if he would like a job at Decorous Enterprises.

That approach was implemented nearly seven years ago on a college campus. That was then; this is now.

Richard never took his focus off his Renaissance man, who eventually became not only his right-hand man at Decorous Enterprises but also his best friend. He felt this man was more like a family member to him, somewhat like—get this—Richard being his older brother.

Michael wore an exhausted expression before turning his gaze back to his computer.

"So," Richard began to ask him again, in a more cheerful tone this time, "are you coming to the party or what? We're all waiting on you."

"No. Not tonight. I'm still trying to figure out as to–"

Richard cut him off: "Don't be a moron. You have done enough work for this company to sustain us for a decade." He then turned to the woman on his left. "Do you see that handsome young man over there?" He removed his arms from around the woman's waist, then continued: "He made this company two hundred fifty-three million dollars today."

Michael slightly shook his head, barely noticeable, feeling a bit embarrassed because Richard was sharing their financial profit margin with those strangers while under the influence of alcohol.

As Richard left the two women standing at the doorway, he staggered over to the desk and leaned his mouth to Michael's ear. "Craig had sent his regards, based on your likes. So go ahead. Just pick anyone you want," he whispered, looking towards the doorway. "Exotic looking, aren't they?" he paused. Then he added, "I like the one on the left, so pick the brunette. She's a keeper."

No comment. Michael kept his lips sealed, gazing at the two lovely women. He wasn't sure which Craig Richard was referring to. Was it Craig Sullivan, the owner of Splash nightclub in South Beach, or Craig Donaldson of Model Quality Introduction, known for his top-notch glamorous ladies from coast to coast? It was probably for the best, as they didn't look ordinary, but rather extra and extraordinary. They were A-class women, flawless and built for the showcase. However, Michael would have to decline Craig's generosity because he was tied up at the moment. Perhaps later, but not now.

Both women smiled.

Michael smiled back, but it was insincere.

"Yeahhh," Richard dragged, cheering him on. Then he added, "That's what I'm talking about. Now get up and let's go out there and party with them." He then reached over and turned off the computer.

"Hey!" Michael turned it back on. "I'd told you that I'm working on something."

"Yeah. But not right now you are." He turned the computer off again.

Michael sat there, feeling more bothered than disturbed. He remained silent for a few seconds before deciding, "You are right. I do need a break." His facial expression brightened. "Just give me a second here so I can log off. I don't want to lose what I have gathered so far."

"Now, I have you as an associate here." Richard looked at the doorway. "He's going to the party," he repeatedly pointed to himself and the females, "with us." He then winked at them before turning back to Michael. "So come on then. You're holding us up."

"A few more seconds," he said while typing on the keyboard. Okay … Here … Weeee … Go!" Within a second, he pulled the flash drive from his computer and placed it in his briefcase.

"That's more like it," Richard began to walk away from the desk. "Because I wasn't leaving without you."

"Believe me, I know."

They walked toward the door together, where two beautiful ladies greeted them.

"Oh, shit!" Michael expressed himself not only through words but also through facial expressions.

"What is it?"

"I forgot to email Mr. Wilson regarding the contract specifications we drafted for him."

"You could do that tomorrow. Don't worry—"

"No. I can't: I promised to fix it for him as soon as possible." Michael turned around, heading toward his desk. "It'll only take me a few seconds.'

Richard and the two women stood there, waiting.

Michael looked up and noticed. "You all can head out to the party. I'll be right out in a few seconds behind you."

"Are you sure? You're not just pulling my leg?"

"No, of course not." Michael logged back onto his computer and took a seat. "And while you're out there, have your secretary, Donna, make me a double shot of Brandy."

"I got you." Richard smiled and left the office with the two women at his side.

After a brief moment, Michael realized everything was back to normal. "B-three to F-seven," he whispered. Then he said, "Checkmate." He pressed the Enter key while standing up. He grabbed his briefcase and blazer, then quietly walked to his office.

A few people were in the hall, enjoying themselves as they celebrated the company's profits, with music drifting from the front area.

Michael stayed close to the wall and sneaked up the corridor to the elevator. He made it there safe: Unnoticeable.

Then, suddenly, he heard a woman shout, "Hold the door for me!" as she stuck her hand inside the elevator cart to prevent it from shutting on her.

Shit!

It was Donna Bushwick, Richard's assistant.

Donna Bushwick was a young, attractive woman in her early thirties and a single mom. She was Black, with perhaps a hint of Asian or Hispanic ancestry, likely of Cuban descent. She had a buxom figure, a sweet caramel skin tone, and hazelnut eyes. She wore a navy-blue pantsuit paired with a white blouse. Her long, dark hair hung down her back.

Although Donna was attractive and single, Michael had never tried to flirt with her like most of the other guys at Decorous Enterprises. Michael just wasn't interested in her. Perhaps it was because he had never dated outside of his race. He wasn't racist, but his preference leaned toward white females—milky white females—especially those with red curly hair.

"Thank you for holding the door."

"No problem." He was still pushing the elevator button for the garage level before and after she had entered the elevator cart.

The elevator door closed finally.

It grew quiet briefly until Donna asked him, "So I imagine you are not staying for the party?"

"Of course. I'm staying," he thought of something quick before she would snitch on him. "I would like to grab something out of my car."

"Ohhh …" She looked at his briefcase.

He ignored her gesture by casting a glance at his wristwatch. It was four minutes to midnight.

The elevator opened.

They both tried to exit the elevator simultaneously, colliding slightly with one another. They froze.

"I thought ladies were first?" Donna joked with a little laugh.

"Oh, I'm sorry." His facial expression said something else. Then he held his hand outwards, as if sweeping trash out. "Please."

She rolled her eyes at him, exiting the elevator. "You asshole," she murmured.

Of course, he heard her, but he didn't care. She was being Donna, he thought.

Within a few minutes, as he entered his Audi R8 car and pulled off, he observed Donna on a cell phone.

As expected.

He exited the parking lot, drove down the street, and turned left on Biscayne Boulevard.

Then, suddenly, his iPhone began to ring. He looked at the caller ID.

His face showed a hint of a wry smile. He decided to take the call on the fifth ring. "Hello."

It was Sophia. "I can't believe you stood me up all night," she damn near sounded as if she wanted to cry. And you didn't have the decency to call me in advance and let me know that you weren't going to show up tonight."

Michael began to gather up his thoughts, then tried to give it a shot: "It's not like–"

She cut him off: "Please don't give me another one of your lame excuses again. I don't deserve that from you."

"Listen." He jumped onto I-95 North. "I had a terrible day today. And to hear you bickering in my ear will not help here."

Silence grew over the phone line.

Then, after a short moment, Sophia asked more leisurely. "What happened to you today?"

He slowly shook his head. "Do you remember that project I have been working on for the past three months?"

"Yeah, of course, how could I?" She had been surfing with him since he stood her up for the past three, if not four, months straight. "You're talking about the cyber-phone, right?'

"Yeah." He stuck his head inside the glove compartment to grab a Chinese menu from out of there. "It didn't go through today as planned. Because, come to find out" – he looked at the order menu in his hand – "Those Chinese bastards already came up with the same concept and designed it already."

"Oh, I'm sorry to hear that."

"One point four billion dollars down the drain."

The phone line grew quiet again.

Then she asked, "So what about Richard? How is he taking it?"

"He's taking it hard. He was looking forward to the deal to come through for the company."

"Do you think I should give him a call?"

"No!" he quickly barked. Then he said, "Don't bother yourself. I just got off the phone with him a few minutes ago, and he informed me that he was calling it quits for the night, not wanting to be disturbed." Then, at that precise moment, he received a text. He looked at the screen at about the same time Sophia was saying something to him, but he wasn't paying any attention to her. He read Richard's text message.

Answer your damn phone or bring your ass back to the office!

Michael got back on the phone. "Hey, Sophia."

"Yes."

"I have to call you back: I have to go."

"No. Don't go. I have something to say to you, and it will only take me a minute."

Author's Contact Info

An idiot once told me that if you can't see the brighter side of life, polish the dull side to make it shine. There is some truth in that, but I beg to differ in some respects. For instance, in a dysfunctional relationship, if someone chooses to stay, there's no polishing, just running. Run as fast as you can!

If you would like to offer a suggestion,
Please feel free to comment or express any criticisms about my book.
Feel free to address this with the giving info below:

bitterbrother321@gmail.com

Keep in touch with Davis via the web:

YouTube: @bitterbrother321

Facebook: @bitterbrother321

X: @bitterbrother3

Instagram: @bitterbrother321

Tik Tok: @bitterbrother321

Snapchat: @bitterbrothere32

Twitch: @bitterbrother321

About the Author

Davis Zebrowski is a traveler who pursues knowledge. When he is not confined in a straitjacket in a padded cell—running in circles—he enjoys browsing through his imaginary bookshelf of encyclopedias to learn more about eccentric psychiatrists. At this moment, he is observing you from a distance, perched in a tree with binoculars.